mem

THE INFERNAL DEVICE

Professor Moriarty, erstwhile Mathematics professor, is not 'the greatest rogue unhanged' that Sherlock Holmes would have one believe, but rather an amoral genius — and the only man Holmes has ever been bested by. *The Infernal Device* takes Professor Moriarty from London to Stamboul to Moscow and back, Sherlock Holmes close on his tail, until they both join forces to pursue and capture a man more devious and more dangerous than either of them has ever faced before . . .

Books by Michael Kurland
in the Linford Mystery Library:

THE TRIALS OF QUINTILIAN
VICTORIAN VILLAINY

MICHAEL KURLAND

THE INFERNAL DEVICE

Complete and Unabridged

LINFORD
Leicester

First published in Great Britain

First Linford Edition
published 2013

A catalogue record for this book is available
from the British Library.

ISBN 978–1–4448–1798–0

Published by
F. A. Thorpe (Publishing)
Anstey, Leicestershire

Set by Words & Graphics Ltd.
Anstey, Leicestershire
Printed and bound in Great Britain by
T. J. International Ltd., Padstow, Cornwall

This book is printed on acid-free paper

Prologue

He who has one enemy
will meet him everywhere.
— Ali Ibn-Abu-Talib

The urchin proceeded cautiously through the thick London fog. Occasionally he paused to peer at the brass numbers on a brick gatepost or puzzle over a street sign.

Stopping at a brick house fronted by a high wrought-iron fence, he carefully compared its address with that on the envelope clutched in his grimy hand. Then he mounted the steps and attacked the door with his fist.

The door opened, and one of the largest men the lad had ever seen stared stolidly down at him. 'There is a bell,' the man said.

'Werry sorry,' the lad said. ''As I the 'onor of knocking up sixty-four Russell Square? Is you Professor James Moriarty?'

1

'I am Mr. Maws, the professor's butler.'

The lad considered this for a moment, then he backed up a step and announced, 'I 'as a envelope for Professor James Moriarty what I is supposed to 'and 'im personal.'

'I'll take it,' Mr. Maws said.

The lad backed up, ready to run. 'I is supposed to 'and this 'ere envelope to Professor James Moriarty 'imself, and not to nobody else.'

Mr. Maws squatted down to approximate the boy's height. 'But I am the professor's butler,' he said. 'I stand in the position of loco habilitus to Professor Moriarty under the common law. Giving me the envelope is the same as giving it to Professor Moriarty himself. That's my job, you see.'

'Gor!' the urchin said, unconvinced.

'Here,' Mr. Maws reached into his waistcoat pocket and pulled out a shilling, holding it between his thumb and forefinger. 'It's my job to pay for them, too.'

'Coo!' the lad said. 'A bob!' He stared at the coin in fascination for a moment, then quickly exchanged it for the envelope and ran off down the street.

Mr. Maws took the envelope inside and carefully closed and bolted the door before further examining it. It was of stiff yellow paper. Written across the front, in what Mr. Maws took for a foreign hand, was PROFESSOR MORIARTY — INTO HIS HANDS over 64 RUSSELL SQR. On the back, across the flap, was PERSONAL and MOST URGENT. Mr. Maws sniffed it, squeezed it, and held it before a strong gaslight before putting it on a salver and bringing it into the study.

'Letter,' he said.

'I thought the first post had come,' Professor Moriarty said, without looking up from the worktable where he was slowly heating a flask of dark-colored liquid over a spirit lamp.

'A young ragamuffin just delivered this by hand,' Mr. Maws explained. 'Incidentally, sir, the gentleman with the prominent nose is still lurking across the way in Montague Place.'

'Ah!' Moriarty said. 'So we still interest Mr. Sherlock Holmes with our little comings and goings, do we? Good, good.' He took the flask off the fire and set it aside. 'Just raise the blinds, will you, Mr. Maws? Thank you.' He pinched a pair of pince-nez glasses onto his nose and examined the envelope. 'Of Eastern European manufacture, I should say. Meaningless of itself — so much is being imported these days. But the handwriting has a definite foreign flavor. Look at that 'F.' Let's see what's inside.'

Moriarty slit the envelope open along the top with a penknife and removed the stiff sheet of paper folded within. The message was block-printed in the same hand as the envelope:

MUST AT ONCE MEET WITH YOU REGARDING TREPOFF MATTER. YOUR AID URGENTLY SOLIC-ITED. WILL CALL THIS EVENING. TAKE ALL CARE.

V.

'Curious,' Moriarty said. 'The writer assumes that I know what he's talking

4

about. Anything about a Trepoff in the popular press, Mr. Maws?'

Mr. Maws, an avid reader of the sensational dailies, shook his head. 'No, sir,' he declared. 'It is a puzzler, sir.'

'It does present a few interesting features,' Moriarty admitted. 'Hand me down my extra-ordinary file for the letter 'T,' will you?'

Mr. Maws went to the shelf and removed the appropriate volume from the set of clipping-books in which Professor Moriarty kept note of those items and events that, although seemingly commonplace, his keen intellect had perceived were actually out of the ordinary. He handed the thick book to the professor.

'Hm,' Moriarty said. 'It looks as though T were ready for a subdivision. Let me see.' He flipped through the volume. 'Theodora the ant-woman. The Thanatopsis Club. Tropical poisons. The Truth-seekers Society. Nothing under Trepoff.' He put the volume down. 'Well, there is nothing to be gained in speculation when we shall soon have the facts.'

The doorbell rang, and Mr. Maws went to answer it, while Moriarty took the letter over to his worktable and contemplated the shelf of stoppered reagents.

'A package, sir,' Mr. Maws said, returning to the room with a small, carefully wrapped box. 'Likely from the same person.'

Moriarty glanced at the carefully printed address. 'Similar,' he said, 'but not the same. Now why — of course!' He turned to his butler. 'Who delivered this?'

'A small, very fair-looking gentleman, sir.'

'What did he do? Did he just hand it to you?'

'He inquired if this was the right residence, sir. And then he unwrapped a carrying-string and handed me the package. He did ask me if it would be delivered to you right away.'

'I'm sure he did,' Moriarty exclaimed. Grabbing the package from Mr. Maw's hands, he pitched it through the closed front window, knocking out several panes of glass.

The box exploded before it hit the

ground, taking out the rest of the window and sending glass shards and fragments of wood and brick flying back into the room.

Moriarty's hand went numb. He looked down to discover that a sliver of glass had ripped through the sleeve of his smoking jacket and sliced into his upper forearm. Bright red blood pulsed through the wound, soaking the sleeve and dripping onto the hardwood floor.

'Very interesting,' Moriarty said, pulling the handkerchief from his breast pocket to staunch the flow of blood.

1

STAMBOUL

What is Fate that we should seek it?
—Hafiz

Constantinople, the city of a hundred races and a thousand vices, was split in half by that thumb of the Bosporus known throughout recorded history as the Golden Horn. On one side, Stamboul, outpost of Asia; on the other Galata and Pera, terminus of Europe. A floating bridge connected Galata and Stamboul. The Galata side was European and nineteenth century. The men wore top hats and gaiters, and the ladies favored French bonnets and French perfumes; the hotels had gaslight and indoor plumbing.

Stamboul was Roman and Byzantine and Turk and Arab; ancient and timeless. It smelled of Levant. The men wore turbans and fezzes and the women were veiled. Caravan drivers from Baghdad spread their goods in the Covered Bazaar, and one ate only with one's right hand.

An early morning fog covered the Golden Horn, with here and there the mast of a caïque poking through, and the great dome of St. Sofia looming out on the Stamboul side. From the breakfast veranda of the Hotel Ibrahim in Pera, Benjamin Barnett peered out over the mist boiling below and tried to pick out landmarks that matched the sketches in his guidebook. 'Nothing looks right,' he complained to his table companion. 'I can't line it up with the book. And I sure can't read the street signs. I guess I'd better hire a guide.'

'If you are determined to go,' Lieutenant Sefton said, folding his two-day old *Times* carefully and putting it to the right of his plate, 'I suppose I'd better come along. Show you the ropes and all that.'

'Thanks a lot for the offer,' Barnett said, attacking the last bit of egg on his plate, 'but I think I can take care of myself.'

'No doubt,' Lieutenant Sefton said, eyeing the stocky, self-composed young American. 'You Yanks seem to make a fetish of taking care of yourselves. Comes from living on the edge of the frontier, I shouldn't wonder. Outlaws and Red Indians and all that.'

'Um,' Barnett replied, trying to decide if he was having his leg pulled. He had first met Sefton four days before when he boarded the Simplon Express in Paris, and during the entire three-day trip the tall, angular officer of Her Most Britannic Majesty's Navy had not displayed anything resembling a sense of humor.

Barnett's employers, the *New York World*, had sent a coded telegram to him in Paris. Royce's Complete Telegraphers' Phrase Code made for stilted communications, but it saved money. And a two-penny newspaper saved all the money it could.

GYBUT CONSTANTINOPLE UHWOZ NONKE
UKHOX TYDYC FOWIC ADGUD WORLD

11

Barnett had dug out his leather-bound Royce and written the message out in pencil in his notebook:

Go to Constantinople. Telegraph report on Ottoman testing new submersible. Expences paid. Accreditation waiting.
— International Editor,
the New York World.

The *New York World* was very proud of its coverage of military and naval news. Many of its readers followed the power politics of Europe, as unfolded in its pages, as eagerly as others followed the sports pages.

During these last decades of the nineteenth century Constantinople was a focus of European intrigue. Four wars had been fought in twenty years for pieces of the crumbling Ottoman Empire, and no one dared guess when the next one would start, or which of the great powers would be involved. England, France, Russia, Austria, and Prussia had all lost troops in sight of the clear blue waters of the Sea of Marmara.

Sultan Abd-ul Hamid, the second of that name, and the twenty-ninth Osmanli sultan to rule from the Seraglio in Stamboul since Mohammed el Fatih — the Conqueror — took Byzantium in 1453, would not give up his European possessions easily. He armed his Mamelukes with Maxim machine-pistols, and his Janissaries with Nordenfeldt field pieces. He had Portsmouth Naval Yards build him a battleship, had Krupp Germania Aktiongesellschaft fabricate three gunboats, and now had had the Garrett-Harris submersible boat shipped over from Hartford, Connecticut, for sea trials.

And — to encourage his friends and discourage his enemies — he invited the world to watch.

And the *World* wanted Barnett to watch. So he'd packed two suitcases, sent a note of apology to the young lady of the *Folies* who was to have dined with him, notified his *concierge* to watch his *logement* while he was gone, and made it to the *Gare de l'Est* with forty seconds to spare.

The Simplon express had arrived in

Constantinople the afternoon before, and Barnett had gone right to the American Embassy in Pera. A native clerk informed him that the ambassador was out, the assistant ambassador was out, and the secretary was out.

Barnett waved his telegram at the clerk. 'I'm supposed to have papers to watch the submersible trials. It's all arranged.'

'Return Monday, effendim,' the clerk said, straightening his tie and adjusting his fez. 'The ambassador will be here then. I must close the office.'

'But the sea trials start Saturday!'

The clerk shrugged and closed the window.

Barnett now had no choice but to go to the Sublime Porte in Stamboul, the seat of the Osmanli government, where the necessary permissions could be obtained.

Sefton pushed back his chair and stood up. 'Take my word for it, Barnett,' he said in his clipped, inflectionless voice. 'If I don't come along with you, you're fated to spend the rest of the week warming one of the marble benches in the courtyard. I must go to the Sublime Porte at any rate, to see about my own accreditation.'

Barnett nodded his acquiescence. 'I'm convinced,' he said. 'I just didn't want to put you to any trouble, but as you're going at any rate, I'd be glad of your assistance.'

They left the hotel together and walked down the hill to Galata and the floating bridge. The fog was almost burned off now, and the clear March air smelled of some unidentifiable spice. Lieutenant Sefton pointed out the sights as they walked and told anecdotes of the timeless city. 'I've been away for two years,' he said, 'but nothing changes. Across the bridge in Stamboul twenty years or two hundred could pass, and still nothing would change.'

'Were you here long?' Barnett asked.

'Long enough,' Sefton said. 'I was junior naval attaché to our embassy, then naval attaché. Finally, they decided that I'd gone native and shipped me home.' He laughed, but the memory was clearly a bitter one.

'And now you're back.'

15

'Yes.'

'Excuse me if I ask too many questions,' Barnett said. 'It's a habit that you get into if you're a journalist.'

'Quite all right,' Sefton said. 'Actually, I'm here on the same business you are: the sea trials of the Garrett-Harris submersible. I seem to have become the Royal Navy's submarine expert.'

'Ah!'

Sefton bounced his walking stick against the sidewalk. 'The Royal Navy, you understand, has no interest in submarines.'

'No interest?' Barnett asked.

Lieutenant Sefton nodded. He evidently got a great deal of perverse pleasure from telling this story. 'The Holland submersible was tested in New Haven, Connecticut, last year, and I observed. My report was favorable. I strongly suggested purchasing one and beginning our own testing program for the craft.

'The report went all the way up to the First Lord of the Admiralty. He scribbled 'Of what use is a boat which sinks?' across

16

the cover and sent it back, and that was the end of that.'

The street they were following ended in a steep flight of stairs, below which the blue waters of the Golden Horn danced and shimmered in the late morning sun. Off in the distance two great buildings rose out of the haze on the Stamboul side. The dome of the Mosque of the Sultana Validé shimmered directly in front of them, and off to their left, gleaming white across the water, the *suleimanieh*, the gigantic and ancient mosque of Soliman, straddled a tall hill and frowned out over both the Golden Horn and the Sea of Marmara.

They descended the stairs and each paid his penny to the white-robed toll collector. The bridge was as crowded, Barnett thought, as the Bowery on a Saturday afternoon. And such people as were never seen on the streets of New York: Persians in flaring red robes and tall, conical hats; Circassians with curled blond beards, wearing long, black caftans and bearskin caps . . . Four black Turks trotted by with an ebony and ivory sedan chair on their shoulders. A veiled harem girl stared soulfully through the gauze curtains at Barnett, and then giggled as the chair passed.

'I'm getting a peculiar feeling as we cross this bridge,' Barnett told Sefton. 'It's hard to explain, but it's as though we were going, step by step, backward in time.'

'The nineteenth century has yet to reach Stamboul,' Sefton agreed, 'for all that it's almost over. For us, it's 1885. For them' — he pointed with his stick at three women in front of them wrapped in layer after layer of concealing linen — 'who is to say what year — what age — it is. As they reckon time, it is the year 1302 of the Hegira. These young ladies are *halaiks* — slave girls — belonging to the harem of some emir, and the two tall black gentlemen escorting them are eunuchs from his court.'

'Well!' Barnett said.

The Sublime Porte, a connected maze of palaces and gardens surrounded by a high wall, contained the palace of the sultan's chief minister, the grand vizier, along with the ministries of foreign affairs and war. Lieutenant Sefton led the way into the palace and took Barnett through a series of offices and waiting rooms. In each he spoke to someone, a few lire notes changed hands, and they were forwarded to the next.

Finally, they were taken to a richly appointed room on an inner courtyard of the palace. 'We have arrived,' Sefton said, sinking into a gold-brocade overstuffed armchair. 'The Captain Pasha himself is going to see us.'

'The Captain Pasha?'

'The Osmanli equivalent of the First Lord of the Admiralty,' Sefton explained, darting his eyes around the room like some great hawk.

'Was it really necessary to bribe all those people to get here?' Barnett asked.

Lieutenant Sefton focused his gaze on Barnett. 'You are serious,' he decided. 'My dear man, those weren't bribes. You're in the Levant. Simple gratuities, incentives. Thus we arrived in this office in slightly over an hour instead of two weeks. This despite the fact that the

Captain Pasha actually wants to see us.'

'I wasn't making a moral judgment,' Barnett assured him. 'This sort of thing exists in the States. It's just the openness of it here that surprises me. A Tammany politico would take you in the back room with the lights turned down low. And he'd have four relatives and a judge all ready to swear that he was somewhere else at the time.'

'Our Western ways are slow to take hold here,' Lieutenant Sefton said, 'no matter how hard we try to show them the superiority of our methods.'

A very short, very wide man waddled through a door at the far end of the room. He wore a fur-trimmed green robe, under which yellow boots peeked out as he walked. His face was creased in a permanent smile. 'Ah, my dear, dear Captain Sefton,' he said, with a pronounced British accent, crossing the room with his arms outstretched. 'My heart leaps with pleasure that you have been able to return to Constantinople.'

'Your Excellency,' said Sefton, jumping to his feet and pulling Barnett with him.

'It is good to see you again. I am pleased that my government has once more sent me here to watch and learn from the master.'

The Captain Pasha waved a pudgy hand of disclaimer at the praise and turned to Barnett. 'And you must be the American correspondent, Mr. Benjamin Barnett.' He took Barnett's hand and pumped it with the enthusiasm of one who is unaccustomed to the ritual of hand-shaking and still finds it faintly amusing. 'We are honored at your presence here, sir. A representative of the press of your great democracy is always welcome.'

'The honor is mine, Your Excellency,' Barnett said, keeping to the spirit of the exchange. 'It gives me an occasion to acquaint myself with your remarkable city.'

'Ah, yes,' the Captain Pasha said. 'Constantinople, the jewel of cities. You are lucky to have Captain Sefton as your guide. He knows the city as few Europeans do.'

'Lieutenant,' Lieutenant Sefton said pointedly.

The Captain Pasha turned around, his hands in the air, his fingers waggling in horror. 'No!' he said. 'It cannot be! A man of your talent and intelligence still only a lieutenant? I will not permit it! Come, I offer you an immediate commission in the naval service of Sultan Abd-ul Hamid. You shall come in as a full commander. Captain next year. In five years you shall be *oula*, in ten, *bala*. Guaranteed. My word.'

Sefton gave a polite half-bow. 'Every man knows the worth of your word, Excellency. I am disconsolate that I cannot accept your offer.'

'And why not?' asked the Captain Pasha. He flipped his hand at the outside world. 'They do not appreciate you. I do. You will have a career of honor and reward in a navy that values your ability. And remember that Sultan Abd-ul Hamid is an ally of your Queen Victoria. There can be no dishonor in fighting in the cause of an ally. I give you my most solemn word,' he said seriously, 'that if we ever declare war upon Great Britain I shall release you from your service.'

'I shall consider your words, Excellency,' Lieutenant Sefton said, 'and I thank you for them. Even though I am afraid that it can never be.'

'Never be?' the Captain Pasha chuckled. 'You should not use such terms. Is it not written that no man's eye can pierce the veil that hides the face of tomorrow?' He turned to Barnett. 'My secretary will bring you the documents you need. I shall arrange for you both to have places on board His Supreme Highness' steam yacht *Osmanieh*, from which to observe the trials. May Allah, in His Infinite wisdom, assure that we meet again soon.'

The Captain Pasha left as abruptly as he had entered. A moment later his secretary came in and handed them each a thick gray envelope sealed in red wax bearing the device of the star and crescent. Then a tiny pageboy in an ornate red-and-gold uniform escorted them through the maze of hallways to the outside world.

Lieutenant Sefton glanced at his pocket watch. 'It is still early,' he said, 'although we do seem to have missed our lunch hour. Would you like to see the Covered Bazaar? It's quite fascinating, really. We can have a bite to eat on the way, if you like.' He led the way through a complex of narrow, twisting streets and alleyways. Barnett followed, looking this way and that at the exotically unfamiliar city he was passing through.

They'd been walking for about ten minutes when the mellifluous chanting of the *Mu'adhdhin* sounded from the towering minarets all over Stamboul, calling the Faithful to afternoon prayer. Within seconds the streets were virtually empty as the locals went inside to perform the prescribed ritual.

Then, over the chanting, came the sound of many running feet. A tall European turned the corner a block away and headed toward the square at a dead run, coat-tails flying. A second later a gang of Arabs boiled around the corner behind him, waving a variety of weapons, intent on catching up.

'I say,' Lieutenant Sefton said, 'an Englishman seems to be in trouble.

Barnett put his notebook away and

took off his jacket. 'He might be French,' he said.

'Nonsense, man — look at the cut of those trousers!'

Folding his jacket carefully, Barnett put it on the rim of the fountain. Long experience at bar-room brawling had taught him that bruises heal, but ripped jackets must be replaced.

Lieutenant Sefton twisted the handle of his stick and slid out an eighteen-inch blade. 'The Marquis of Queensbury wouldn't approve,' he said, 'but those chaps aren't gentlemen.'

'I don't suppose you have another of those pigstickers concealed about your person, do you?' Barnett asked, eyeing the approaching mob and the assortment of curved knives they were waving. He picked up his jacket again and wrapped it around his arm. The custom governing bar-room disputes on the Bowery limited the engagement to fisticuffs and an occasional chair or bottle, but — other places, other habits.

'Here,' Sefton said, tossing him the body of the stick. 'It's rolled steel under the veneer. Feel free to bash away with it.'

'Thanks,' Barnett said, hefting the thin steel tube. The tall stranger had almost reached them, and the mob was close behind. Holding the truncated stick like a baseball bat, Barnett advanced to the attack.

2

MORIARTY

*He is a genius, a philosopher,
an abstract thinker.*
— *Sherlock Holmes*

He ran down the Street of the Two
Towers, closely pursued by six men in
dirty brown burnooses. One of them had
been following him since he left his hotel,
and the six together had attacked him as
he left the shop of a dealer in ancient
brass instruments a few blocks away. He
was deciding among the four most logical
means of escape when two men in
European dress, waving menacing weapons, raced to his aid. In an instant, he
stopped running and turned around to
face his attackers, his feet firmly planted
and his arms together and extended in
the baritsu defense posture.

The Arab nearest him leaped, curved blade high in the air, and brought it down in an overhand arc aimed straight at his temple. With a deceptively easy-looking twist of his body he moved aside, grasped his assailant's knife-arm as he passed, and pinned it behind. The Arab made the mistake of trying to twist free, and he screamed with shock and pain as his shoulder joint pulled out of its socket.

Then Barnett and Sefton reached the scene. The lieutenant, using his sword-stick like an épée, took two of the Arabs on in classical Italian style, his left hand raised languidly behind him. Barnett, swinging his stick freely in both hands, rushed at the others.

One of the attackers yelled out a few words in a guttural language, and his comrades broke off the fighting and raced away in as close to five different directions as they could manage in the narrow street. Lieutenant Sefton, who had downed one of the men with the first thrust of his blade, raced after another, yelling at him to stop and fight.

'Pah!' the tall man spat, straightening

up and glaring after the retreating figures. 'Amateurs! I am insulted.'

'Excuse me?' Barnett said, trying to catch his breath.

Moriarty dusted himself off. 'Thank you for your assistance,' he said. 'I seem to have lost my hat.'

Lieutenant Sefton chased the retreating Arab to the corner before giving up. 'Too big a head start,' he lamented, returning to the square. He took the body of his swordstick back from Barnett and returned the blade to its scabbard. 'Are you all right, sir?'

'Yes,' Moriarty said. 'Except for a slight rent in the jacket sleeve and the loss of my stick and my hat. I owe you gentlemen a great debt. Your assistance alleviated a troublesome situation.'

'Glad to help,' Barnett said briefly. He personally thought it might have been a bit more than 'troublesome,' but he held his tongue. Traditional British understatement, he decided.

'Couldn't allow a fellow Englishman to be molested by cutthroat Arabs without doing something,' Lieutenant Sefton said.

'My pleasure, I assure you. I am Lieutenant Auric Sefton, Royal Navy. My companion is Mr. Benjamin Barnett, an American.'

Moriarty shook hands with both of them. 'From the great city of New York, I perceive,' he told Barnett. 'Although most recently from Paris. And a journalist, if I am not mistaken.'

'Why, that's quite right,' Barnett looked his amazement.

'Of course it is. I am Professor James Moriarty. I think we could all use a chance to catch our breath. Come, there's a small coffee shop a few blocks from here. If you would care to accompany me, it would be my pleasure to offer you a cup of that thick brew which the Turk, in his wisdom, calls coffee.'

'Why did those chaps attack you?' Sefton asked.

'I have no idea,' Moriarty said. 'Let us go to the coffee shop, where I can sit down. I think I lead too sedentary an existence. My wind isn't what it should be. I promise I'll answer your questions there. Oh — one last thing . . . ' Moriarty bent over the body of the downed attacker and gave it a perfunctory examination. 'All right,' he said, straightening up. 'It is as I thought. Let us go.'

The tables at the coffee shop were arranged outside on the sidewalk, under a wide awning. Barnett and Sefton instinctively picked a table with a bench against the wall, where they could sit facing the street. Moriarty calmly sat facing them across the postage-stamp-sized table. 'My usual preference is also the seat with the, ah, view,' Moriarty told them, smiling grimly. 'But with you two stalwart gentlemen guarding my rear, I feel confident that there will be no surprises. Is it to be *shekerli* or *sade*, gentlemen?'

'What's that?' Barnett asked.

'Sweet or bitter,' Sefton explained. 'The coffee.'

'Oh,' Barnett said. 'Sweet. Very sweet.'

The waiter was a short, wide man, sporting a great handlebar mustache and swathed in a white apron. He approached his European customers and performed an impressive dumb show to indicate that whatever language they spoke, he didn't.

Moriarty spoke to him in Turkish, interrupting him in mid-gesture, and his face lit up. A minute later he was back at the table, making the coffee in the customary small brass pot over a charcoal burner.

'Your knowledge of the language is excellent,' Lieutenant Sefton complimented Moriarty. Have you been in Constantinople long?'

'On the contrary,' said Moriarty. 'I have been here for but three days. I leave tomorrow.'

Lieutenant Sefton leaned forward. 'And you haven't been here before?'

'Never.'

'Then where did you learn Turkish?'

'I have developed a system for learning languages,' Moriarty said. 'I confess that Turkish was something of a challenge for the system; I never expected to have to use it. When I learned that I had to go to Odessa on business, I couldn't resist arranging to spend a few days here in Constantinople, both to see the city and to practice my Turkish.'

'Then you are a professor of languages?' Barnett asked.

Moriarty shook his head. 'My degree is in mathematics. When I was younger I held the Chair of Mathematics at a small provincial university, but I am no longer so employed.'

'You don't know who attacked you?' Lieutenant Sefton asked, getting back to the matter at hand. 'We should probably report the ruffians to the authorities.'

'I have no idea,' Professor Moriarty said. 'I came out of a shop and two of them attempted to propel me into an alley, where the others waited. I broke away. Aside from the fact that they were amateur assassins, and definitely not Arabs, I know nothing whatever about them.'

'Why do you say they were not Arabs?' Lieutenant Sefton asked. 'They looked like Arabs to me.'

'Such was their intent, but there were a few small details they missed,' Moriarty said. 'One of them called to the others, and he did not speak Arabic. And the characteristic butternut color of their skin

33

— was greasepaint.'

He pulled out his pocket handkerchief and displayed a dark brown stain across one corner. 'The gentleman you left hors de combat was wearing this. I suspected it, so I ran the handkerchief across his chin.'

Lieutenant Sefton took the handkerchief and examined the stain. 'Curiouser and curiouser,' he said. 'So it was more than just an attempted robbery. It did seem to be quite a pack to be hounding one retired professor of mathematics.'

'Yes,' Moriarty said dryly. 'I thought so myself.'

'Tell me, Professor,' Barnett said. 'I don't want to seem to pry into your affairs, but you're not here, by any chance, to watch the sea trials, are you?'

'Sea trials?' Moriarty asked, sounding puzzled.

'The Garrett-Harris submersible boat,' Barnett explained. 'Day after tomorrow.'

'No, gentlemen, I have nothing to do with the trials. I would find it fascinating to watch them, but I cannot stay. My business in Odessa calls me away tomorrow.'

'Say!' Barnett said. 'I meant to ask: how did you know I'm a journalist, and from New York?'

Moriarty touched his finger to his ear. 'If you could hear yourself,' he said, 'you wouldn't have to ask the second part of that question. As to the first: the notebook in your inner pocket, the sharpened pencils in your breast pocket, the writing callus on your right forefinger — all point in a certain direction. And to verify my deduction, I had only to look at the signet on your ring. The New York Press Club sigil is not unfamiliar to me.'

'I see,' Barnett said, fingering the ring Moriarty had mentioned and nodding his head slowly. 'And Paris? How did you know I had come from Paris?'

'Your shoes, sir,' Moriarty said. 'Unmistakable.'

The waiter brought over a small plate of candies. 'Try one,' Lieutenant Sefton said, shoving it over to Barnett *'Rahat loukoum*. Call them Turkish delights in England. Go with the coffee.'

'I've heard of them,' Barnett said, sampling one of the small squares. It was a sweet gel of assorted fruits, which did indeed go well with the thick Turkish coffee.

Professor Moriarty took a small leather case from his pocket. 'Allow me to give you gentlemen my card,' he said. 'I expect you both to look me up at your earliest opportunity.'

Barnett took the proffered pasteboard and looked at it:

James C. Moriarty, Sc.D.
64 Russell Square
Consulting

'Consulting?' he asked.

'Consulting,' Moriarty affirmed.

Lieutenant Sefton examined the card at arm's length. 'I say,' he said. 'At what do you consult? Who consults you?'

'I answer questions,' Professor Moriarty explained patiently. 'I solve problems. Very occasionally I perform services. My rates vary with the difficulty of the task.'

'Is there much demand for such a

service?' Barnett asked.

'I am never at a loss for commissions and my rates are quite high. Of course, I am paid only for success.'

'You mean you guarantee success?' Lieutenant Sefton asked, incredulously.

'No man can guarantee success at any task. What I do is minimize the chance of failure.'

They had one last cup of coffee together before separating. Barnett and Lieutenant Sefton offered to walk the professor back to his hotel, but he refused. 'I do not anticipate any further trouble,' he said.

'I hope you're right,' Lieutenant Sefton said. They shook hands, and the professor strode off.

'Queer cove, that,' Sefton commented thoughtfully as he and Barnett started back to the Hotel Ibrahim. 'Do you suppose he's anywhere near as intelligent as he thinks he is?'

Barnett pondered, then: 'I reckon he is, Lieutenant,' he said. 'You know, I just reckon he is.'

3

DEATH

He who commands the sea commands everything . . .
— *Themistocles*

It was cold, damp, foggy, and uncomfortable — altogether as one would expect on a small caïque in the Bosporus just after dawn in mid-March. 'They can't find the yacht,' Lieutenant Sefton announced after the boss *caiquejee* yelled to him in Turkish.

'Why can't they find the yacht?'

'Because it isn't in sight.' Lieutenant Sefton waved his hand at the fog. 'Not much of anything in sight.'

The boss *caiquejee*, a small, swarthy man with immense biceps and a mustache that seemed to curl around his ears, started an earnest, profound discussion with Lieutenant Sefton that involved much pounding on the oarlock and gesticulating. 'What's happening?' Barnett asked Sefton at the first pause in the discussion.

'There are two problems,' Lieutenant Sefton said. 'Firstly, although Turkish is our only common language, my friend here speaks it worse than I do. It seems to be a tradition in the Stamboul docks that all the *caiquejeem* — oarsmen — are recruited from somewhere in Eastern Europe. Secondly, they want to return to the dock now. I'm trying to convince him that they were hired to take us to the *Osmanieh* and that their job isn't done until they find it, wherever it is.'

The boss *caiquejee* said something slowly and distinctly to Barnett, then wiped his mustache carefully with his sleeve and spat into the sea. His companion nodded and spat out the other side of the boat. They both glared at Barnett.

'What's happening now?' Barnett demanded.

'They want you to know they are not

39

afraid of you,' Sefton explained.

'Why,' Barnett asked with a sinking feeling in his stomach, 'should they be afraid of me?'

'When my friend here suggested that we could swim out to the *Osmanieh* if we wanted to find it so badly, I told him of your reputation.'

The two *caiquejeem* spat again, almost in unison.

'My reputation?' Barnett asked.

'Yes. I told them you were a cowboy from America. They know about cowboys.'

'Wonderful,' Barnett said. 'What's that noise?'

'Noise?' Sefton asked.

The boss *caiquejee* clapped his hands together. '*Mujika!*' he yelled, slapping his assistant on the back. He turned to Barnett with a wide, black-toothed grin. '*Mujika!*' he insisted, holding his fists clenched with the thumbs sticking straight up and wobbling them in front of him.

'Bells,' Sefton said. 'Ship's bells. It must be the yacht.'

The *caiquejeem* bent to their task with renewed vigor, and soon the sharp lines of the steam-yacht *Osmanieh* materialized before their eyes through the fog. Two smartly uniformed seamen aboard the yacht lowered a boarding ladder as the caïque pulled alongside.

'Aha!' The boss *caiquejee* said, as Barnett stepped past him to grab the ladder. 'Bang, bang!'

Barnett started. 'What the hell?'

'Bang, bang!' the *caiquejee* repeated, shooting his finger at Barnett. 'Buffalo Beel. Beely de Keed. Whil'Beel Hitkook. Bang, bang!' He grinned and slapped Barnett on the back. 'Cowboy!'

'Yes, yes,' Barnett said, smiling back weakly. 'That's right.'

With this encouragement, the *caiquejee* broke into an expansive statement, accompanied with chest-thumping and a lot of wiggling of fingers.

'Well,' Lieutenant Sefton said, staring back down at them from halfway up the ladder. 'I wrought better than I knew. It appears that you have a friend for life, Barnett.'

'What's he saying?' Barnett demanded.

'He says that he has a brother in Chicago, so he knows all about cowboys. His brother writes once a month. He, himself, hopes to move to America where all men are soon rich and they wear six-shooters.'

'Well, I guess we're all brothers under the skin,' Barnett said vaguely, as he climbed up the ladder.

The officer at the head of the ladder checked their papers and passed them on to a midshipman, who took them aft to the main cabin.

There were about twenty other guests in the cabin, mostly from the press and diplomatic corps of European countries. Red-robed servants wearing long, curved-toe slippers walked silently about, passing out cups of coffee and small breakfast cakes. Some minutes later, when the last of the invited guests found their way through the fog, the yacht got underway and the Captain Pasha came down to talk to the group. He spoke of the Osmanli naval tradition, and of Sultan Abd-ul Hamid's desire to live in peace with all his neighbors. He spoke of world trade and water routes, and of the strategic position of the Bosporus. He urged them to eat more of the little cakes, and assured them that they would be impressed with the day's display.

'Awfully confident, don't you think?' Lieutenant Sefton murmured to Barnett. 'From my past experience with submersibles, they'll be lucky to get the thing running at all on the first trial. Either it won't start, or it won't sink, or it will sink only bow-first or upside down.'

'I thought you were pro-submarine,' Barnett said.

'Pro-submarine? Is that an Americanism, or merely journalese? Yes, I am impressed by the potential of the craft. When the designers get all the mechanical problems solved and the beasts become a bit more dependable, they'll be invaluable to the navy.'

'How will they be used in warfare?' Barnett asked.

'They will primarily be used for scouting and messenger service, as well as for guarding harbors and fleets at anchor and such duty.'

'What about attacking other ships?' Barnett asked. 'I kind of picture them sneaking up on battleships and sinking them.'

Sefton shook his head. 'That's a common misconception — fostered, if I may say so, by the sensational press. You must take into account the limitations inherent in the device. First of all, they can never be used in the open ocean; they are too fragile and their range is too limited. Secondly, a submersible could never go against a modern capital ship. It would have to get too close to launch its torpedo. It would be vulnerable to the ship's gun battery. One shell from even a six-inch gun would sink any submersible, whereas it would take a dozen Whitehead torpedoes to do any significant damage to a ship of the line.'

'You disappoint me,' Barnett said. 'I thought the submersible was the weapon of the future.'

'Oh, it is,' Sefton said. 'Properly employed by an imaginative commander, submersibles would have a decisive effect on the outcome of any naval battle. They will eventually change the complexion of naval warfare.'

The fog was clearing now, and the foreign observers were called on deck by a Turkish officer. There, a hundred yards off the port beam, rode the Garrett-Harris submersible boat. It looked like a giant steel cigar, and rode so low on the water that the deck was awash and only the small conning tower was clear of the waves. The craft rocked and rolled alarmingly with every swell that washed over it, but there was something very businesslike in the look of the riveted steel-clad deck, and an ominously efficient look to the streamlined, cigar-shaped hull.

Sultan Abd-ul Hamid came onto the flying bridge of the Osmanieh, causing an instant swell of whispering among his foreign guests. It had not been known that he would be present, and the diplomats aboard were trying to decide what his presence signified, so that they could send portentous reports to their governments.

The sultan waved his hand at the two men perched on the wet deck of the submersible, and they popped open a hatch and scrambled below.

'The test commences,' announced the Turkish officer.

A spray of foam churned up from the rear of the Garrett-Harris as the four-bladed screw turned over, and the ship moved forward cleanly through the sea.

Barnett took out his notebook and a pencil and stared pensively at the retreating craft.

The ironclad cigar cut through the water with nary a ripple on either side to mark her passage, he wrote. *Slowly she sank beneath the waves until but one slim tube connected her with the surface, and then that, too, disappeared. Now only the slight phosphorescence of her wake marked her passage beneath the surface of the Bosporus.*

The Turkish officer rang a small bell to get their attention. 'You are about to witness a major happening in naval warfare,' he announced solemnly. 'When, during the American Civil War, the Confederate States' submersible *Hunley* sank the Union *Housatonic* it used a torpedo affixed to a long lance. But the Garrett-Harris boat has solved the problem of launching mobile projectiles from under the water. It is equipped with a device to enable it to fire one of the new design sixteen-inch Whitehead torpedoes without coming to the surface. The torpedo will then unfailingly propel itself to the target. Please observe!'

Barnett took up his pencil:

Now the slim vision tube returns to the surface, almost invisible in the slight swell. The Garrett-Harris moves into position to line up on its unsuspecting target. There is a pause while the target sloop sails into the perfect spot for the launching of the Whitehead torpedo, which carries a dummy warhead but in wartime would be filled with eighty pounds of high explosive. Now, with the sloop perfectly lined up — with twenty-five members of the international press and diplomatic corps watching from along the rail of the royal yacht Osmanieh, and Abd-ul Hamid II, Sultan of the Osmanli Empire, himself watching from the bridge —

A giant plume of water shot up from the hidden submersible. As the sound of a tremendous explosion reached the yacht, the little undersea boat threw itself out of the water bow first and then fell back, breaking in half as it hit. For a second the two halves floated separately, and Barnett thought he saw someone inside the forward half scrambling to get out; then a wave closed over the halves and they disappeared from view.

The underwater shockwave hit the yacht, which bobbed and tossed violently for a few seconds, knocking several people down. Water from the explosion plume fell back, soaking those on deck and adding to the general confusion. Barnett saw some activity at the rear of the yacht, where sailors were trying to heave a line to someone who had been washed overboard by the wave. Finally the man grabbed it, and they hauled him back up.

Nothing was to be seen of the Garrett-Harris submersible or its two operators.

A motor launch took the assembled foreigners back to the quay on the Stamboul side of the Golden Horn. They were assured by an expressionless captain of marine that a statement would be issued later by the proper authority.

Barnett and Lieutenant Sefton walked back to their hotel. 'What do you suppose happened?' Barnett asked.

'It blew up,' Sefton said.

'That much is clear,' Barnett agreed, trying not to look annoyed, 'but how?'

'It could be faulty venting of the gasses from the electrical accumulators,' Sefton said, 'but personally I doubt it.'

'What, then?'

'A deliberate act of subversion by foreign agents.'

Barnett took out his notebook. 'I was

49

hoping you'd say that. Pray, continue.'

'I'm sorry, but I can't possibly be quoted on this,' Lieutenant Sefton said. 'You'll have to get some Turkish authority to say it. But that shouldn't be too difficult.' Sefton seemed nervous and distracted. 'Excuse me, old chap,' he said as they reached the Hotel Ibrahim. 'I must dash off now. See you at dinner, what?'

'Very good,' said Barnett, himself a little distracted by the need for sending an immediate cable to the *World* outlining what had happened. He settled himself at one of the small desks in the writing room to compose a message. The idea was to be as brief as possible. A long cablegram would follow, night rate, detailing the story, but this would serve to put the editors on guard for it and give them time to decide how much space it deserved. Barnett poised his pencil over the paper.

GARRETT HARRIS SUBMERSIBLE DE-STROYED BY EXPLOSION DURING TRIAL ESPIONAGE SUSPECTED MORE FOLLOWS
BARNETT

That was too long. He tried again:

SUBMERSIBLE SPY EXPLODED TESTING MORE

BARNETT

There. That was the sort of economy of expression — and of the paper's money — of which the *World* cable editor approved. It was even briefer than he could do with the Royce Telegraphers' Code. He got a cable blank from the front desk and wrote it up, then called for a pageboy to deliver it to the cable office. He would work on the story after dinner, probably long into the night, and get it into the cable office before the rate change at eight the next morning.

Lieutenant Sefton returned in time to join Barnett for dinner, but his thoughts were clearly elsewhere. Barnett thought that Sefton looked both worried and pleased.

'Do you want to tell me about it?' Barnett asked finally, over the pudding. He described his interpretation of the lieutenant's expression to him.

Sefton thought it over. Then he said, 'Yes, I think I do want to tell you about it. I wish to enlist your aid. Can you be discreet?'

'Half a newsman's job is not telling what he knows,' Barnett said, pulling in his chair. 'Otherwise his news sources will dry up.'

'Will you swear to keep this a secret until I tell you otherwise and only reveal as much as I say you can?'

'Yes — unless I get it from another source,' Barnett said.

'Fair enough,' Sefton agreed. He leaned back on his elbows and smiled. It was the first time Barnett had ever seen him smile. 'I am a spy,' he said.

Barnett was conscious that Sefton was watching his reaction, so he did his best not to react. 'How interesting,' he said. 'Why are you telling me?'

'As I said, to enlist your aid.'

'I thought you people never asked outsiders to assist.'

'There are no hard and fast rules, and right now I desperately need your help. So I ask.'

'You didn't have anything to do with the submersible blowing up this afternoon?' Barnett asked.

'No. On my honor. I would have done my best to prevent it, had I known. The Turks are our allies for the moment. We don't do things like that for practice, you know.'

'What sort of help do you need — and why should you ask me?'

'A man is to deliver some information to me later tonight I do not altogether trust him. I would like you along to watch my back. There should be a good story in it for you.'

'One I can use?'

'Oh, yes. But I shall ask you to suppress some small points, such as my involvement.'

'You fascinate me,' Barnett said. 'I assume it involves the Garrett-Harris.'

'Correct'

'Why can't you get help from one of your own people?'

'There is no one else within a thousand miles.'

'Your embassy?'

'They know nothing of this. They would disapprove. The Foreign Office, under Mr. Gladstone, does not approve of gentlemen reading other people's mail.'

'Who do you work for?'

'The Secret Service.'

'We have one of those.'

'I know.'

'Nobody,' Barnett said, 'has ever accused me of being a gentleman. I'm your man.'

'Good.' Sefton nodded his satisfaction. 'I must go now. There is some other business I have to transact this evening. Can you meet me in my room at twelve o'clock?'

'Midnight it is,' Barnett said cheerfully.

He spent the three hours until midnight writing the first draft of his story.

It was five minutes to twelve by Barnett's pocket Ingersol when he closed his writing portfolio. He splashed some water on his face, put a fresh collar on, and slipped into his jacket. After a moment's consideration he picked up his stick and tucked it under his arm. It had no blade concealed in the shaft, but it was stout ash and would serve to turn a knife.

He walked down the hall to Lieutenant Sefton's room and tapped softly on the door. There was a brief scuffling sound from inside the room, and then silence. Barnett tapped again. The door swung open at his touch this time. The room was dark except for a reading lamp by the bed. In the yellow glow of the lamp Barnett saw Lieutenant Sefton lying supine across the coverlet. His head was off the side of the bed and blood from an open wound at the temple was spurting onto the polished wood floor.

For a moment Barnett was frozen with shock as the scene registered on his brain. Then the meaning of the still-flowing blood came through: Sefton must still be alive! Barnett rushed over to the bed and pulled Lieutenant Sefton's head gently back onto the sheet. He ripped off one of the pillowcases to make a bandage.

There was a faint scraping noise behind him. He turned . . .

4

ODESSA

Politics is a way of life.
  — Plutarch

The room was large. Sunlight from the two floor-length casement windows fell into a tessellated parallelogram across the marble floor, intersecting the great oak desk in the room's center, but leaving the corners in perpetual dusk.

Fifteen feet off the floor, a narrow balcony ran around three of the walls. The ceiling was lost in gloom.

Moriarty sat in a shortened chair in front of the desk and waited. Eventually a man entered through a small door in the far wall. '*Sdravsvoitye, Gospodine* Moriarty,' he said, taking his place behind the great desk. '*Kak vye pojyevoitye?*' He was a slender man, still young, but his face was lined with his years and what he had seen and done. He wore a thin mustache, which looked as though he had put it on for the occasion.

'*Nye panyemi po-Russkie?*' the man said. 'You do not speak Russian? I am sorry. My name is Zyverbine. I am in charge of the Foreign Branch of the *Okhrannoye Otdelenie*, the Imperial Department of State Protection. You come to us highly recommended. Would you tell me something about yourself?'

'No,' Moriarty said. 'You already know everything you need to know about me.'

Zyverbine suppressed a smile. He touched a concealed stud on the desk and the top drawer slid open. He removed a folder from the drawer. 'Moriarty,' he said, reading from the folder, 'James Clovis. Born in 1842 in Bradford-on-Avon, Wiltshire, of Thomas Moriarty, headmaster of the Bradford School, and his wife, nee Anne DeFauve, a woman of French extraction. Has an older brother, James Francis, a booking agent for the Great Central Railway, and a younger brother, James Louis, a major in the

Royal Gloucestershire Foote, a regiment which has the traditional privilege of remaining covered when in the Queen's presence.

'James Clovis Moriarty enrolled at the University of Aberdeen at fourteen, living with an uncle, Paul DeFauve, in that city, Paul DeFauve,' he went on. 'Your mother's brother. Teaches music and tunes pianos. Now living in Bath.'

Moriarty laughed, which seemed to displease Zyverbine. 'That is not accurate?' he demanded.

'Quite accurate,' Moriarty admitted. 'You have impressed me with your ability to cull the public record and make files. Now, could we get on with this?'

Zyverbine closed the file and replaced it in the drawer. 'I am not altogether sure that you are the man for this job,' he said.

Moriarty shrugged. 'That is your affair. You paid my passage to come out here and listen. I came out here, prepared to listen. I am neither impressed with nor intimidated by your stage setting. I suppose it serves some purpose in dealing with the children that usually face you across this desk.'

'Stage setting?' Zyverbine put his hands on the desk, the slender white fingers pressed into the polished wood.

'This room,' Moriarty said, waving his hand. 'The artful gloom. The vast empty space. The shortened legs of this chair to make me lower than you. It is all stage setting. Reading me the file to intimidate me with your wealth of sterile facts. I'm not impressed. If you have a job for me, tell me what it is, and let's get on with it.'

Zyverbine moved his foot, and the door in the far wall popped open. 'Bring another chair,' he directed the brown-suited man who appeared in the doorway. 'You're right,' he told Moriarty. 'We of the *Okhrana* spend much of our time trying to intimidate everyone we deal with, including one another. Ridiculous, is it not?'

Moriarty sat himself in the new chair of normal height. He remained silent until they were once again alone in the room. Then: 'What do you want me to do?'

'Bear with me for another moment,' Zyverbine replied, lacing his fingers under his chin. 'I have a few questions for you. Having paid your way here for this interview, we have the right to ask them.'

A scraping sound came from the balcony, Moriarty did not look up. 'Proceed,' he said.

Zyverbine nodded. 'What do you know of explosives?'

Moriarty considered. 'Of the chemistry,' he said, 'I know what is known. Of the history, I know very little. Of the utilization I have a complete knowledge in some specialized areas.'

'Such as?'

'I can blow open a safe without harming its contents,' Moriarty said. 'But I could not, without further research, destroy a building or a bridge. I am more familiar with the use of nitroglycerine than nitrocellulose or picric acid.'

'Ah!'

'Zyverbine!' a harsh voice called from the balcony above Moriarty. '*Sprosy yevo ob anarkhistakh!*'

'What do you know of politics?' Zyverbine asked, without looking up or acknowledging the voice.

'The subject does not interest me.' Moriarty said.

'Do you not feel that any one form of government is superior to another?'

'I have never seen it demonstrated to be so.'

'Do you believe that sovereigns rule by the will of God or the sufferance of the people?' Zyverbine asked.

Moriarty thought about this for a moment. 'We are of different religions,' he said finally.

'Forget dogma,' Zyverbine said flatly. 'Whether you are Orthodox, Roman, or a Protester is of no importance for the subject of this conversation.'

'I am an atheist,' Moriarty said.

This remark was greeted by an extended silence from Zyverbine and the unseen one above.

'*Ateyst!*' the unseen one said finally, '*Bezbozhnik!*'

Zyverbine looked up. He and the unseen one had a brief, intense conversation. Then there was the sound of a door slamming on the balcony.

Zyverbine transferred his gaze to

Moriarty. 'That is not in my file,' he said.

'That is not my concern.'

'A man is about to enter this room,' Zyverbine said, leaning forward. 'Stand up when he comes in. Bow when I introduce you.'

Moriarty shrugged. 'As you say.'

'I wish I had phrased that question differently,' Zyverbine said, 'although I commend your honesty. It does not make one whit of difference to me whether you believe in one god or twelve. You would seem to be the best man to handle this job, and your private beliefs are not my concern. But the Grand Duke is certain to feel differently.'

'A grand duke,' Moriarty said. 'Of the royal line?'

'Of course. You will respect his incognito.'

'Naturally. And I can appreciate his concern for religion. One who claims to rule by the will of God must dislike even the thought of atheists.'

The man who entered the room was as tall as Moriarty but with massive shoulders and a barrel chest beneath his severely cut gray sack coat. His hair was gray, but his square-cut beard was pitch black and his eyes were light blue.

Zyverbine jumped to his feet. 'Professor Moriarty, may I present Count Brekinsky,' he said.

Moriarty stood and gave a bow that managed not to look too much like a parody. 'Your Grace,' he said.

'Yes, yes,' Brekinsky said. 'Sit down. Professor Moriarty, I am a blunt man. I have a question for you.'

Moriarty remained standing. 'Ask,' he said.

'Why do you do what you do?'

'For money.'

The man calling himself Count Brekinsky held out his left hand toward Zyverbine. 'The file!'

Zyverbine pulled Moriarty's file from the drawer and handed it across the desk.

Brekinsky studied it. 'Our information is that you control the greatest criminal organization in Great Britain.'

'Not so,' Moriarty said. 'There is no such organization. I have some men in my employ; never more than ten or fifteen.

Occasionally the acts they perform are contrary to the laws of the land. The other, ah, criminals that your informant would have me controlling merely consult me from time to time. If my advice is useful, they pay me for it. I in no way control their actions or give them orders. That is not my concern.'

'But they pay you for this advice?' Count Brekinsky asked

Moriarty nodded. 'That is my concern,' he acknowledged. 'I sometimes describe myself as the world's first consulting criminal.' There was a hint of a smile on his face.

'You think of yourself as a criminal?' Brekinsky asked. 'Does not this bother you?'

Moriarty shrugged. 'Labels,' he said, 'do not bother me. The fact that I am, on occasion, in conflict with the laws of my country does bother me, but it is the laws that must give way. I live by my own ethical and moral code, which I do not break.'

'You have a right to live beyond the law?' Zyverbine asked.

'If I do not get caught.'

'And yet you consider yourself — trust-worthy?' Brekinsky asked.

'When I give my word,' Moriarty said, 'it is never broken.'

Brekinsky tapped the file. 'Our records indicate that you are trustworthy,' he said, clearly doubtful.

'One does not have to believe in the God of Abraham and Moses to keep his word,' Moriarty said.

'Ah,' Brekinsky said, grabbing at the phrase. 'Then you do believe in some sort of deity?'

'I am willing to admit of the concept that there is a guiding force in the universe,' Moriarty said, choosing his words carefully.

'I will interpret that as a belief in God,' Brekinsky said. 'I could not return to Moscow and tell the Tsar, my brother, that we have employed someone in this matter who does not believe in God.'

'He is acceptable?' Zyverbine asked.

'Yes,' Brekinsky said. 'He is acceptable. I pray God he is acceptable! You may tell him.'

'Very well, your Grace.'

Brekinsky stuck out his hand, and Moriarty took it. 'You are shaking the hand of a Romanoff,' Brekinsky said. 'We have long memories for good and evil.' He turned and left the room.

Moriarty sat down. 'Well?' be said to Zyverbine.

'Russia and Great Britain have been to war three times this century,' Zyverbine said, 'but each time it has been a minor conflict, of marginal concern to the real interests of either country.'

'Yes,' Moriarty said. 'So?'

'A full-scale war between the two countries would be a horrible thing. The world's greatest land power against the world's greatest sea power. It would go on for years. Millions of people would die. It could turn into a global conflict, pulling the other nations of the world irresistibly into its vortex.'

'Yes.'

'It is possible that one man, in England now, could cause this tragedy. He is a madman. He calls himself Trepoff.'

'Trepoff!' Moriarty said 'I have seen the name.'

'Indeed?' Zyverbine said.

'Yes. I received a communication from someone wishing to speak to me concerning one 'Trepoff,' who said he would call in the evening. It seemed to assume some prior knowledge of the matter that I did not have. Shortly after the note, I received a bomb. The man never called.'

'So!' Zyverbine said, clasping his hands together. 'Was the note signed?'

'The letter 'V' was affixed to the bottom.'

'Vassily!' Zyverbine exclaimed, nodding almost imperceptibly. 'Vassily!'

'Vassily?' Moriarty asked,

'Yes. We did not know that he had tried to seek your aid, although it was from him that we first got your name. He was our best agent in England. He is dead.

'Some weeks after warning us of Trepoff's presence in England, and of his intentions, Vassily Vladimirovitch Gabin, known in London as Ned Bunting, the street artist, died of drinking poisoned soup.'

'I'm sorry,' Moriarty said.

'His widow received the Imperial Order of Merit, Second Class, and a pension of thirty roubles a month,' Zyverbine said.

'Very thoughtful,' Moriarty said.

'I understand Vassily was a very good street artist. They paint directly on the pavement, do they not?'

'They draw on the pavement,' Moriarty told him, 'with colored chalks. A very transitory art form.'

'Zyverbine sighed. 'Transitory,' he said. 'Impermanent The epitaph of a spy.'

'Tell me about this Trepoff,' Moriarty said. 'The man has evidently already tried to kill me once, and was undoubtedly responsible for Bunting's death as well. I'd better at least know what he looks like.'

'I wish I could help you,' Zyverbine said. 'There is no man who knows what Trepoff looks like. He has at times disguised himself as an old man, a youth, and even a woman, and gone undetected each time.'

'I see,' Moriarty said. 'Can you tell me anything about him? How is he going to bring about a war between Russia and Great Britain?'

'I don't know,' Zyverbine said.

'As I somehow suspected,' Moriarty said.

'It is, perhaps, not as stupid as it sounds,' Zyverbine said. 'Tell me, Professor, how much do you know of Russian history?'

'What any educated Englishman would be expected to know,' Moriarty said, 'which is to say, practically nothing.'

'The history of my country over the past thirty years,' Zyverbine said soberly, 'has been written in blood. When Tsar Alexander II ascended the throne in 1855 and liberalized the policies of his father, Nicholas, he was rewarded by increasingly frequent assassination attempts. He dissolved the hated Special Corps of Gendarmerie, and in 1866 the nihilist Karakozoff shot at him in St Petersburg. He reduced the power of the Secret Third Section, and in 1867 the Polish anarchist Berezowski attempted to assassinate him in Paris. He later abolished the Third Section, and the nihilist Solovioff

69

attempted to murder him on April 14, 1879.

'The *Okhrana* attempted to infiltrate these nihilist groups and to protect the life of the Tsar, but although we had fair success, it was too late. On March 13, 1881, as he was passing a cheese factory on Malaya Sadova Street, on the way to visit his former mistress, the Princess Catherine, a white handkerchief was waved by the nihilist Sophya Perovskaya and two bombs went off by his sledge.'

'I remember reading of the assassination,' Moriarty said, 'although not in such detail. The bombs did the job, then?'

'The first bomb killed two of the Tsar's Cossack guards. Alexander dismounted to go to their aid, and the second bomb killed him.'

'That was four years ago,' Moriarty said.

Zyverbine stood up. 'Four years ago, Alexander III became Tsar of all Russians,' he said, crossing himself, 'and we of the *Okhrana* took a blood vow to protect him and his family against anarchists, nihilists, and revolutionaries.

We intend to keep that vow.'

'Very commendable, I'm sure,' Moriarty said. 'Trepoff is, then, a nihilist?'

'On the contrary, Professor Moriarty,' Zyverbine said. 'Trepoff is the leader of the *Belye Krystall* — the White Crystal, a group of right-wing fanatics within the External Agency of the *Okhrana*.'

'You mean that this Trepoff, who murdered your best agent in England — and who, incidentally, tried to kill me — is himself an agent of the *Okhrana*?'

'Unfortunately,' Zyverbine said, sitting back down and staring across the great desk, 'that is exactly what I mean.' He held his hands out, palms up. 'You must understand, the *Okhrana* is unlike any organization you are familiar with. For one thing, the *Okhrana* consists of tens of thousands of people — a population larger than that of many small countries. Most of them work for the Internal Agency.'

'Russians spying on other Russians.'

'That is right,' Zyverbine said. 'Indeed, even the External Agency is mostly comprised of Russians spying on other

Russians. Over the past twenty years many thousands of Russians have left their homeland. Among them were many anarchist intellectuals fleeing the *Okhrana* and taking their plots with them. Many of them — indeed most of them — have settled in London. There are a few in Paris and one small group in Berlin and some old men in Vienna; but most of the younger, more active anarchists are gathered in the East End of London.'

'I know of them,' Moriarty said. 'In fact, it would be hard not to. They are said to create all sorts of problems for the police. They have established their own private clubs, which are the gathering places for Eastern European revolutionaries, nihilists, socialists, and other political activist types that the police believe to be troublemakers.'

'Indeed,' Zyverbine said. 'Tell me, in your country, what is the prevailing opinion of these emigres?'

'I would say it is mixed,' Moriarty replied, thoughtfully. 'Most Englishmen would approve of their ideals, as they conceive them to be: freedom, social justice — high moral goals. And yet they go around shooting grand dukes and bombing trains, and that sort of thing is frowned upon. There is also a strong belief among both the police and the criminal classes that the anarchists support both themselves and their movement by robbing banks, also frowned upon.'

Zyverbine nodded and looked satisfied. 'Just so!' he said.

'This pleases you?' Moriarty asked.

'Of course,' Zyverbine told him. 'We work very hard to create this image. Not, you understand, that it isn't true. We just emphasize here, expose there' — he touched the air with his forefinger at different imaginary points — 'and show these people up for what they are.'

Zyverbine paused before he went on. 'Trepoff, of course, is more difficult to deal with, and the damage he could do to our relations with your great nation is grave indeed. Which is why we have called for you. Will you take the job, and what are your terms?'

'I don't believe,' Moriarty said, 'that

you have, as yet, defined the job.'

'True,' Zyverbine admitted 'We have been talking around it. Well — to the point: we have discovered that Trepoff is determined to so discredit the Russian Émigré community in London that your country will be forced to deport them all. He plans to commit some act that is so heinous, so atrocious, that your English citizens will rise up and force your government into taking such action.'

'Why?' Moriarty asked.

'The anarchist heads in London wag the tails in Moscow and St. Petersburg,' Zyverbine said. 'When the next attempt is made on the life of Alexander III, it will almost certainly come on orders and plans from London.'

'If they are ejected from London,' Moriarty said, 'they will merely settle elsewhere.'

'Our goal is to keep them in motion,' Zyverbine said. 'This makes it harder for them to plan or to raise money, and easier for us to infiltrate their organizations.'

'I see,' Moriarty said.

'But what Trepoff and the *Belye*

Krystall are planning . . . ' Zyverbine shook his head. 'A major outrage is not wise. It is too dangerous, too full of pitfalls. Who can tell what will happen if the plan backfires?'

'If he is caught,' Moriarty said, 'or if the *Okhrana* itself is otherwise implicated . . . '

'At the least, a terrible revulsion of feeling in Great Britain against Russia,' Zyverbine said. 'At the most — war!'

'I understand,' Moriarty said.

'You must also understand that the Tsar, my master, is a great friend of Great Britain and your Queen.'

'Three wars in the past sixty years,' Moriarty reminded Zyverbine.

'His father.' Zyverbine shrugged. 'Besides, they were mere differences of opinion. But they have created a climate where England distrusts Russia. One little mistake — '

'The mistaken blowing up of one battleship,' Moriarty suggested.

'Exactly! And so Trepoff must be stopped.'

'Can't you recall him?' Moriarty asked.

'The *Belye Krystall* is a secret organization within a secret organization,' Zyverbine said. 'They are fanatical in their beliefs and actions. Even the Tsar himself could not order Trepoff to stop. He believes that he acts for the greater good of the state and expects no reward beyond the successful completion of his task. In fact, he would gladly sacrifice his life to accomplish his objective. Such men are infinitely dangerous.'

'Have you considered informing Scotland Yard or the British Secret Service?'

'And tell them what?' Zyverbine demanded. 'That a representative of the Russian Secret Police is planning to commit a violent crime against an unknown objective and we'd be obliged if they stopped him? First of all, it would make us look like fools; and second of all if they didn't catch him, they would always suspect that we had planned it that way. No. This way, if he isn't stopped, there is always the chance that he'll get away with it — and we'll have to settle for that.'

Moriarty rubbed his slender hands

together. 'I must confess that I find the problem an intriguing one,' he said. 'You want me to discover one man, whom you cannot describe, out of the population of Great Britain, before he commits an unknown crime of magnificent proportions.' He thought for a minute. 'I suppose he speaks fluent English?'

'Like a native.'

'Good, good,' Moriarty said. 'An intriguing problem, indeed. You must tell me what is known of this man and his methods. I assume something is known.'

'We have an extensive dossier on Trepoff and the *Belye Krystall*,' Zyverbine said. 'Of course, much of it is guesswork, rumor, unconfirmed reports, gross exaggeration, and deliberately misleading facts planted by sympathizers.'

'Better and better,' Moriarty said. 'This case will give free rein to the processes of logic — the one touchstone by which one can infallibly separate truth from fiction. I think I can promise you that, given sufficient time before he attempts this outrage — and I do not need much time — Trepoff will be apprehended.'

'Then you will work for us?' Zyverbine asked.

'I shall.'

'I will get you the dossier,' Zyverbine rose from his desk.

Moriarty held up his hand. 'First,' he said, 'there is the matter of my fee.'

5

A BARGAIN

Have the courage to live.
Anyone can die.
— *Robert Cody*

The mud-faced warder peered in through the small, barred window in the cell door. 'Is here,' he announced, positively.

'Who's here?' Barnett asked, squinting into the bright square of light framing the warder's face. 'The American minister? Did the *World*'s lawyer show up?'

'Is here,' the warder repeated. Then he stomped away down the corridor.

It seemed hours before he returned, followed by a tall man in a black frock-coat. The warder worked the heavy bolt on the door and pulled it outward on its ancient hinges. 'Go in,' he said. 'I wait.'

Barnett's eyes took a moment to adjust

to the light from the gas lamps in the corridor that now flooded into his unlit cell. 'Professor Moriarty!' he exclaimed, recognizing his tall visitor. 'What are you doing here?'

'I have come to talk with you.' He looked about. 'There is no chair?'

'Here,' Barnett said, moving to the far end of his wooden cot. 'Sit here, please.'

'Very well,' Moriarty said, sitting on the cot next to Barnett.

'How did you get here?' Barnett demanded.

'I bribed the governor of the prison,' Moriarty said. 'It seems to be the way they do things here.'

'Yes, but I mean why?' Barnett asked. 'That is, I'm delighted to see you. If you've come to help me, I'm over-whelmed.'

'I would say that I've come to help you. Tell me what happened. How did you end up in here?'

Barnett nodded and thought for a moment of how to put the last few weeks into words. 'Lieutenant Sefton — the gentleman who came to your aid with me

— was murdered in his room the evening after the submersible was destroyed. He was a British agent — a spy. He evidently had some information about the destruction of the Garrett-Harris. He asked me to aid him and I agreed. I was to meet him in his room at midnight, and we would proceed to some undisclosed destination. I had the impression that it would be wise if I came prepared for trouble, so I brought my walking stick.

'When I arrived at the door to Sefton's room, it must have been almost midnight. I heard a scuffling sound from within. The door opened when I pushed at it, and I entered. Sefton was lying across the bed with a great wound in his skull. The window was wide open. There was nobody else in the room — or so I thought at the time.

'I rushed to the bed to aid Sefton, who was still alive, but barely. Suddenly someone struck me from behind, and I fell, unconscious, to the floor.'

'You saw no one?'

'I neither saw nor heard anyone. Were it not for the evidence of the bump on the

81

back of my head, I'd have no reason to believe that there was anyone else in that room.'

'And then?'

'When I came around — it couldn't have been more than a few minutes later — the room was full of men. The night manager, the floor man, and several guests were all milling about, waiting for the police to arrive. I immediately tried to go to Lieutenant Sefton's aid. He was so far gone now that I couldn't tell whether he was still breathing, but nothing had been done to staunch the flow of blood from his head wound.' Barnett lowered his head into his palm and began sobbing softly, this one dreadful memory overcoming his already fragile composure.

'Yes,' Moriarty prompted. 'And?'

'And they wouldn't let me!' Barnett said without looking up. 'Those moronic — those incredible idiots wouldn't let me touch him. They thought that I'd struck him, you see. So they held me back when I attempted to go to him, and by the time a doctor arrived, he had bled to death!'

'How do you *know* Lieutenant Sefton

was a spy?' Moriarty asked.

'He told me so.'

'Ah. Continue.'

'When the police arrived they searched me. They found my walking stick on the floor, with blood on the ferrule, and they found several papers in my jacket pocket that appeared to be sections of the plans for the valving mechanism of the Garrett-Harris submersible.'

'You, of course, have no idea how they got there.'

'They weren't there when I left my room,' Barnett insisted. 'Whoever struck me on the head must have shoved the papers into my pocket; although why anyone would want to do such a thing is beyond me.'

'The motives of men,' Moriarty said, 'are often quite beyond rational explanation. Although, in this case, the reason seems quite clear.'

'Not to me,' Barnett said. 'I've been beating my brains trying to figure it out for these past weeks.'

'A doubtful way to induce profitable ratiocination,' Moriarty commented dryly. 'However, continue. You were accused of this crime?'

'This crime?' Barnett laughed hoarsely. 'I was accused of the crime of murdering Lieutenant Sefton *and* of the crime of being a spy. For good measure, what they'd also like to believe is that I blew up their precious submersible. That's what they've been trying to get me to admit when they question me, hour after hour, until I think I'm going mad.'

'There was a trial?' Moriarty asked.

'You could call it that,' Barnett said. 'I wanted to wait until I could get legal help, but they weren't buying that. Three days after the murder I stood before a magistrate. I asked for the American minister to aid in my defense. An American counsel came as a spectator; the minister was otherwise engaged. I asked the *World* — my paper — to get me a lawyer. He hasn't shown up yet. Meanwhile, I was tried and convicted in something like three hours, and I've been here ever since.'

'The trouble is, you see, that they also believe you to be guilty.'

'You mean the American minister and my paper? How can they?'

'Why not? You were found alone in the room with Sefton. There were signs of a struggle. Obviously you fought over the plans, you struck him with your stick, and then he knocked you unconscious before falling back in a swoon on the bed. After all, the plans were in your pocket.'

'But the open window?'

'It was inspected by the police. Nobody leaped to the ground — or at least, there were no marks.'

'But what would I want with the plans?'

Moriarty shrugged. 'What do spies ever want with the plans, or the papers, or the treaties, or whatever they steal? In any case, that's of no concern to the police.'

'So you think my people are not going to help me?' Barnett asked.

'They are going to forget about you as rapidly as is decently possible.'

'But you believe me innocent?' Barnett asked. 'And you are willing to help me?' He shook his head and stared at the wall. 'How can anyone help me?'

'I know you to be innocent, as it happens,' Moriarty said. 'And I can help you.'

'How?' Barnett asked.

'First you must realize that I am your last hope,' Moriarty said. 'And then you must agree to my terms.'

'What is it that you want? No — first tell me how you know me to be innocent.'

'As you may remember, when you saw me last I told you I was going to Odessa.'

'Yes.'

'While there I had access to some secret files of the Russian government — never mind how. What I read in the files, combined with some knowledge of my own, led me to the conclusion that you were not guilty of the murder of Lieutenant Sefton, the theft of the plans, or the destruction of the Garrett-Harris submersible.'

'But then — you heard of all this in Odessa?'

'No, I heard of it quite by accident when I arrived back in Constantinople. But the chain was immediately clear to me.'

'I see,' Barnett said. 'Well, then, couldn't you take this information to the proper authorities and convince them of my innocence?'

'You misunderstand,' Moriarty said. 'I cannot get your conviction overturned by appealing to any authority. My conclusion is based on an assortment of random facts, connected only by my inference. No authority is going to release a convicted felon because of a chain of inference concocted by a defrocked professor of mathematics. Besides, you must understand that the Osmanli authorities have a strong vested interest in seeing that you remain guilty of these crimes: they have already so informed Sultan Abd-ul Hamid, and one does not easily confess an error to the Shah of Shahs.'

'Well then,' Barnett said, 'for my own piece of mind, tell me: What is your evidence?'

Moriarty took a large handkerchief from an inner pocket and fastidiously wiped his hands. 'Before I left London,' he said, 'someone tried to kill me. Then

again, when I arrived here in Constantinople, as you know, an attempt was
made.'

Barnett nodded. 'I thought you didn't
know why you were attacked.'

'Not at the time,' Moriarty said. 'But
when I arrived in Odessa I discovered
that the Russian principal I had come to
see wished to hire me to apprehend a
dangerous man who is fanatically devoted
to the Russian cause.'

'The Russians want to hire you to catch
someone devoted to their own cause?'
Barnett asked.

'I will explain at some future time — if
ever,' Moriarty said. 'For the moment,
accept the fact.'

'Go on,' Barnett said.

'The Russian agent was aware that an
attempt had been made to solicit my aid
before I left London,' Moriarty said. 'It
clearly was he who tried to kill me, both
in London and here.'

'Okay,' Barnett said.

'Therefore, he followed me here. He
did not follow me to Odessa, since I was
taken aboard an Imperial steam-frigate

for the trip there and back. Therefore, he was in Constantinople when the submersible exploded. Therefore, he was in Constantinople when Lieutenant Sefton was murdered and you were blamed.'

'You have seen him?' Barnett asked.

'I have no idea who he is or what he looks like. It may not have been the subject himself, but one of his henchmen. I am assured that he has henchmen.'

'But why would this mysterious man have done this thing to me?' Barnett demanded.

'Ah, he did not do this to you,' Moriarty said. 'He did this to the Ottoman Empire, the traditional enemy of Russia for these past hundred years. You merely happened along at the opportune moment.'

'To be charged with murder.'

'Yes.'

'You mean that on the spur of the moment, without preparation, he was able to arrange for the destruction of the Garrett-Harris submersible and the theft of the plans?'

'Why not? I could have done the same.'

Moriarty refolded his handkerchief and replaced it in his pocket. 'I must assume that Lieutenant Sefton somehow became aware of this agent's activities, and that is why Sefton was killed. I assure you that the casual murder of one man means no more to our Russian friend than the swatting of a fly.

'The sections of the plans were thrust into your pocket to give the authorities a convenient scapegoat, so they would look no further for the culprit. And this was successful. I imagine he took those plans he thought would be useful and left you only with those he didn't need.' Moriarty smacked his hands together. 'All this executed, as you say, on the spur of the moment. The man is capable, courageous, and cunning. Truly a fit antagonist.'

'I'm convinced,' Barnett said. 'So how do you plan to get me out of here, and what do you want from me in return?'

'I plan to arrange for your escape,' Moriarty said, 'and quickly, before the authorities tire of attempting to obtain from you information which you do not

90

possess. For on that day you will die.'

Barnett shuddered. 'Cheerful,' he said.

'What I want from you,' Moriarty told him, 'is two years of your life. I would like to employ you. I shall endeavor to remove you from this place, and in return you will work for me for two years.'

'Why?'

'You are good at your profession, and I have use for you.'

'And after the two years?'

'After that, your destiny is once again your own.'

'I accept!'

'Good!' Moriarty stood up and looked around the cell. 'Bear up and be patient! You shall not be here much longer.' He shook hands with Barnett and then strode out of the cell.

The stocky warder slammed the door behind him, and Barnett heard the heavy bolt sliding into place.

★ ★ ★

It was scant minutes after dawn, and the sun was still pushing its way up out of the

91

Black Sea as the *Mu'adhdhin* was preparing to call the faithful to Friday morning prayer. Five brown-clad monks came down the Street of Venyami the Good and presented themselves at the East Gate of the ancient Prison of Mustafa II. 'We have come to shrive such of the prisoners as are of the Christian faith,' the spokesman for the monks told the gate guard in heavily Greek-accented Turkish. 'It is Shrove Friday.'

The guard smiled, a wide smile that showed both his teeth. 'I would be glad to be of assistance,' he said, giving a palms-up shrug, 'but I have not the authority.'

One of the monks produced a thick parchment, folded and creased many times, and handed it to the spokesman, who passed it through the bars to the guard. 'Within here is the authority,' he said.

The guard unfolded the parchment, holding it open with both hands, and examined the cursive writing within, first with one eye and then with the other. 'I'll have to show this to the Captain of the Guard,' he decided finally. 'I cannot make heads nor tails from it.'

'But certainly,' the talkative monk agreed.

The guard thrust the parchment out through the bars. 'Come back at eight,' he said. 'The captain makes his rounds at eight.'

'Too bad,' the monk said, shaking his head slowly. 'We cannot wait. Tradition demands that we begin now, so we shall have to go to another prison.'

'Too bad, indeed,' the guard agreed, smiling his tooth-exhibiting smile.

'We shall have to pay to someone else the traditional gatekeeper's fee.' The monk took a small ornate purse from his robes and shook it so the coins within jingled.

'The gatekeeper's fee?'

'The traditional gatekeeper's fee,' the monk agreed. 'Legend has it that Simon, our patron saint, knocked three times and was not admitted, and then he paid the gatekeeper and he was admitted. This was the gatekeeper's fee.'

'How much is this traditional gatekeeper's fee?'

'Two gold medjidié.'

'Hold on! Wait right here. Perhaps I can . . . The captain might be . . . You just wait right here. I won't be long. Don't go away.' The guard closed the wooden door behind the ancient iron bars and disappeared within.

The talkative monk turned to his four silent, brown-cowled friends. 'Ah,' he said, 'the power of the almighty medjidié.' Three of them nodded under their deep cowls, the fourth remained still and silent.

It was no more than a minute before the guard returned, bringing with him a short, surly man with a wide, bristling mustache who was busily buttoning the last few buttons on his gold-striped dark blue trousers. 'Now, now,' the short man said, adjusting his wide gold sash, 'who are you people? What's the story I hear? Where is this document? Where are these supposed gold medjidié? You're not trying to bribe an officer in the performance of his duty, now, are you?'

'You are the Official of the prison?' the

monk asked, respectfully.

'I am the Captain of the Guard,' the captain said.

'We are monks of the Simonite order,' the monk told him. 'We celebrate a sixteen-hundred-year-old ceremony: the Shriving of the Prisoners. Every year on Shrove Friday we go to a different prison and shrive those prisoners who are Christian, or those of other faiths who wish to be shriven. We ask three times to be admitted, and then pay the traditional gatekeeper's fee. We enter and shrive the prisoners. Then we pay the Official of the Prison one of the gold medjidié for each prisoner we have shriven. Please, who is the Official of the Prison?'

The Captain of the Guard stroked his mustache. 'I am,' he announced finally. 'You say you have an authority?'

The monk handed the parchment to the captain, who spread it open and studied it. 'This is an authority to visit prisons in the service of your religious practice?' the captain asked.

'That is correct.'

'It is signed by Sultan Bayezid II?'

'Correct.'

'Four hundred years ago?'

'Just a trifle more than that.'

'This is still good?'

'It has never been rescinded.'

'You have, perhaps, something more recent?' the captain pleaded, seeing the promised gold dissolving before he had even a chance to taste it. 'I cannot permit you to enter the Prison of Mustafa II on a four-hundred-year-old authority.'

'Well, then,' the monk said, reaching doubtfully into his robes, 'there is this.' He handed through the bars an official-looking document with etched red borders, stamped, sealed, notarized, embossed, impressed, and triply signed.

'Why, this is signed by the Grand Vizier, the Commander of Prisoners, and the Djerrah Pasha!' the Captain of the Guard said. 'There'll be no trouble about your shriving the prisoners.'

'Ah, well,' the monk said, 'if you prefer these recent signatures to that of a four-hundred-year-old sultan, so be it.'

The captain shook his head. 'You religious people,' he said tolerantly. 'Wait,

I will get four guards to accompany you. We cannot afford any trouble. Some of these men are desperate.'

'Very good of you,' the monk said.

The captain called forth four guards and then opened the gate. 'Enter,' he said.

'May we be admitted?' the monk asked.

'Didn't I just tell you to enter?' the captain said.

'May we be admitted?' the monk asked.

'What's the matter, don't you understand Turkish?' the captain said. 'Now, look — '

'May we be admitted?' the monk asked again.

A great light dawned on the gate guard. 'Only if you pay the fee,' he said, winking at the captain.

'Here you are,' the monk said; 'two gold medjidié.'

'Enter,' the gate guard said.

'Ah!' the captain said.

The five monks entered the prison in a close group, with two guards in front of them and two behind. The captain led the group across the courtyard and into the corridors that housed the prisoners. Then he fell behind and watched as the group went from cell door to cell door calling in Turkish and Greek, 'Are you Christian? Do you wish to be cleansed of your sins?' Occasionally the call was made in French and English, and if the captain thought that strange he said nothing. Every time a prisoner responded and the cell door was opened, he mentally added one more gold medjidié to the growing count.

Because the prisoners were bored and any activity was a welcome novelty, many of them conceived a sudden desire to be cleansed of their sins. The monks slowly worked their way down the corridor, stopping at door after door, shriving the damned. Devout Musselmen and Zoroastrians did not admit them, neither did the paranoid nor the catatonic, but most of the prisoners welcomed the monks and the diversion they represented

Two or three of the monks would enter the cell when bidden by the prisoner and close the door behind them. The other monks would kneel outside the cell door and pray for the prisoner's soul. The monks spent between three and ten minutes inside each cell they entered.

For the first hour the guards kept a close watch on the monks, one of them going into each cell along with the shrivers; but as time passed and nothing remarkable happened, they relaxed their vigilance and grew bored, squatting together to talk when the monks entered a cell.

It was well along in the third hour before the Simonites reached Benjamin Barnett's cell. 'Do you want to be cleansed of your sins?' came the call from the corridor.

Barnett, who had been dozing, woke with a start as the ghostly voice boomed through the cell: 'Do you want to be cleansed of your sins?' this time in French. He looked around wildly before realizing that the voice came from someone with his mouth close up against the cell door.

'What do you want?' Barnett called.

There was a rattling and thumping, and the cell door opened to admit three men in brown robes who seemed to glide into the room joined at the shoulders. Barnett had a glimpse of another two kneeling in front of the cell before the door swung closed.

'Quick!' the nearest monk whispered in French. 'Remove your garments!'

'What?'

'The Professor Moriarty sent us. Remove quickly your garments. We are to exit you from this place.'

Without further discussion Barnett stripped off the few gray rags that the prison authorities had given him. 'What are you going to do?' he asked. 'I am chained to the wall.'

'We have prepared ourselves for that eventuality,' the monk told him. 'However, we must hasten ourselves.'

The three monks separated from each other, and an amazing thing happened; the monk in the middle silently folded up and collapsed until there was nothing left of him except a bundle of brown clothes on the floor.

Barnett gasped and took an involuntary step backward. He didn't know what he had expected to happen, but it surely wasn't this.

'Hush!' the monk on his left whispered sharply, putting his forefinger to his lips.

'Mon Dieu, but I am sorry!' the other monk said. 'I should have paused to realize how startling that would appear if unwarned.'

'What happened to him?' Barnett demanded, pointing to the empty robes.

'Ah, but you see there was no 'him,'' the monk said. 'He was merely simulated by wires in the robes artfully manipulated by my comrade here and myself. Now he and you are about to merge.'

'No time for talk,' the left-hand monk said, whipping a pocket razor out from his robes and twisting it open. 'To work!'

The other monk took two small phials from inside his robes and handed one of them to Barnett. 'This is a vegetable oil,' he said. 'Apply it to all parts of your beard and rub it in. This will facilitate the shaving of your face.'

Barnett carefully and thoroughly anointed his three weeks of stubble with the oil while the monk stropped the razor on a small piece of leather sewn to his sleeve. Then he tested the blade on the back of his hand, nodded approval, and approached Barnett. 'Move not your face,' he warned.

Barnett held his face motionless while the monk artfully applied the razor. The other monk crouched on the floor and unstoppered his second phial. 'Hold still your feet,' he said.

'What are you doing?' Barnett demanded, unable to look down.

'Applying oil of vitriol to the link connecting your foot to this chain,' the monk told him. 'It will take a few minutes. Hold still!'

When the one had finished shaving Barnett he took a rag and spread grease over Barnett's face. 'Darken your skin,' he said. 'Remove prison whiteness.'

Two minutes later, Barnett, in brown robes, his face deeply concealed by the cowl, his feet in worn monk's sandals thoughtfully provided by his escorts, walked out of his cell. For another ten minutes, the group continued through the prison, chanting and praying and shriving. Then, the circle completed, they arrived back at the East Gate and paid the head tax to the Captain of the Guard, carefully counting out each gold medjidié into the palm of his hand.

'In Simon's name we bless you,' the speaking-monk said.

'Come back soon,' the guard captain replied, transferring the gold to a leather purse.

'Next Shrove Friday,' the monk said. 'You have my word.'

6

64 RUSSELL SQUARE

To trust is good;
not to trust is better.
　　　— Verdi

Barnett arrived at 64 Russell Square
rolled inside a 600-year-old Kharvan rug.
He was unrolled in the butler's pantry by
the two men who had brought him, working under the direction of a tall woman in
a severe black dress. 'Very good,' she told
the men as Barnett unfolded from the
rug. 'Now take it into the front parlor.
Mr. Maws will tell you what to do with it.'

Barnett stood up and did a couple of
knee-bends to get the blood circulating in
his legs again. 'Hello,' he said.

The woman extended a slender hand.
'I am Mrs. H,' she said. 'Professor
Moriarty's housekeeper. You are Mr.

Benjamin Barnett.'

'That's right,' Barnett said, taking the hand.

'You'll be wanting a bath. Come with me.' She led him up two flights of stairs. 'This will be your room,' she said, opening a door in the hall to the left of the landing. 'The bath is across the way. Fresh linens on the bed and towels on the washstand. There's hot water. I'll have a bath drawn for you while you get out of those garments. Leave them outside the door and I'll see that they're disposed of.'

Barnett looked down at the filthy laborer's garb the monks had supplied him with before he left Constantinople. It had not gained anything in cleanliness in the weeks he had been crossing Europe. 'But Mrs. H,' he said, 'I have nothing else to wear.'

'Your clothing,' she told him, 'is in that wardrobe and in this chest of drawers.'

Barnett pulled open the top drawer of the chest. Inside were a row of starched white shirts. A brief inspection convinced him that they were his own, from his Paris flat. 'How did these get here?' he demanded.

'Express,' she said. 'I'll see to your bath.' And with a satisfied nod, she turned and left.

An hour later, scrubbed, clean-shaven, and immaculately dressed for the first time in over a month, Barnett was taken by Mrs. H to see Professor Moriarty. 'He's in his basement laboratory,' she told him, leading the way. 'We do not disturb him there unless it is important, but I have instructions to bring you in as soon as you're presentable,' Mrs. H told him,

After two turns in the narrow stairs they crossed a door that led onto a landing overlooking a large, cement-floored basement room, which had been turned into a modern laboratory. Low wooden tables were spread in a circle about the room, leaving the central area bare. On one table, a series of retorts and gathering-tubes were clamped in place over small Bunsen lamps. On another, a complex arrangement of lenses and mirrors was fastened to a revolvable wooden stand ready to twist into motion

106

at the turn of a crank. The cabinets along the walls were furnished with every conceivable sort of chemical and physical apparatus that Barnett was familiar with, and many that he was not.

After a while Moriarty looked up from his writing. Then he stoppered the inkwell and put down the pen. 'You look a good deal better than the last time I saw you,' he told Barnett. 'Welcome to London and my household. I trust you had an acceptable trip.'

'Not very,' Barnett said, going down the last few steps and crossing the room to Moriarty's desk. 'I was smuggled across the Bohemian border in a caravan of wagons loaded with fresh-clipped wool being taken to be combed and washed. The smell was indescribable.'

'It kept away the border guards,' Moriarty said.

'I was carted across Rumelia with four other people in a pox-wagon,' Barnett said.

'Nobody tried to stop you,' Moriarty commented.

'From Bosnia through Austria we

became a traveling team of acrobats. I couldn't tumble, so I caught the others and held them up. My shoulders and my legs still ache.'

'Nobody ever looks at the low man,' Moriarty said.

'In Italy we finally caught the train,' Barnett said. 'It was a fourth-class local. Have you ever traveled fourth class from Trieste to Milan?'

'You would have attracted attention in first class with your clothing,' Moriarty said. 'And you would have attracted more attention trying to buy other clothing.'

'In Milan we became part of a circus and spent a couple of weeks reaching Paris. I cleaned the animal cages in the menagerie.'

'It sounds like an enriching experience,' Moriarty said.

'And they wouldn't let me go to my apartment in Paris.'

'Does it strike you as brilliant for an escaped felon, wanted for murder, to stroll over to his apartment to collect his clothes?' Moriarty took a small notebook from his pocket and consulted its pages.

'In Rumelia you picked a fight with the wagon driver,' he said, 'a fact that I find incomprehensible, since you had no language in common. On the train outside of Milan a farm woman accused you of stealing a chicken, and you argued with her until the conductor was called.'

'I didn't steal her chicken,' Barnett said. 'It squeezed through the wicker cage and flapped its way out of the carriage. It's a wonder she didn't lose the other six.'

'And as I pointed out, in Paris you had to be restrained from going to your apartment to get a change of clothes.'

'You should have told me that you were having all my things brought here,' Barnett said. 'How did you manage to get by the concierge?'

'I had a letter from you,' Moriarty said dryly, 'authorizing my agent to remove your belongings. You paid her an extra month's rent in lieu of notice.'

'I did?' Barnett said. 'I see.' He looked around for a chair. 'May I sit?'

'Of course,' Moriarty said. 'There is a stool under that table. Pull it over.'

Barnett retrieved the long-legged work stool that was lying on its side, set it up, and straddled it a few feet from Moriarty's desk. 'You were having me watched as I crossed Europe,' he said.

'The three who accompanied you are in my employ, as you should have surmised,' Moriarty said. 'They conceived it to be part of their function to send me a report on your behavior. Actually, there are many favorable points in the report. I would like to have seen the way you smiled and mumbled inanely at that Austrian border guard until he gave up and let you through. And you acquitted yourself quite well in dealing with the conductor on that Italian train, although you should have arranged things so that he was never called.'

'That woman called me a thief,' Barnett protested.

'There is no magic in epithets,' Moriarty said. 'You don't have to ward off their effects by disputing them.'

'I suppose you're right,' Barnett said, grudgingly.

Moriarty returned the notebook to his

pocket. 'I am satisfied that, if induced to exercise discretion, you would be a competent and useful assistant to me. Are you ready to discuss the terms of your employment?'

'I'd like to know what the job is,' Barnett said. 'I have gathered over the past few weeks that you are no ordinary professor. What is this consulting business of yours?'

'First we must have an understanding. All else is open to discussion, save this one thing only: you must never divulge anything that you learn while in my employ — not about me, my associates, my activities, my comings and goings, my possessions, my household, nor indeed anything at all related to your employment. This ban does not terminate when and if your employment terminates, but is to continue throughout the remainder of your life. And beyond.'

'Beyond?'

'Words outlive people. You must not keep a diary or write an autobiography or memoir that in any way touches upon the time you spend with my organization.'

'That's quite a ban,' Barnett said.

'Can you keep it?'

'I reckon so.'

'Regardless of whether you agree or disagree with any of my activities, whether you find them in opposition to your religion or ethics or even morally repugnant to you?'

Barnett gave a low whistle. 'That is quite a ban!' he said.

'Can you keep it? Can you give me your unqualified word?'

'Well, about these, ah, morally repugnant acts — if I find any of your activities to be offensive to me, am I obliged to engage in them myself?'

'Certainly not, by no means. It would not be to my interest to employ a man for a job he finds offensive.'

'Well, with that understanding I guess I can keep my mouth shut about your doings. And I confess that with this preamble you've got me mighty curious as to just what these doings might be.'

Professor Moriarty slipped a pair of pince-nez glasses onto his nose and peered through them at Barnett. 'You swear to keep your silence?' he asked.

'Cross my heart, Professor,' Barnett smiled broadly..

'There is less humor in this than you think,' Moriarty said, 'for I shall hold you to that oath. So think on it seriously and give me a serious answer.'

Barnett raised his hand. 'You have my word, Professor Moriarty, that I shall never speak of your affairs to anyone. I swear this on the sacred memory of my mother.'

'That completely satisfies me. As you become privy to my affairs, you will see why I require such an affirmation from all my associates. And you will also see how seriously I regard it.' He took a pocket-watch from his waistcoat pocket and snapped it open. 'We shall regard your employment as commencing now,' he said. 'It is five past two in the afternoon of Tuesday, May fifth, 1885.'

'Is it?' Barnett asked. 'I had quite lost track of the days.'

'On the hour of two p.m. on May fourth, 1887 — which will be, I believe, a Wednesday — you are quits with me.

Until then you are in my employ at a salary of — let me see — how much were your New York City employers paying you?'

'Ten dollars a week,' Barnett said.

'I shall make it five pounds a week,' Moriarty said, 'if that is satisfactory.'

'Satisfactory?' Barnett laughed. 'Why, that's well over twice as much. Very satisfactory!'

'And then, of course, there's your room,' Moriarty said. 'Since it is at my request that you'll be living in this house, I can't very well charge you rent. So you may consider your room and such meals as you eat here as complimentary. And incidentally, I think you'll find Mrs. Randall a more than adequate cook.'

'Then you want me to keep that room?'

'Is it satisfactory?' Moriarty inquired. 'If so, I would have you keep it.'

'Exactly what is my position to be in your organization?' Barnett asked. 'And exactly what sort of organization do you have?'

'I solve problems,' Moriarty told him. 'I am a consultant, taking on my clients' problems for a fee. Some of them are purely cerebral, and I solve those by sitting in my study, or working in my laboratory, or taking a long walk through London; I find walking very stimulating to the mental processes. But other problems require deductive or inductive reasoning from facts, from evidence; and that evidence must be assembled. And each glittering fact must be tested, like a gold sovereign, to see if it rings true.'

'I see,' Barnett said.

Moriarty smiled, 'By which you mean you do not see. But you soon will.' He removed his pince-nez glasses, cleaned them with a piece of flannel from his desk, and then replaced them firmly on his nose. 'Your hours are to be those required to accomplish your assignment, when you have one,' he continued. 'In recompense, when you have no assignment you are free to do as you like whatever the time of day. We have not allowed the concept of 'office hours' to infiltrate our little domain.'

'That's agreeable,' Barnett said. 'I much prefer that scheme, as a matter of fact. Do you have anything for me now?'

'Anything for you . . . ' Moriarty rubbed his chin with his left hand. 'I think you'd better use the first few days to get acquainted with my household and my organization. If you need anything, ask Mrs. H, the housekeeper, or Mr. Maws, the butler. I shall arrange to have someone show you around the rest of the organization and introduce you to those whom you should know or who should know you.'

'Very good, Professor. And I haven't as yet had a chance to thank you for rescuing me from that Turkish jail. You saved my life!'

'I think we shall both benefit from your, ah, timely release,' Moriarty said. He offered Barnett his hand, which was firmly taken. 'Welcome to my employ, Mr. Barnett.' With that, Moriarty dismissed Barnett and returned to his scientific note taking.

Barnett returned to the ground floor and hunted up Mrs. H, who was in a small room off the pantry. 'You're in my office, Mr. Barnett,' she told him as he looked curiously around the room. 'What may I do for you?'

'I was wondering if it was too late to get some lunch,' he asked her. 'I spent the morning wrapped up in a rug.'

'Go into the dining room, Mr. Barnett,' she said. 'I shall see that you are served.'

'Thank you, Mrs. H,' he told her. 'I appreciate it.'

'Humpf,' she said.

Barnett retreated to the dining room, where he was shortly served a large omelet with jam, by a somber-looking maid-of-all-work who curtsied before scurrying out of the room. He found the omelet excellent, and as he sat eating in comfort for the first time in over a month, he fell to musing over his recent past and his probable future.

Working for Professor Moriarty for the next two years promised to be quite interesting. Barnett still didn't have any clear idea of what Moriarty did, or what his role would be, but he had formed the notion that it wasn't quite proper and might be quite exciting. And Barnett, at just twenty-eight, was of the opinion that a bit of impropriety and a dash of adventure were the salt and leavening that made the loaf of life worth eating.

When Barnett had finished his omelet and was beginning to wonder what to do next, the hall door opened and a small, almost tiny man wearing a natty fawn-colored suit and yellow spats and carrying a spotless brown bowler tucked under his left arm glided into the room. 'Afternoon, afternoon,' he said. 'Permit me to introduce myself. The name is Tolliver; 'Mummer' Tolliver, they calls me, or just 'the Mummer.''

'I'm Benjamin Barnett,' Barnett said.

''Course you are,' Tolliver said. 'And welcome to our little ménage, I says. The professor, he asked me to show you around, seeing as how you're to be a fellow resident.'

'Oh,' Barnett said. 'You live here, then?'

'Up in the attic. I've got my little room up there. Closer to the sky, you know.' He pulled out one of the chairs and reversed it, then straddled the seat and leant his chin on the top bar of the straight back. 'First off, I should tell you who else shares this impressive abode with us. There's the professor himself, of course; and Mr. Maws, the butler; and Mrs. H, the housekeeper; and Mrs. Randall, the cook; and Old Potts.'

'Old Potts?'

'Right. He has a room in the basement, he has. Spends his days blowing glass and suchlike for the professor's scientifical experiments.'

'He's really into this science stuff, then?' Barnett asked.

'	'Course he is. He's a genius, the professor is. A scien-bleeding-tifical genius. He's always writing things and figuring things, you know. And he studies little things that you can only see under a microscope, and great tremendous things like the distance from here to the Moon or the Sun. A couple of years ago, when we was out at his cottage on Crimpton Moor, he had a couple of us measure off five miles professional-like with instruments so he could set up some sort of apparatus and determine the proper distance of the Moon and Mars and some stars what he thought might be closer than the others.

'And then he gets into the technical stuff, all about waving lights, even though there isn't any ether, and nobody alive has any idea of what he's talking about, but it for certain does make you feel important just to listen to him.'

'But he doesn't do that all the time,' Barnett said. 'I mean, this other business takes up most of his time, and the science is just a hobby. Is that right?'

'I'd say it was the other way 'round,' the Mummer said. ''Course he does spend most of his time on these here activities what make the money and employ the services of the likes of you and me. But this is the hobby. The experiments is really his life. He's told me many a time that if he's ever to be remembered for his time on this earth, it will be for the science stuff and his theories.'

'What about the rest of the household?'

'I'll bite,' the Mummer said. 'What about it?'

'Mrs. H, the housekeeper, for example. What's her real name?'

'You'd best ask her that.'

'I have.'

'You're a braver man than me, then.'

'What about Mr. Maws?' Barnett said. 'Why is he called 'Mr.'? I've always understood that butlers were called simply by their last name.'

'That is correct, so they are. Except, 'course, below stairs, so to speak. The other servants in a household always call the butler 'Mr.' — at least, to his face.'

'But everyone seems to call Mr. Maws 'Mr. Maws.''

''Course they do,' the Mummer said. 'He was called Mr. Maws by all when he were in the fancy, back around fifteen years ago.'

'The fancy?'

'Prizefighting, Mr. Barnett. Gentleman Jimmy Maws went twenty-three rounds to a decision for the bare-knuckle heavyweight championship of England. Unofficial, of course, since it were illegal at the time. That was back in 1872, I believe. Mr. Maws won the championship and six months' penal servitude for engaging in an illegal prizefight contest.'

'I'm impressed,' Barnett said.

★　★　★

Mummer Tolliver devoted the next few days to showing Barnett around Professor James Moriarty's London and introducing him to the people he would be dealing with in Moriarty's service. Although very few people were in his constant employ, the professor had associates all over the city. There were those in every social class and profession, and in almost every institution, guild, club, and business who were ready to do Moriarty a service or repay a favor.

In a cellar below a warehouse in Godolphin Street, almost in the shadow of the great tower of the Houses of Parliament, Barnett met Twist, London's most deformed beggar and the head of the Mendicants' Guild — an organization with rules as strict and as strictly enforced as those of the British Medical Association or the Queen's Dragoon Guards. It was Twist and his corps of wretches who enabled Moriarty to make good his boast that he had eyes on every street corner in London.

Twist looked Barnett up and down with his one good eye — the right one had a great patch over it — and then shook his head doubtfully at the Mummer. "'E's fly?' he demanded.

'He's fly,' the Mummer insisted. 'The professor sprung him from quod in Araby. He's to be the professor's principal. 'Course he's fly. Who says he ain't?'

Twist took the patch from his right eye and stared up at Barnett with it, as though seeking confirmation for what his left eye had shown him. The right eye had a milky-white disc covering most of the cornea, and Barnett found it very disconcerting to have it staring at him. He was having trouble following the conversation, but he didn't want to ask for an explanation for fear it would make Twist think him a complete outsider.

Twist replaced the patch, stared thoughtfully for a minute at Barnett's shoes, and then nodded. 'If the professor says you're fly,' he told Barnett, 'that's jonnick with me. 'As the Mummer 'ere given you the office?'

''Course I hasn't,' the Mummer

123

interjected. 'I leaves that to you, as always. It's not my place.'

''E's right,' Twist said to Barnett. 'It's my place and it's my privilege.' He hobbled over to a table in one corner of the large cellar, which was filled with low wooden tables and lower wooden benches. 'We'll do it by the book,' he said. 'And 'ere it is.' He opened a large, ancient ledger and turned the pages slowly and carefully until he reached the last one with writing on it. 'They are those,' he said, 'as think I'm the oldest thing around 'ere, but this book is far older than any living man. It's the Maund Book and all as 'ave ever been members of the London Maund, which we now call by the appellation of the Mendicants' Guild, are signed by they name, or they mark, and sealed with they thumb into this book. This book was opened in 1728, in the second year o' the reign of George the Second.'

Barnett went over and, with Twist's permission, examined the book, turning a few pages and peering at the ancient leather binding and the lists of signatures and strange hieroglyphics. He noticed a squiggle with a straight line over it and two'X's at each end, and 'the Connersty Barker, his mark,' written after. Each signature had a strange brown blob at the end, which Barnett decided was the thumbseal Twist had mentioned. 'Absolutely fascinating,' Barnett said. 'You have a piece of history here.'

'Ain't it the truth!' Twist said, pleased at the observation. 'And they's nobody what gets to see it without I say so.' He produced an inkstone and poured a few drops on it from a bottle under the table. 'Gin,' he explained, pulling a goose feather from a cubbyhole. With a couple of quick swipes of his pocketknife he created a passable point, which he rubbed into the gin-moistened ink. 'What moniker?' he asked.

'How's that?' Barnett said

'What moniker?' Twist repeated. 'You can't use your own, you see.'

'Oh!' Barnett said, as the light dawned. 'Moniker! Nickname! But I've never used one.'

'Why'nt you jolly him one?' the

Mummer suggested.

Twist considered. 'Got it,' he said. 'We'll moniker 'im after 'is quod. You go in the Maund Book as 'Araby,' if that's jonnick with you.'

'Sounds fine,' Barnett said, wondering what all this was leading up to.

Twist carefully and painstakingly wrote the date at the start of the line, twisting his head around so that his left eye could watch what his right hand was doing. Then he handed the quill to Barnett. 'Write your moniker or make your mark,' he instructed.

Barnett wrote 'Araby' neatly after the date and then, staring at it and feeling it looked naked by itself, added 'Ben' after it. 'Araby Ben,' he said. 'How's that?'

'Good,' Twist said, taking back his quill. He took Barnett's right thumb with his left hand and, with a sudden gesture, jabbed a long brass pin into the ball of the thumb.

'Hey!' Barnett yelped, jerking his hand back.

'Squeeze out a couple of drops of

blood,' Twist said, sticking the pin back into the lining of the filthy waistcoat he was wearing. 'Then press your thumb after your moniker.'

Barnett dutifully squeezed his thumb until two drops of his blood pooled on top. 'You should be careful with that needle,' he said. 'You could give someone blood poisoning.'

'I've pledged 'alf an 'undred men with this selfsame needle,' Twist said, 'and ain't none of 'em dead yet, barring a couple who've swung.'

Barnett made his thumbprint in the book, and Twist closed it. 'Yer a member now,' he said.

'Give him the office,' the Mummer said.

Twist struck a pose. 'You see what I'm doing?' he asked Barnett.

'No,' Barnett said, seeing nothing unusual in Twist's appearance beyond his deformity.

'Right enough,' Twist said. 'But any o' your fellow members of the guild would see right off that you was passing them the office.' He held up his left hand. 'Left 'and,' he said, 'with the thumb protruding, as it were, from between the first and second fingers. Not a natural pose, but not queer enough to be noted.'

'I see,' Barnett said.

'If you 'ave a message what you want delivered, but you're under the eye of some busy, or somefing of the kind, just give the office when you pass a street beggar. If 'e returns it, give 'em the message or drop it somewhere in 'is sight.'

'Twist here will have it within the hour,' the Mummer said with as much pride as if he'd invented the system himself. 'And the professor in another.'

Barnett nodded. Although he couldn't imagine what possible use such an elaborate signaling and message-carrying system could be to Moriarty, he was impressed. 'You certainly have evolved an efficient system,' he said.

''Course it is,' the Mummer said. 'E-bloody-ficient.'

'Don't forget your moniker, now,' Twist said. 'That's the name I knows you as. Good meeting you, Araby Ben. Good luck to you.'

They walked to the corner, where the Mummer hailed a passing hansom cab. 'One last stop, Guv,' he said, giving the cabby an address in the East End.

'I may be mistaken, since I'm not too familiar with London,' Barnett said as the hansom moved out to enter the stream of traffic, 'but we seem to have gone back and forth across London today in a great zigzag. Aren't we going back now in the direction we came from only a couple of hours ago?'

'Traveling roundabout London is the best way to get to know the city,' the Mummer told him.

Half an hour later their hansom pulled into Upper Swandam Lane, which despite its name was not much more than an alley sitting behind the wharves lining the north side of the Thames to the east of London Bridge. 'See that slop shop, cabby?' the Mummer called to the driver perched over their heads. 'Right to the other side of that, if you please.'

The cabby pulled past 'Abner's Nautical Outfitters, Uniforms for all Principal Lines' and stopped before the unmarked door on the far side. The Mummer tossed him a shilling and hopped down. 'Here we are,' he told Barnett. 'Come along.'

Barnett climbed out of the cab and stepped gingerly through the muddy street to the sidewalk. In the late afternoon light the building he faced seemed to have a strange and exotic character. Three stories high, it was constructed from ruddy bricks that might have seen service in some ancient Celtic fortress and then lain buried for two thousand years before being resurrected for their present use in this Upper Swandam Lane façade. There were no windows on the ground floor, and those on the second and third were fitted with great iron shutters, crusted with layers of maroon paint. The front door, large enough to pass a four-wheeled carriage when opened, was similarly of iron, and featureless except for six iron bands bolted to it in a crisscross pattern and a small window at eye level, not more than four inches square.

'What is this place?' Barnett asked, staring up. 'It looks like the treasure house of some Indian maharaja, who's in London buying modern plumbing supplies for his palace.'

The Mummer looked at Barnett's face, as though half afraid he might have said something funny. And then, reassured, he went and stood in front of the great iron door.

Inside of half a minute the peephole in the door opened and someone within examined them carefully. Barnett wondered: How did he know we were out here?

A small door, which had been artfully concealed by the pattern of iron bands in the large door, sprang inward, and a Chinese boy in his mid-teens, wearing a frock coat and a bowler hat, nodded and smiled at them from inside.

'Mr. Mummer,' he said, 'and, as I trust, Mr. Barnett. Please enter.'

The Mummer nodded Barnett through the door and then stepped in after him. 'Afternoon, Low,' he said. 'Where's your dad?'

The youth had closed the small door and slid two heavy bolts silently into place. 'Come,' he said. They were in a large room filled with orderly rows of packing cases one atop the other. Two gas mantles affixed to stone pillars near the door were lit, but out of their circle of harsh light the area quickly receded into gloom and then into utter black. It was impossible to judge the size of the room, but Barnett sensed it was immense.

The Chinese youth picked up a lantern and led them down the aisle to an iron staircase and then preceded them up to the next floor.

At the top of the stairs they passed through an anteroom into a medium-sized room that was fitted out like an antique store or a curio shop. The iron shutters were thrown back on the two windows and the late afternoon sun shone directly in, illuminating some of the finest Oriental furniture and pottery that Barnett had ever seen. A teak cabinet and several brass-fitted teak traveling chests were along the wall. In the middle of the room a large walnut table inlaid with ivory dragons at the four corners attracted Barnett's attention. He had a slight knowledge of Chinese furniture, which was in vogue in Paris at the moment, and he had never seen anything so fine. And the dragons were representations of the Imperial dragon — forbidden to anyone not of Manchu blood.

'I never thought I'd say this about a piece of furniture,' Barnett said, 'but this is the most beautiful thing I've ever seen.'

The boy nodded and smiled. 'My father's,' he said. 'Come.' He led the way past rows of delicate vases with the traditional patterns of long-defunct dynasties to another staircase, and they followed him up to the third floor. Second floor, Barnett reminded himself. Here it was ground floor, first floor, second floor. When in London . . .

This floor was again one long room, but a row of windows and a mosaic of skylights in the ceiling flooded it with what was left of the daylight. The room was divided into sections: one held several large tables and drafting boards; another had a small furnace or forge resting on a stone slab; across the room was a complex of interconnected chemical apparatus on a scale several times larger than that in Professor Moriarty's basement laboratory. The whole center area had been cleared out and the floorboards scrubbed clean, and long bolts of white silk were laid out on it in a complex pattern that meant nothing to Barnett. Several men in white smocks and felt slippers were crouched on different parts of the pattern industriously sewing one section of white silk to another section of white silk. It looked to Barnett like make-work in a madhouse.

It was then that Barnett noticed the tall, stoop-shouldered figure of Professor Moriarty hovering about one of the drawing boards. He held a pencil in one hand and a large gutta percha eraser in the other, and he alternately attacked a paper pinned to the board with one and then the other. Standing at his right shoulder, peering intently at the drawing growing under Moriarty's hand, was a tall, thin, elderly Chinese in a sea-green silk robe. Every time Moriarty drew in a line or wrote down a figure, the Chinese gentleman ran the fingers of his left hand along a small ivory abacus he held in his right and then murmured a few words into Moriarty's left ear.

With the Mummer tagging close behind him, Barnett strode across the room to join Moriarty.

'Ah, Barnett,' Moriarty said, glancing up from his work, 'Tolliver. Just on time, I see.'

' 'Course,' the Mummer said.

'Mr. Benjamin Barnett,' Moriarty said, 'allow me to introduce Prince Tseng Li-chang, a former minister from the court of the son of Heaven to various Western nations, and quite possibly the finest mathematical mind of the nineteenth century. Mr. Barnett, as I mentioned, is a journalist.'

Prince Tseng bowed. 'Professor Moriarty has told me something of your travail, Mr. Barnett,' he said in a deep, precise voice. 'I trust you shall find your period of association with Professor Moriarty to be a stimulating and rewarding experience. He has an incisive mind, quick as a crossbow dart; it is only his occasional companionship that makes my years of exile tolerable.'

Barnett's journalist's ear perked up. 'Exile?' he repeated.

Prince Tseng nodded sadly. 'My step-cousin-in-law, the Empress Dowager Tz'u-hsi, who rules China through her adopted son, the Emperor Kuang-hsi, has no use for Western ways. She chooses to believe that if you ignore the barbarians at the gates and insult their envoys, they will go quietly away. I advised her otherwise and she did not wish to listen. Soon she no longer wanted to see me or tolerate my presence. I was allowed to request the privilege of residing elsewhere.'

'And so the Empress Dowager has lost a valuable advisor,' Moriarty said 'And I have gained a trusted friend.'

'Say,' Barnett said, 'if you don't mind my asking, what is all this?' He swept his hand around to indicate all the diverse activities that filled the room.

'This is my factory,' Professor Moriarty said. 'On the floor below, Prince Tseng manufactures antiques, while up here I create dreams.'

'Two conundrums,' Barnett said.

'Not at all, not at all,' Prince Tseng said. 'Here, look!' He went to a ring set into the floor and pulled it up, opening a three-foot-square trapdoor, which led down to the floor below. Squatting by the opening, he gestured down. 'There you see my workshop. There are my skilled artisans engaged in recreating the T''ang, the Sung, the Yuan, and the Ming dynasties through representations of their art. Very precise representations.'

Barnett gingerly approached the square hole in the floor. Directly below, a row of young women with kerchiefs tied around their heads sat before a long table. Each of them was painting patterns on a piece of unfired pottery with a fine Chinese brush.

'There is a great demand for the antiquities of my country, Mr. Barnett,' Prince Tseng said. 'It is a vogue — a fad. Unfortunately, very few of these objects have left my country. But the demand must be filled, must it not?' He dropped the trapdoor back into place and stood up.

'That's very interesting,' Barnett said.

'Not all that interesting, Mr. Barnett,' Prince Tseng said. 'It's very mundane, really. It's what I must do to finance my work.'

'You mean all this?' Barnett asked, gesturing around the room.

'No, sir. My work takes place in my homeland.'

'All this,' Professor Moriarty interrupted, 'is mine. My responsibility entirely. Prince Tseng is good enough to aid me with the calculations and with his scientific insight, but the project is mine.'

Barnett looked around the room again. The workers seemed to have tacitly agreed that it was time to quit for the day; they had gathered at a row of wooden lockers and were exchanging their smocks and slippers for street clothes. 'I hope this doesn't appear a naive question,' Barnett said, 'but just what is going on in here?'

'You see before you,' Moriarty said, indicating the neat mounds of white silk with a wave of his hand, 'the beginnings of what is to become the world's first aerostat observatory,'

'Aerostat — '

'An aerostat is a balloon that is filled with some gaseous substance which makes it lighter than air,' Prince Tseng said.

'Yes,' Barnett said. 'Of course. My Uncle Ben was a balloonist in McClellan's army during the Rebellion. After the war he used to give exhibition balloon rides at county fairs. I helped him for a summer, and he taught me a bit about ballooning. It's the juxtaposition of the two words that puzzled me. Does an aerostat observatory observe aerostats or observe from an aerostat?'

'Ah!' Moriarty said. 'Our journalistic friend possesses both a practical knowledge of ballooning and a rudimentary sense of humor. A valuable assistant, indeed. I don't trust a man without a sense of humor. For your enlightenment, Barnett' — Moriarty swiveled one of the large, wheeled chalkboards around, revealing a drawing pinned to the reverse side — 'this is what the apparatus will look like. It is designed to rise up into the comparatively tranquil air that prevails four or five miles above the earth. It will carry an astronomical telescope of special design and a crew of five: two to work the aerostat and three to perform the experiments and observations.'

The drawing, a carefully-lined rendering, showed a cluster of balloon gasbags surrounding a central core that must have been the telescope. An elongated, closed gondola was suspended below, and various pieces of equipment, the purpose of which Barnett could not even guess at, were shown affixed to the sides of the gondola.

'Trapped as we are beneath a vast ocean of air that randomly refracts, reflects, and otherwise distorts the rays of light which pass through it,' Moriarty said, 'we cannot hope to observe properly, much less understand, the universe which we are immersed in and are a part of. And until we manage to understand properly at least the fundamental laws by which the universe is run, we cannot hope to begin to understand ourselves: our design, our function, and our purpose, if any.'

'Surely,' Barnett said, 'you can't hope to loft a telescope of any appreciable size with a bunch of balloons.'

'True,' Moriarty said, returning the chalk board to its original position, 'but my calculations indicate that once above nine-tenths of the Earth's atmosphere, a five-inch refractor should achieve a clarity of vision that not even a twenty-inch one achieves on the ground. The twenty-inch has more gathering power, it is true, but in many cases that merely serves to make the blur brighter. Every astronomer has had the experience of having his field of vision become crystal-clear for just one instant, so the nebulosity he is staring at is as sharp as if etched on glass. But before he can put pencil to paper, the atmosphere has again transformed the image to a wavering, flickering blur too indistinct to understand correctly.'

'What do you hope to accomplish with your aerostat telescope?' Barnett asked.

Moriarty shook his head. 'I may discover the innermost secrets of the universe,' he said. 'Or then again, I may discover that through some hidden flaw I

141

failed to anticipate, I get no usable information at all from the apparatus. As a very old friend of mine once told me, There is no shame in playing the cards that have been dealt to you as long as you play them to the best of your ability.' It was, of course, in another context.' Moriarty looked around him. 'Well, we seem to have done everything we can for today, gentlemen,' he said. 'Let us return to Russell Square and see what Mrs. Randall has prepared for us in the way of a supper. I seem to remember Mrs. H saying something about mutton before I left the house. May I invite you to dine with us this evening, Prince Tseng?'

Tseng Li-chang bowed. 'I think not, Professor,' he said. 'Many thanks for inviting me, but I think my son and I had best stay in this evening and partake of our own poor repast. He has lessons to do, and I could profitably use the time.'

'Just as you say,' Moriarty said. 'I shall see you, then, within the week. Tolliver — go over to the cabstand on Commercial Road and see if you can pick us up a growler. We'll be downstairs.'

'Have it here in half a minute, Professor,' the Mummer said, and the little man darted back down the stairs, his jacket flapping.

* * *

As the four-wheeler headed placidly toward Russell Square, Moriarty crossed his arms, lowered his chin onto his clavicle, and sank into a deep reverie. His eyes were open, but it was clear that his thoughts were elsewhere. Mummer Tolliver settled in one corner of the gently swaying growler, whistling to himself while rolling a half-crown back and forth along the backs of his fingers. He obviously was prepared to continue this occupation indefinitely.

Barnett stared out the window at the passing London scene. He had several disquieting notions to consider.

'You're right,' Moriarty said suddenly, interrupting his thoughts. 'I am a criminal. Does this distress you?'

'I'm not sure,' Barnett said. 'I haven't really . . . ' He looked up in astonishment.

'How the devil did you know what I was thinking.'

Moriarty chuckled dryly. 'My attention returned from the abstruse world of mathematics to the interior of this growler,' he said, 'to find you staring out the window. Then you glanced surreptitiously at Tolliver several times and back out the window. As we were passing Newgate Prison at the time, it was not hard to surmise the general outline of your thoughts. The process of association is almost unavoidable, I have found. Tolliver has recently told you of his criminal background, and the sight of Newgate reminded you of this.'

'I recall something like that going through my head,' Barnett admitted.

'Then you looked from Tolliver to me, glanced back out the window, stared at your feet, and shuddered slightly. You were considering the possibility of your new association putting you back behind stone walls. I briefly thought it might be merely a memory of Stamboul, but the shudder was too prolonged for that — so you were clearly viewing a return to the life of a felon. Therefore, you are afraid that your new employment might meet with disfavor in the eyes of the authorities. You have decided, or perhaps deduced, that I am a criminal.'

Barnett leaned back in the leather seat and stared at Moriarty. 'What a weak chain of inference!' he said.

Moriarty smiled. 'In science,' he said, 'the test of validity is reproducibility. Keep that in mind, Barnett, as we march into the future together.'

The occupants of the four-wheeler remained silent for several minutes. Then Moriarty said, 'Now about my, ah, criminal activities. Do you regret accepting employment with a criminal?'

'I don't know, Professor. There are crimes, and then there are crimes.'

'A brilliant observation,' Moriarty commented. 'Am I to understand by this that there are some crimes you would condone and others you would find opprobrious?'

'I think that's true of everyone,' Barnett said.

'Not so!' Moriarty said. 'Most individuals in our enlightened society would neither commit nor condone any crime. They would cheerfully allow a child of twelve to starve to death working twelve hours a day over a shuttle-loom for a shilling a week; but then that is not a crime.' He raised his hand. 'But just let — Wait a second! Do you hear that?'

'I hear nothing wrong,' Barnett said, listening intently. 'As a matter of fact, I can't hear anything over the horse's hooves.'

'Indeed!' Moriarty said. 'And the horse has just gone over wooden planking, such as is installed in the street to cover a temporary excavation for sewer lines and the like.' He tried the door handle. 'And, as there is no such excavation on the direct route to Russell Square, I deduce we have taken the wrong turning. We are now on Grey's Inn Road, I believe.'

'Perhaps the jarvey knows a shortcut,' the Mummer suggested, from his corner of the four-wheeler.

'And perhaps he's fixed the door handles so we won't fall out and hurt ourselves,' Moriarty said.

'How's that?' the Mummer said. He tried the handle on his side and found it immoveable. 'Why, that bloody barsted,' he said, his voice raised in indignation. 'What's 'is game?'

'Now, now, Mummer,' Moriarty said, 'don't lose your aitches; it's taken you long enough to acquire them.'

'What's happening?' Barnett asked. 'Won't the doors open?'

'They won't. And what's happening is that we're being abducted,' Moriarty said, 'like in one of the popular novels. Although I don't believe your virtue is in any danger.' He wiggled a finger at Tolliver. 'I thought I warned you about taking the first cab in the rank.'

'Wasn't any rank,' the Mummer said. 'The growler was proceeding down the bloody street and I hailed him.'

'Indeed,' Moriarty said. 'How convenient.' He rapped on the roof of the four-wheeler with his stick. 'Cabby!' he called. There was no response. Barnett wondered whether he had expected one.

Moriarty leaned forward in his seat,

resting his chin on his hands, which were laced over the ivory handle of his stick. 'This seems inane,' he said. 'They surely can't expect us to just sit here until the carriage arrives at some secret destination. My first inclination is to do just that, to learn who we are dealing with. But our mysterious adversaries will surely try to do away with us, growler and all, at the first opportunity. I'd suggest we exit from this clarence cab lockbox as expeditiously as possible. Mummer, remove that window and try the outside knob.'

'It don't roll down, Professor,' the Mummer said.

'I didn't suppose it would,' the professor said. 'Break the glass!'

The Mummer took a cosh from his belt and broke the glass out of the window on his side of the four-wheeler, while Moriarty used his stick to do the same on the other side.

'It don't open from the outside neither,' the Mummer called.

'Remove the rest of the glass,' Moriarty said, 'and get out the window. Fast!'

There were a couple of thumping

noises from overhead, and Barnett saw the cabby swing off his seat and drop to the street, where he fell, quickly regained his feet, and disappeared from view as the four-wheeler continued to move on at an accelerated pace.

'Whatever's going to happen is going to happen now,' Barnett cried. 'The jarvey's just left us.'

The cab jounced and clattered down the street, lurching madly from side to side as the tempo of the horse's gait changed from a placid trot to a frenetic gallop.

'I rather think the jarvey did something to annoy our steed as a parting gesture,' Moriarty said, knocking the remaining shards of glass out of the window on his side. 'Thus enhancing an already interesting experience. Mr. Barnett, if you would make your way to the street through this window . . .'

Barnett looked out at the pavement, which was passing under the wheels of the cab at a dizzying speed. Then he glanced across the cab at Tolliver, who was already most of the way out of the window on his side. He shrugged. 'This will ruin my suit,' he said. Grabbing the leather strap above the door, he swung his legs out the window, twisted through, and dropped.

The cab swerved just as he let go, and he fell heavily on his side and slid across the cobblestones. A second later, Moriarty followed him out the window, hitting the ground feet-first, and then rolling forward in the baritsu manner to absorb the impact before coming neatly to his feet again.

The cab, now bouncing and clattering wildly behind an increasingly frenzied horse, barely missed a carter's wagon to its left and then careened into a lamppost on the right. Bouncing off the lamppost, it twisted over until it was riding on just two wheels. The traces gave way under the twisting force, and the horse, suddenly freed, raced off down the street. The four-wheeler righted itself again, now heading directly toward a bank on the corner. As it reached the curb, it exploded in a cloud of black smoke, sending wood and iron fragments hurtling through the air to clatter against the walls and breaking windows up and down the block. Barnett instinctively covered his face with his arms, but miraculously none of the fragments touched him.

When most of the debris had come to rest, Barnett got up and dusted himself off. His leg burned where he had scraped it, and his good French frock coat and trousers were now suitable only for the dustbin, but there seemed to be no other damage done. He looked around and saw Moriarty crossing the road to where Mummer Tolliver was lying. The Mummer's tiny body, one leg twisted at an unnatural angle, lay quite still. Somehow, despite the explosion debris and dust all around him, Tolliver's checkered suit and yellow spats were still neat and spotlessly clean, but his face was covered with blood.

Moriarty knelt by the Mummer and cleaned his face off with his pocket handkerchief. Cautiously he straightened the twisted leg and then undid the Mummer's tight high collar and loosened his cravat. 'He's breathing,' he told

151

Barnett. 'Let us get him home.'

'Shouldn't we take him to the nearest hospital?' Barnett asked.

'St. Bartholomew's is probably the closest hospital,' Moriarty said. 'And my house is quite a bit closer, a good bit cleaner, and has most of the facilities.' Lifting Tolliver as gently as he would a small child, Moriarty rose. 'Flag down that cab,' he directed Barnett. 'We'll stop at the house first, and then you go on to Cavendish Square and bring back a physician named Breckstone. He's the only man in London I'd trust to treat anything more complicated than a head cold.'

Barnett hailed the growler, which was busy trying to turn around and avoid the blocked far end of the street. A uniformed policeman came around the corner at a dead run as they boarded the cab. 'Here, here,' he yelled, continuing past them toward the wreckage. 'What's all this?'

7

THE SCENT

*When you have eliminated
the impossible, whatever remains,
however improbable, must be the truth.*
— Sir Arthur Conan Doyle

'I have been remiss,' Moriarty said. 'I have allowed my own interests and desires to distract me from an assignment which I accepted in all good faith, just because there is no one here to prod me into activity. While I have been concerning myself with anomalies in the orbit of an asteroid, Trepoff has been planting his infernal devices about me with the assiduity of a British gardener setting roses.'

'How is the Mummer?' Barnett asked, in part to find out and to get Moriarty off a line of self-abasement that Barnett found uncomfortable.

'Doctor Breckstone was here again this morning, before you descended,' Moriarty said, with a hint of reproach in his voice. 'The haematoma over the right parietal has somewhat subsided and it looks as though there is no underlying fracture. Aside from a severe headache, which Doctor Breckstone feels should subside in a day or so, and some minor abrasions, Tolliver is none the worse for his experience. You might go up and see him.'

'I shall,' Barnett said.

'Good. He refuses opiates for his headache, so he remains quite querulous. I don't like him snapping at the maids, and Mrs. H is far too busy. Go and let him snap at you for a while so he won't take it out on the domestic help.'

'I'm glad to discover that I have some useful function in this establishment,' Barnett said, smiling ruefully. 'I was beginning to think that you had nothing for me to do.'

'On the contrary, I have a great deal for you to do,' Moriarty said. He ceased pacing and sat down in the large leather chair behind his desk. 'I have been giving some thought to the Trepoff problem, and you figure prominently in my plans.'

'Say, Professor,' Barnett said, 'just exactly who is this Trepoff you keep talking about?'

'Trepoff is the man who blew up our clarence cab last evening. He is the man who committed the crime you were accused and convicted of in Constantinople.'

Barnett thought about this for a minute. 'Trepoff is the fellow the Russians want you to catch,' he said.

'That's correct.'

'Who is he?'

'Nobody knows,' Moriarty said. 'Let me explain.' And inside of ten minutes he had told Barnett all that he knew of Trepoff and the *Belye Krystall*, withholding nothing. It was Moriarty's usual practice to burden his associates with no more information than they needed to perform their tasks, but on the Trepoff matter, there was, so far, not sufficient information to be selective about it.

'It's a fascinating problem,' Barnett said when Moriarty had finished. 'I don't see how to get a handle on it: finding a man you've never seen and can't identify in the midst of the world's largest city in time to prevent him from committing an unknown atrocity.'

'It is a challenge,' Moriarty admitted. 'Although it is only the time constraint that makes it interesting. Any population can be sifted through for one individual member, given sufficient time. I have already begun several lines of inquiry. I confess I should have done more.'

'I'll say,' Barnett said.

'Moriarty stared steadily at Barnett. 'Perhaps your keener intellect has grasped some fact that has eluded me,' he said. 'You have some suggestion to make?'

Barnett ignored the implied sarcasm and give a considered answer: 'There are areas in London where Russian émigrés are known to congregate. That's probably the place to start.'

'Quite right,' Moriarty said. 'And that is, indeed, where I began. There are nine revolutionary clubs run by expatriate

Russians in the East End, of which the Bohemian Club seems to be the most popular. The center for intrigue, however, is a smaller establishment called the Balalaika. Behind and above the public rooms at the Balalaika are a complex of private rooms, in which all manner of scheming and plotting against every government in Europe would seem to go on. The owner, a Mr. Petruchian, has agreed to aid us, and one of my agents is now stationed behind the bar.'

Barnett whistled softly. 'You got the owner of an anarchist bar to help you? What do you have on him?'

'Petruchian is not himself an anarchist, you understand — merely the proprietor of a club. And while he might not be averse to an occasional bombing in St. Petersburg or Vienna, he is a loyal citizen of Britain. When I explained to him — after I had established my bona fides — that an atrocity was planned against his adopted homeland, he was eager to help.'

Barnett would have been fascinated to find out how Professor Moriarty had established his 'bona fides,' but instead he asked, 'Have you found anything?'

'Precisely nothing.'

'Do you know what you're looking for?'

'It would be enough to discover someone who is whispering of plots against some target here in Britain. Trepoff is probably recruiting his men from among the ranks of the genuine anarchists, but if so, he is being too subtle for me.'

'Well, he certainly knows where you are,' Barnett said.

'A fact that I have been hoping to put to good use,' Moriarty said. 'I have managed to trace three of the men who attempted to kill me, including last night's jehu. But they've all been hirelings, who know nothing of their employer.' He slapped his hand down on the desk vehemently. 'It is time to go on the offensive,' he said, 'before the man manages to kill one of us by sheer luck.'

'You said you have something for me to do,' Barnett said. 'What is it?'

'Ah, yes,' Moriarty said. He leaned forward across the desk. 'I want you to go to Fleet Street,' he said, 'and reacquaint yourself with your profession. I want you to become familiar with all the important dailies. Get to know the journalists who work for them.'

'Easy enough,' Barnett said, 'except for one thing — what do I tell them I'm doing there, and who do I say I am?'

'Your name is Benjamin Barnett,' Moriarty said, 'and you are going to open a news bureau. An American news bureau, I rather think. Rent an office in the area and hire a competent secretary; you'll need one for my plan in any case. Put a sign on the door. Something on the order of: 'Barnett's Anglo-American Telegraphic News Service.' I leave the exact wording to you.'

'What happens when some random Turkish newsman or government official happens on the name 'Benjamin Barnett'?' Barnett asked.

'Ah, yes,' Moriarty said. 'That's the other thing I wished to see you about. I have good news for you: you are dead.'

'What?'

'As far as the Ottoman government is

concerned, you are dead. Shot while trying to escape, or something very like that. So the Gurra-Pasha reported to the Sultan, and so it shall be.'

'Why would he do that?' Barnett asked.

'Better not look a gift Pasha in the mouth,' Moriarty said. 'I would assume he was trying to cover up the escape to protect his reputation. He waited a couple of weeks to make sure you were really gone and then officially notified Abd-ul Hamid Khan the Second, Sultan of Sultans, King of Kings, Shadow of God upon Earth, that you were killed while escaping. Thus he managed to please himself, Abd-ul Hamid, and you all at once, and hurt nobody. Would that all human intercourse were that simple.'

Barnett nodded. 'Such a short life,' he said, 'but lived to the full. I shall have to get the copy of the *New York World* that has my obituary and see what they have to say about me.'

'A unique opportunity,' Moriarty agreed. 'I trust you will not be disappointed.'

'At any rate that is certainly good news

— but how many people would say that after being informed of their own deaths?'

'Anyone of whom the report was in error, I fancy, would at least be amused. For the others I will not venture to speak.'

'There's no chance that someone seeing my name or encountering me will report it to the Ottoman government?'

'There's every chance it will be reported. And no chance the report will be anything but studiously ignored. Would you like to be the one who informs the King of Kings that you had made a slight mistake in regard to the death of a prisoner?'

'I see what you mean,' Barnett said. 'Now, back to Fleet Street. I am to open a news service. What sort of news?'

'Anything out of the ordinary,' Moriarty said. 'I feel sure that there are many stories that come into a newspaper every day that are not used because they prove to be insufficiently interesting or questionably factual.'

'That's so,' Barnett said. 'I'd say less than half of the stories that come over a city desk ever see print.'

'And one class of these unused stories would be the unique event that looks as though it would be newsworthy if more information could be developed, but that additional information never comes to light — is that so?'

'Right,' Barnett agreed. 'Someone comes up with one fascinating fact that looks as though there is a great story behind it, and you investigate it and get nowhere. And you never know for sure if there was anything there or not. You can't use the story because you have insufficient information.'

'These are the stories,' Moriarty said, 'in which I wish you to be most interested. This is where the spoor of Trepoff is to be found. You must look for the merest hints and traces, for this man will most assuredly cover his tracks with the cunning of a jungle beast.'

'But what am I to look for?' Barnett asked. 'How can I tell when one of these stories relates to Trepoff?'

'You must first eliminate those incidents which cursory investigation will show do not relate to Trepoff or the *Belye*

Krystall. What is left you will write up and put into a notebook. I shall periodically go through the notebook and tell you which items warrant further consideration. Investigate bizarre crimes, seemingly senseless cruelties, and insane acts; look for the unique masquerading as the commonplace.'

Barnett shook his head. 'I'm sorry, Professor, but I'm still not clear on what sort of thing it would be most profitable to look at. Perhaps if you could give me some example . . . '

'Rather than an example,' Moriarty said, thinking, 'let me give you an analogy. Trepoff is like a general in some field army preparing for a battle. He will have his scouts out surveying the land; he will have training exercises for his troops; he will be preparing his logistics and supply; his spies will be probing for the enemy's weak points; his armorer may be preparing and testing weapons; and so on. I'm sure you can extend the analogy yourself well into the ridiculous. And each of these activities will leave a trace for the observer who knows what he is looking for — and looking at.

'Our problem is that we don't know precisely what we are looking for, so we shall have to examine a mass of inconsequentia to establish the relevance of what we are looking at. Can you follow this rather stretched metaphor?'

'I think so,' Barnett said. 'I hope so.' He stood up.

'Good!' Moriarty said. 'Other members of my organization will be out searching for data, each in his own specialized way, but I am very hopeful of the journalistic approach.' He looked up at Barnett narrowly. 'Be careful!' he said. 'Remember that in this game murder is an acceptable move.'

★ ★ ★

Barnett found office space on the top floor of a small building on Whitefriars Street, just south of Fleet Street. He equipped it with a desk, a Grandall typewriter, a box of pencils, two reams of yellow paper, and a wastepaper basket, and felt at home. After much thought he

found a sign painter and had him inscribe
'American News Service' across the door
with 'B. Barnett' in much smaller letters
under it.

The next step was to establish his bona
fides. There was no point in faking
something that could just as easily be
legitimate. He made up a list of New York
and Boston newspapers that might take
filler material from him — he'd worry
about the rest of the country later. To
start with, he sent a cable to his last
employer, the *New York World:*

NOW WORKING FOR AMERICAN NEWS
SERVICE COMMA LONDON STOP WILL
YOU TAKE NEWS AT SPACE RATES
PLUS CABLE CHARGES QUESTION-
MARK WE PAY FOR QUERY COMMA
YOU SPECIFY INCHES
BENJAMIN BARNETT

Within four hours, the fastest turnaround
time Barnett had ever seen on the
transatlantic cable, he had his reply from
the *World*, signed by Hardesty Gores, the
managing editor himself:

165

Barnett read the cable and scribbled a short reply for the boy to take back.

I DIED
BARNETT

The next morning, when Barnett arrived at the office to supervise the hanging of curtains and a few other necessary amenities, another cable from the *World* awaited him:

WANT EXCLUSIVE YOUR PERSONAL STORY STOP WILL TAKE TO ONE HUNDRED INCHES SPACE RATES
GORES

So there was his first account. And an interesting challenge it would be, too, to write the story of his incarceration and escape without violating the terms of his agreement with the professor. He'd have to work on that one.

Barnett sent cables to the other papers

on his list and turned his attention to getting to know the editors and journalists of Fleet Street. Within the next two days, Barnett had consulted with the city editors of the *Daily Telegraph*, the *Daily News*, the *Standard*, and the *Times*. Under the pretext of doing a series of articles for the American market on crime in metropolitan London, he arranged to have access to the newspapers' clipping files and to be apprised of current happenings by messenger once a day. Newspapers tend to be very responsive to the requests of outside journalists who are not direct competitors. It was a cheap and effective sort of broadcasting.

Within a week, Barnett had replies from eleven East Coast dailies to the effect that they were willing to see his queries and buy from him at space rates if he had anything that interested them. 'I have,' he told Professor Moriarty over dinner, 'quite inadvertently established myself in a business. I'm going to have to go out and hire that secretary you suggested just to keep up with the legitimate stories, not counting the research I'm doing for you. I didn't think it would be so easy.'

'You must be considered a good journalist by your American peers,' Moriarty suggested.

'I don't think that's it,' Barnett said. 'Not that I'm not a good journalist — but I think what these papers see is the notoriety value of my byline. Something like this: 'Mr. Barnett, our London correspondent, is the man who recently conducted a daring escape from a Turkish dungeon after being tried and convicted for the murder of a British naval officer. A murder he claims he did not commit. Full details in our Sunday edition'.

'You see,' Barnett went on. 'where I come from, a woman who killed her lover with a nickel-plated revolver last year was acquitted of the crime when she told the jury that he had lied to her. And then she went on a vaudeville singing tour that took her to twenty-seven cities. Despite a voice like a bullfrog, she packed the house at every stop.'

Moriarty put down his fork and stared at Barnett. 'So, the moral of it would have to be, 'When in America keep nickel-plated revolvers out of the hands of women who can't sing'.' Then he chuckled and returned his attention to his pudding.

Barnett put an advertisement in the next morning's *Daily Telegraph* for a 'secretary for a small news-office, conversant with the operation of typewriting machines. Reply to Box 252, Telegraph.' He arranged for a messenger to deliver the replies to his office. By that afternoon's post he had sixteen replies, and by the following morning when he arrived at the office, eighty-seven.

He piled them all up on top of his new desk and settled down to go through them. He found that a good many of the applicants eliminated themselves through unacceptable vagaries of grammar, syntax, or spelling. He counted the letters remaining: fifty-two. He had no interest in interviewing fifty-two people, so what next?

As he sat frowning, there was a knock at the door. Barnett looked up. More applications, no doubt. He put his pencil down. 'Come in.'

The office door opened, and a young lady entered. Barnett watched her come in, then stood up politely. And then he fell in love. This was not unusual, although it was the first time since he had reached London. Barnett had fallen in love every other day in Paris, and at least once a week in New York. But each time it was a new and unique emotion. Still, it had happened enough that he was able to control the emotion and not allow it to interfere with his conduct.

'Excuse me,' she said, 'are you Mr. Barnett?'

'Indeed I am, Madam,' he said. 'How may I assist you?' It wasn't what he wanted to say, he told himself, wishing for poetic words and romantic images to come springing to his lips — but none did. So he merely smiled foolishly at the young lady and waited for her to speak.

'I have brought your mail,' she said, holding forth a packet of letters in her daintily gloved hand, 'from the *Daily Telegraph*.'

'Oh,' Barnett said. He took the letters

and dropped them on top of the others. 'Thank you.'

The girl set herself firmly before the desk, took a deep breath, and said, 'I should like to apply for the position myself. Of secretary. In this office.'

'Oh,' Barnett said. 'I see. Here, take a seat, why don't you? How interesting. Ah . . . ' He plopped back down into his chair as she sat herself in the straightback wooden chair by the side of the desk. 'I'm sorry if I seem surprised,' he said, 'but I hadn't expected to see anyone until tomorrow at the earliest. How did you get here, by the way? And what is your name?'

'I am sorry if I surprised you,' the girl said. 'My name is Perrine, Miss Cecily Perrine. I was quite determined, when I saw your advertisement, to apply for the position before anyone else had a chance to. To get the jump on them, as they say. So I took the liberty of ascertaining who had placed the advertisement. And then I came here under the pretext of bringing you your mail.'

Barnett looked at the girl, trying to

pierce the depths of the clear blue eyes that met his gaze without coyness or shyness. Her oval face was framed with light-brown curls under her straw bonnet. And she seemed totally without artifice. Which, Barnett reflected, was probably the highest form of artifice of all.

'Why do you want the position?' he asked.

'I want to be a journalist,' she said, 'to work for a newspaper. But none of them will take me seriously. So when I saw the advertisement for a position in a small news-office, I decided to try for it. I thought that if I could get a start as a secretary, I might get a chance . . . I suppose it was silly . . . ' Her voice trailed off and she looked away. Barnett could see that her hands were clenched and white, although her face was flushed. She was in the grip of some strong emotion, and she was not acting.

'There are lady journalists,' Barnett said.

'Journalists!' she scoffed, her jaw setting. 'There are ladies, sir, who write dainty little pieces about social teas, and

172

soirees, and whether the Dowager Duchess of Titipu wore mauve or lavender to the last garden party at Balmoral. That, sir, is not journalism, and you know it!' Then she looked suddenly stricken. 'Oh, I'm so sorry. I can't help it. But none of the daily papers will hire a woman even as a secretary. If you knew how many times I've heard that a newsroom is no place for a lady.'

'You will have to learn to control your emotions,' Barnett said gently.

'You're right, of course,' Miss Perrine said, taking a deep breath and standing up. 'Thank you for your time.'

'I have three more questions for you, Miss Perrine, if you don't mind,' Barnett said.

She sat slowly back down. 'Yes?'

'Why do you want to be a reporter?'

She thought about it for a moment. 'I don't exactly know,' she said. 'When I was twelve — I think — I told my father I wanted to be a journalist and he laughed and asked me why. And I said something like, 'Because they find out the truth and then they tell people.' I had just read one of Mr. Dickens' novels where one of the characters was a journalist and I was impressed. It was a man, of course, but at the time that barrier didn't seem insurmountable.'

'That's as good a reason as I've heard,' Barnett said. 'The only one better was advanced by a man named McSorley who covered the police beat for the *New York Daily American*.'

'And what did Mr. McSorley say?' the girl asked.

'He said they were paying him twelve dollars a week,' Barnett told her, 'and that was more than he could make shoveling coal.'

Miss Perrine thought about that for a minute, possibly trying to decide whether or not Barnett was making fun of her. 'This man McSorley,' she said, 'didn't have to fight for his job.'

Barnett smiled. 'My second question is, how did you manage to get here to apply for the position? The address, after all, is a box number, and the *Telegraph* is not supposed to give out the name or address of the box holder.'

'It was simple enough,' she told him. 'I went to the window and told the clerk I was picking up the mail for Box Two-Three-Two. He said he understood it was to be sent on. I told him that that was the problem. I said we had expected far more replies than we had received and I wanted to make sure they were going to the right address. So he pulled the card and read me the name and address printed thereon. I assured him that it was right, took the few letters that had come since the last messenger, and here I am.'

'I see,' Barnett said. 'Very effective. And my third question is: Can you spell?'

'Quite precisely,' she said.

'Very good. Now tell me, do you still want the job?'

'Well,' Miss Perrine looked around the office. 'Quite frankly, Mr. Barnett, this is not how I pictured my introduction to journalism. This office, at the moment, seems quite innocent of any connection with any newspaper. Would you mind telling me, Mr. Barnett, exactly what the American News Service does, and what my duties would be?'

'We are a brand new company, Miss Perrine,' Barnett said. 'So new, in fact, that I use the editorial 'We,' as I am, at present, the sole proprietor and only employee of the American News Service. But from such humble beginnings, Miss Perrine, may come a great news organization.

'We gather news for our clients, which are American newspapers. Therefore, we try to anticipate what sort of news would appeal to the American reader. Once a day we will cable a query sheet with a precis of each story to our clients. They then specify which stories they are willing to pay for, and we send them.'

'It sounds interesting,' Miss Perrine said. 'Although I'm afraid to imagine what sort of stories the American newspapers are interested in. Where do you get your stories, Mr. Barnett? You don't just cull the London dailies, do you?'

'I'm developing connections with the city editors of several of the larger papers,' Barnett replied. 'They will supply the basic facts — for a fee, of course. If the story seems to warrant it, there are several free-lance reporters I can hire to develop additional facts. I also do reporting work myself, but at present I have a private client who will take up much of my time away from the office.'

'A private client, Mr. Barnett?'

The incredulous question made Barnett realize how strange the idea of a news bureau having a private client sounded to anyone with even a rudimentary notion of how such a business worked. 'I am engaged in, ah, research, Miss Perrine, among the indigent and criminal classes in London. A private charitable foundation is supplying the financing.'

'How fascinating!' Miss Perrine said. 'You will have to tell me all about it!'

'I certainly shall,' Barnett agreed. 'Now as to your duties. At first they will be mainly secretarial, but as the service expands there will be an increasing amount of in-house journalistic writing to be done. If you can handle the work, it's yours.'

'There's the matter of remuneration,

Mr. Barnett,' Miss Perrine reminded him.

'True,' Barnett said. 'What is the standard rate for secretarial help around here?'

'I believe that a capable secretary would command fifteen to twenty pounds a quarter. That is, a woman would. A man, of course, would get more. Say twenty-five or thirty pounds.'

'Well, why don't we flaunt custom, Miss Perrine, and start you at twenty-five pounds a quarter. I have a feeling that your initiative and intelligence will prove invaluable to this organization. Perhaps even more than if you had been a man.'

Miss Perrine gave Barnett a searching look, but his answering gaze was innocence itself. 'Very well,' she said. 'When do you want me to begin?'

'You do use a typewriter, don't you?' Barnett asked.

Miss Perrine looked disapprovingly at his machine.

'The Grandall is a good typewriter,' she said, 'but I prefer the Remington.'

'As I shall need my own machine at any rate, I was planning to get a second. It shall be a Remington, as you say.'

'Thank you, Mr. Barnett.'

'As for starting, right now would seem a suitable time.'

'Very good. What would you have me do?'

Barnett indicated the pile of letters on his desk. 'Answer these,' he said.

★ ★ ★

Cecily Perrine proved to be more than Barnett could have hoped for. He had advertised for a secretary and he had found a wonder. She handled the business side of American News Service so well that it almost immediately ceased being merely a front for Barnett's other activity and became a profitable enterprise in its own right. Barnett suppressed his infatuation with her as best he could, and replaced it with admiration for her ability.

In the meantime, he was busy with his own task: searching through the crime news, the society pages, the letters to the editors (published and not), and even the agony columns for that hint of the bizarre which might indicate the presence of Trepoff or the *Belye Krystall*.

The bizarre was not hard to find in London, but identifying the elusive hand of Trepoff was another matter. The head of a small child was found in a hatbox in the parcel room of Kensington station. Was Trepoff involved? A man in Walling left his house in the morning, was seen going back for his umbrella, and then disappeared from the face of the Earth. A strange explosion destroyed the house of a Paddington chalk-merchant, who was then found in the cellar, dead of the bite of a giant tropical spider. Was Trepoff involved?

The great safe deposit vaults of the London & Midlands Bank were opened one Monday morning and discovered to be completely empty, with no discernible trace of how the event had happened. The police professed themselves to be baffled in one sentence, and in the next promised an 'early arrest.'

'It really is quite puzzling,' Barnett told Moriarty that evening, 'although I see no sign that our mysterious Trepoff is involved in it. The only set of keys, without which I am assured no man could have opened the vault doors unless he employed sufficient explosive to bring the building down around him, was in the hands of the branch manager continuously from the time he left the bank on Friday until he returned on Monday morning. The time clock on the vault was set by the assistant manager, in the manager's presence, as is their custom, and, indeed, did not release the mechanism until eight o'clock Monday morning. The electric alarm system, which connects with the local police station, was not set off. And the guard, who is locked in for the weekend, saw nothing unusual. Nevertheless, two large vaults have been completely emptied of their contents.'

'It does not concern us,' Moriarty told Barnett. 'Trepoff was not involved.'

'How can you be sure?'

Moriarty was bent over the small worktable in his study, titrating a clear reagent into a test tube half-full of brown liquid. For a time he did not answer, but continued to critically observe the liquid. All at once the brown color faded and the test tube was clear. Moriarty made a note in his notebook and kept watching as the reagent mixed with the now-clear liquid drop by drop. Within a minute there was another change, this one more gradual, until the liquid had turned a deep blue. Moriarty put the test tube aside and wrote a couple of quick lines in the notebook. Then he turned to Barnett.

'The bank manager keeps the keys to his branch — the entire set, mind you — on his dresser while he sleeps. Does this strike you as being a safe procedure?'

'I suppose not,' Barnett admitted.

'Further, he does not share a bedroom with his wife, but sleeps alone. And he is a heavy sleeper. It would be no trick for a clever man to obtain impressions of the keys.'

'I see,' Barnett said slowly.

'The Briggs-Murcheson time clock is a fascinating device,' Moriarty said, going over to his desk and sitting down. 'Mr. Murcheson — Mr. Briggs is deceased

— Mr. Murcheson would no doubt be quite surprised to discover that if a powerful electromagnet is placed in the proximity of the escapement mechanism and the current applied to it is reversed fifty times a second, the clock is speeded up to approximately twice its normal speed. Which means that if the clock were set for, let us say, the sixty-one hours between Friday at seven p.m. and Monday at eight a.m., and someone were to apply such an electromagnet in the appropriate place shortly after midnight Friday, he might expect the timing mechanism to be released at about four-thirty Sunday morning. It could, of course, be reset after someone had gained access to the interior of the vault.'

'This is all just a theory, of course,' Barnett said. 'What of the guard?'

'Theoretically,' Moriarty said, smiling, 'we may assume that the gentleman, as is common with many of his sort, is fond of the bottle. A little laudanum mixed into the flask that he takes to work would effectively render him *non compos mentis* for the required period. And he could hardly be expected to mention it afterward, as it would cost him his job.'

'And the electrical alarm?'

'Ah, yes,' Moriarty said. 'Which goes under the streets to the police station. A workman at the appropriate manhole, several blocks away from the bank, could easily render it inoperative for the required time.'

'I see,' Barnett repeated. And he was now sure he did.

'An aggregate of defenses, when taken together, may sound formidable,' Moriarty said, 'although when individually examined, they may be nothing of the sort.' He laced his fingers together on the desk. 'But let us leave off this theoretical discussion, however fascinating, and get on to more urgent matters. I have some word of Trepoff.'

'You do?' Barnett said. 'What have you found out — and how?'

'I have spent every evening for the last few weeks playing chess at the Bohemian Club and at the Balalaika. The Russians have a passion for chess equaled only by their passion for intrigue. If I may say so, they are on the average better at chess.'

'Weren't you afraid of being recognized? This Trepoff is trying to kill you, after all.'

'He seems to have given up that notion — at least for the time being,' Moriarty said. 'And I took precautions against being recognized. Indeed, I passed you once as you rounded the corner of Montague Place, and you failed to recognize me. I added thirty years to my age and took six inches off my height. You have no idea how tiring it is to appear six inches shorter for hours at a time.'

'Have you made any contacts among the anarchists?' Barnett asked.

Moriarty nodded. 'They trust me. I am an old gentleman who beats them at chess and refuses to allow them to discuss their politics around him because it's all a stupid game and will accomplish nothing. I rant at them about how stupid they are, so they trust me.'

'You speak Russian?' Barnett asked.

'Well enough,' Moriarty said. 'I mostly listen.'

'What sort of people are they?'

Moriarty shook his head. 'They are as ineffectual as children. They talk and talk, they plan, and they argue, hour after hour. They may kill a few people — it is easy to kill — but they cannot form a successful committee. So how can they ever hope to form a government?'

'What did you find out?'

'Trepoff, calling himself Ivan Zorta, has been recruiting from the anarchist community. He has formed a secret group, which does not appear to have a name, made up of three-man cells. He has extorted strong oaths of allegiance from those he has subverted, promising them something big, something earthshaking. And soon.'

'Did you see him?'

'No. Nobody has ever seen him, or so they say over the chess table. That is why I believe Zorta to be Trepoff. That and the promise of something big that he is holding out to his recruits. Also, it is all, except for Zorta himself, a little too visible. Despite all the horrible oaths and vows of secrecy, everyone in the community knows of the organization with no

186

name. Whatever it does will surely be blamed on the anarchists, which is just what Trepoff is trying to accomplish. Now, let's look at your reports for the day.'

Moriarty skimmed over the four sheets of paper Barnett had brought home filled with the day's unusual events. Apart from the mysterious bank robbery, which Barnett now decided to discount, he didn't think there was anything of particular interest.

Moriarty evidently agreed with him, as he didn't pause at any of the items until he reached the last. This he read through twice, and then he put the paper down and tapped it with his finger. 'Tell me about this,' he said.

'It looked to be a fascinating story for a while, but turned out to be nothing in the end,' Barnett said. 'Luckily, all the papers picked up the correction before it got into print.

'The story got out that the Duke of Ipswich's seventeen-year-old daughter was missing under mysterious circumstances. My agent, a reporter for the

Standard, went out to Baddeley, the Ipswich ancestral manor in Kensington, to check on it. The butler answered the door and would not permit a reporter on the premises, but he assured my man that he was mistaken and that there was nothing wrong. My agent went to the local police station and discovered that they had indeed been called some hours before — this was early morning, so make it late last night — and were informed that Lady Catherine, the daughter, was missing. She had been entertaining a small group of friends and they had been playing a game — fish, I believe it is called — that involved much scurrying about and concealment.

'Lady Catherine went out to conceal herself, apparently, and could not be found. After an hour, her friends got worried and went around the house calling for her to come out, but she didn't. So they and the servants organized a systematic search of the mansion, from top to bottom. When they didn't find her — and by now over two hours had passed

— they called in the police.'

'A wise move,' Moriarty noted.

'The butler informed the constable that the house had been locked for the night before Lady Catherine's disappearance. There is a patent burglar alarm on all the doors and windows, and it had been turned on. This had not been set off. So far, a first-class mystery and a first-class story, I'm sure you'll agree.'

'I do,' Moriarty said. 'What is the denouement?'

'Well, just before my agent and the several other reporters who had appeared went racing back to their city rooms, His Grace the Duke of Ipswich arrived back at Baddeley Hall in the ducal carriage and demanded to know what was going on. When he was told that his daughter was missing, he said that on the contrary, he had taken her away himself only two hours before. The duchess, Lady Catherine's mother, is ill and in confinement at her mother's, and the duke and Lady Catherine had driven off to visit. It was a spur-of-the-moment decision of the duke's to take his daughter, and she apparently didn't bother to mention it to anyone in the house. She stayed with her mother while the duke returned home.'

'And the burglar alarms?'

'He has a key.'

'Of course. He would have.'

Barnett shrugged. 'Just an ordinary series of misunderstandings. Luckily, the truth came out before the story was published.'

'The truth,' Moriarty said, 'has yet to come out.'

'What do you mean?'

'Life does not normally attain the qualities of a bad Restoration comedy. When you look at it from the far side of the mirror — that is, as a past event, the implausibility is less evident. But examine the story point by point, as it is supposed to have happened, and see what evolves. The Duke of Ipswich decides to visit his sick wife, who has chosen to be ill at her mother's house. On his way out he sees his daughter, who happens to be hiding from everyone else in the house, and invites her along. They leave, without seeing anyone else, whether friend, guest, or servant. Which has the duke opening and closing his own doors and turning off and resetting his own alarms. Did the duke give any reason for this extraordinary behavior?'

'No,' Barnett said. 'Not that I know of. Is it really that extraordinary?'

'For a duke to open his own front door? I should think so. That's the sort of naiveté that occurs in children's fairy tales. There's a knock on the castle door, and the king goes to answer it. Dukes do not open their own front doors. And if any servant had let them out, he would have mentioned it when the search for Lady Catherine began.'

'So you conclude?'

'That the girl is, indeed, missing. That the Duke was notified of her absence, probably by the abductors, and was rushing back to Baddeley Hall to see if it was true. That he immediately denied her absence because he had been warned by the abductors to do so.'

'Rather a slender thread upon which to hang such a weighty conclusion,' Barnett remarked.

'It will bear the weight,' Moriarty said. 'And there's at least a sporting chance that this is Trepoff's opening gambit.'

'Trepoff! What signs of him are there?'

'None,' Moriarty admitted. 'But yet I see nothing to indicate that it *isn't* Trepoff. And my nose detects the slight odor of the bizarre that makes this one of the few events you've brought to my attention that might involve Trepoff, and therefore it warrants further investigation.'

'Do you want me to get one of my free-lance men out there?'

'He would see nothing,' Moriarty said, 'and you would not see much more. Therefore, we must go together.' He reached for the bell-pull on the wall behind him.

'You mean now?' Barnett asked. 'By the time we get there it will be after ten.'

'If the duke's daughter has indeed been abducted,' Moriarty said, 'then I assure you he will be awake.'

Mr. Maws appeared at the door, and Moriarty told him to go out and procure a four-wheeler. 'See if Clarence or

Dermot are at their stand,' he suggested. 'After our recent experience, I am partial to the jarvey I know. At any rate, have one back here in five minutes if you can. We'll be ready to leave then.'

'Very good, Professor,' Mr. Maws said.

As the four-wheeler, with Clarence atop, proceeded toward Kensington, Moriarty sat stooped like a great hawk, his prominent chin resting on his folded hands above the ivory handle of his stick, eyes narrowed in thought. Barnett, across from him, kept a respectful silence and amused himself by trying to decide what was occupying Moriarty's mind as they sped across London.

After a few minutes Moriarty affixed his pince-nez to the bridge of his nose and turned his gaze to Barnett. 'You have been staring at me for the past ten minutes,' he said. 'Have I suddenly developed a keratosis?'

'No, sir,' Barnett said. 'I apologize. But, to tell you the truth, I was thinking about your attitudes.'

'My attitudes?'

'Yes. Toward people.'

'You refer, I assume,' Moriarty said calmly, 'to my characteristic revulsion toward my fellow man.'

'I wouldn't have put it that strongly,' Barnett said.

Moriarty snorted. 'My fellow man is a fool,' he said, 'incapable of acting twice consecutively in his own interest, for the very good reason that he has only the sketchiest idea of what his interest is, or where it lies. He allows his emotions to override his puny intellect and blindly follows whichever of his fellows brays the loudest in his direction. He firmly believes in the existence of an almighty God, whom he pictures, somehow, as looking a lot like himself, and further believes that it matters to this Creator of the Universe whether He is prayed to in a kneeling or sitting position. He rejects Isaac Newton and Charles Darwin in favor of Bishop Ussher and the Davenport Brothers. He supposes that a planet a hundred times as massive as the earth, and a thousand million miles distant, was placed there solely to predict the outcome of his business affairs or his romantic dalliances. He believes in ghosts, poltergeists, mesmerism, spiritualism, clairvoyance, astrology, numerology, and a hundred other foolishnesses, but isn't sure about evolution or the germ theory of disease.'

'Come, Professor,' Barnett said, 'is not that a bit broad? Surely there are exceptions.'

'Indeed,' Professor Moriarty said, nodding. 'And it is the exceptions who make life interesting.' He took a large handkerchief from his jacket pocket and, removing the pince-nez from his nose, polished the glasses carefully. 'I am not a complete misanthrope, Mr. Barnett,' he said, 'and you must not imagine that I am. Indeed, it must be that on some unconscious level of my brain I am quite concerned about this hypothetical fellow man, or I wouldn't get so angry over his foibles.'

'I thought, perhaps, it was just annoyance at recalling that you, yourself, are one of the creatures,' Barnett said.

Moriarty considered this for a minute. 'So I am,' he said finally. 'I had quite forgotten.'

The four-wheeler turned left off Holland Park Avenue, and Moriarty pulled out his pocket-watch. 'We're almost there,' he said. 'Strike a match, will you?'

Barnett obliged from the small packet of waterproofs he carried to light his occasional cigars.

'Ah!' Moriarty said. 'It is still a quarter till the hour of ten. A bit late for calling, but I have no doubt that His Grace will see us.'

A few minutes later they had turned past the ancient gateposts and were heading up the drive toward Baddeley Hall. Fifty years before, this great three-story Tudor mansion had been the main house to the great estate of Baddeley, surrounded by hundreds of acres of well-managed land. But now Greater London had grown past Baddeley, and most of the managing was done by estate agents who collected the quarterly rents on street after street of semi-detached cottages. It had ruined the duke's shooting — but had enormously increased his income.

Moriarty looked out of the carriage window and chuckled with satisfaction as they pulled around to the great oak doors that were Baddeley Hall's main entrance. 'I was right,' he said. 'The trip was not in vain.'

'What do you mean?' Barnett asked.

'See for yourself,' Moriarty said. 'Every lamp in the house must be lighted, and there are but two vehicles waiting in the drive: a closed landau bearing a crest I cannot make out from here and a hansom. Family friends and advisors, no doubt, come to aid the duke in his time of travail.'

Clarence pulled up to the front steps and they dismounted. 'I don't know how long we'll be,' Moriarty told Clarence. 'I think it wiser if you stay with your vehicle. I don't expect any trouble here now, but there's no point in taking unnecessary risks.'

'That's quite all right, Professor,' Clarence replied cheerily, taking off his bowler and scratching his bald head. 'It ain't all that cold and it ain't raining. I have a flask of tea here, and there's enough light from these here gas fixtures to read the 'Pink 'un' by, so I'm content.' He waved his hat at the horse. 'Maud here gets nervous when I leave her alone at night, anyway.'

'Very good, then,' Moriarty said. He and Barnett mounted the steps together, and Barnett pulled the lion's-head bell-pull by the door. Moriarty took out one of his calling cards and wrote '*Ivan Zorta*' on the back.

The door opened, and a tall man in the Ipswich livery stared out impassively at them. 'Yes?'

'I must see your master on a matter of the utmost importance.' Moriarty said. 'Show him this card.'

The man placed the card on a tray. 'Come in,' he said, taking their hats and Moriarty's stick. 'You may wait in there.'

They crossed the entrance hall under the footman's watchful eye and entered a small reception room. Within a very few minutes a second, shorter but more regal-looking man — Barnett surmised that this was the butler — came to fetch them. 'His Grace will see you now,' he said. 'Please follow me.'

Barnett followed Moriarty down the hall, staring with frank curiosity at his surroundings. This was the first time he had ever been in a duke's residence, and might well be the last, so he wanted to take it all in. The walls were rich, dark oak and hung with ancient family portraits interspersed with occasional pastoral scenes. There was a great, wide staircase, and at its foot, by the intricately carved oak baluster, was a full suit of armor that looked, at least to Barnett's uneducated eye, as though it had once been worn in battle.

'In here, please, gentlemen,' the butler said, showing them into the duke's private study. They entered, and the butler closed the doors behind them.

The duke was a man of medium height and middle age, very stocky, with muttonchop whiskers and a conservatively trimmed mustache. At the moment he was obviously in a fit of passion, which he was suppressing with difficulty and without much success. His face was beet-red, and he was striding back and forth on the edge of his rug with short, stiff-legged steps and flexing a heavy riding crop between his hands.

'Well,' he said glaring at them, 'what is it you want with me?'

'I am sorry to hear about Your Grace's loss,' Moriarty said. 'I know this must be very trying for you, so I shall be brief. To put it as simply as possible, I think I can be of assistance to you.'

'Assistance, is it?' the Duke of Ipswich said, the short whip twisting spasmodically in his hands. 'Very well, then, state your terms.'

Moriarty looked a little surprised at this response, but he continued. 'I need some information first,' he said. 'I need to know how your daughter was abducted, as exactly as possible. I would like to see the scene. I must know whether the abductors have been in touch with you as yet, and if so, what are their terms. I assume they have, since the name I wrote on my card commended it to your attention.'

'Name?' the Duke blinked. He walked over to his desk, picked up Moriarty's card and turned it over. 'Ivan Zorta? This name means nothing to me.'

'I see,' Moriarty said, looking genuinely puzzled. 'Then why — perhaps Your Grace has heard of me in some other context?'

'Must we continue this farce?' the duke demanded. 'State your terms for returning my daughter and they will be met. I know your name.'

Moriarty was silent for a moment, while the duke went back to pacing the floor, his knuckles white around the riding crop. A small sound escaped from the duke's mouth, but whether it was a cry of rage, pain, or anguish, Barnett could not tell. Barnett was horrified at this confusion, and angry that the duke would dare think them capable of such a crime.

'There is a serious misunderstanding, Your Grace,' Moriarty said. 'I assure you — '

'Enough!' the duke cried. 'I have heard enough, I will suffer no more of this. It is with the utmost effort of will that I resist leaping at you, sir, and striking you and your companion down. I was told that it was almost certain that you were the agent of my daughter's disappearance, that anything this dastardly and clever had your mark on it. And now — and now, here you are, sir. Where is my daughter? If you have harmed her, I assure you that there is no place on this earth where I will not hunt you down and destroy you. Mark that, sir!'

'You were told?' Moriarty was astonished. 'Who could have told you such a thing and for what purpose?' He suddenly jabbed an accusing finger at no one in particular. 'Holmes!' he cried, his voice tight with anger. 'You have employed Sherlock Holmes! And he is attempting to earn his undoubtedly impressive fee by convincing you that I am involved in this repulsive crime.'

The door behind the desk opened, and the tall, ascetic figure of Sherlock Holmes stalked in. 'Good evening, Professor,' he said in his expressionless, carefully modulated voice. 'I had, of course, recognized your hand in this crime, but I hardly expected to see you here yourself. Setting an example for your minions, perhaps?'

Moriarty swung around. 'This is outrageous, Holmes! Are you going to give up any semblance of deduction from now on, and merely blame me for every crime in London?'

'In London, Moriarty?' Holmes said. 'Why so limiting? Say rather, in the world, Professor. In the world!' He carefully walked back to the door and closed it. 'But only among friends, you understand, would I say such a thing. And only the best sort of crimes: the clever, evil ones that require a master brain and an utter disregard for common sensibilities or morality.'

'You have already said too much before two witnesses,' Moriarty said, 'and one of them noble. I could have you for slander, Holmes.'

The Duke of Ipswich, who had been growing increasingly agitated as he listened to this exchange, suddenly threw down the riding crop. 'Confound you, you bastard!' he cried, leaping forward.

'What have you done with my daughter?' And as he slammed into Moriarty, his hands reached for the professor's neck.

Moriarty went down before the surprise blow, and the duke was on top of him, his hands around Moriarty's neck and his face apoplectic.

Moriarty took the nobleman's wrists and, with surprising ease, pulled them apart. Then, before either Barnett or Holmes could reach them, he had rolled over and come to his knees. His hands still held the duke's wrists in an iron grip. 'I will release you, Your Grace, when you have calmed down,' he said, his voice even.

The duke took several deep breaths, and then went limp. 'I can't fight you,' he said. 'You have my daughter.'

Moriarty released the duke and stood up, dusting himself off. He reached a hand out for the duke, who ignored it and pushed himself to his feet. 'Your rug is really quite dusty,' Moriarty said, slapping at his trousers. 'You should speak to your staff.'

The duke stood where he had risen,

speechless and trembling. Holmes went over and helped him to a chair. 'You have the upper hand this time, Moriarty,' he said. 'Make your demands.'

Moriarty shook his head sadly. 'For the last time,' he said. 'I know nothing of this crime aside from the bare fact that it occurred. The gentleman with me is Benjamin Barnett, an American journalist, and it is he who informed me that Lady Catherine was missing. I am possessed of some facts — unrelated to the event — that enabled me to develop a theory of the crime. I came here for the sole purpose of ascertaining whether that theory could be correct. If so, I am prepared to share these facts with you and aid you to the best of my ability in apprehending the criminal.'

'Purely for the most altruistic motives, eh, Professor?' Holmes demanded with a sneer.

'Not at all,' Moriarty said. 'It would further my interests.'

'I have no doubt of that,' Holmes said. He turned to the duke. 'It may interest Your Grace to know that the professor's

205

friend here, Benjamin Barnett, is an escaped criminal, convicted of murder by a Constantinople court. There is, unfortunately, nothing the British authorities can do to send him back.'

The duke held his hands out. 'Just tell me how she is,' he implored, his face now ashen and his eyes staring. 'For mercy's sake! Tell me how she is.'

'Your Grace,' Moriarty said, 'I give you my word of honor that I know neither how your daughter is nor where she is. I had nothing to do with her abduction. Nothing. However, I can see that in the present state of affairs I can be of no help to you and you of none to me. If I hear of anything, I shall notify you. Please do not assault my messenger. In the meantime, put your trust in Sherlock Holmes; you cannot do any better. He is, under normal circumstances, an excellent consulting detective. However, in this case, he will not accomplish anything until he rids himself of this ridiculous fixation that I am at the root of every crime that is not immediately transparent to his gaze.'

Moriarty walked to the door and

opened it. 'I think we can find our own way out,' he said. Then he turned back to the duke, who was looking at him with a puzzled expression on his face. 'My advice is not to call in Scotland Yard,' he said. 'This case is beyond them, and they will only bungle it. I hope your daughter is returned to you safely. Good night, Your Grace. Good night, Mr. Holmes.'

He closed the door gently behind him, and he and Barnett walked silently down the long hall. The footman was waiting at the front door for them, with stick and hats.

8

INTERSTICES

As someday it may happen
that a victim must be found,
I've got a little list —
I've got a little list.

— *W. S. Gilbert*

For the next few weeks, having no instructions to the contrary, Barnett busied himself with the affairs of the expanding American News Service. On Wednesday, June 25th, he promoted Miss Perrine — they agreed upon the title of 'Cable Editor' as being the most appropriate — and instructed her to hire an assistant and a messenger boy. Then he purchased two more desks and yet another typewriter. 'If this keeps up,' he told Miss Perrine, as they received confirmation of their forty-third American newspaper account, the *San Francisco Call*, 'we're going to have to search for larger quarters before the end of the month.'

'The offices next door are vacant,' Miss Perrine told him, 'and the rental agent confirms that we can have them as of the first of July.' She put her wide, red-trimmed hat on and carefully adjusted it to the proper rakish angle before pinning it in place. She seemed unaware of Barnett's admiring gaze. 'And, by the way,' she said, 'you are taking me to lunch.'

'You've arranged for the offices?' Barnett asked.

She nodded.

'Without consulting me?'

'Yes.'

Barnett shook his head. 'And quite right, too,' he said. 'Where am I taking you?'

'Sweetings', I think,' she said.

And so he did. And after the waiter had taken their order and gone away, he leaned forward across the table and regarded her steadily through unblinking eyes until she nervously looked away.

'You're staring at me,' she said.

'I am,' he admitted. 'But then, you're well worth staring at.'

'Please!'

'And I was beginning to think you were quite without shame,' he said. Seeing her shocked expression, he laughed. 'You must admit that you've gained tremendously in self-assurance in the past few weeks.'

'That is not the same thing,' she said severely, 'as being without shame.'

'Sorry,' Barnett said. 'That was an ignorant, boorish comment, and I withdraw it.'

'Indeed!' she said. 'As for what you call my increase in self-assurance, that, I suppose, is true. It comes of discovering that I can do the job quite adequately.'

'Quite excellently,' Barnett amended. 'But you told me that when I hired you.'

'Yes,' she said, 'but thinking you can do something, even to the point of moral certainty, is not the same as proving you can do it.'

'Well, you've proven it,' Barnett said.

'You're a born writer and editor. You have an innate word sense, and you write good clean prose.'

'Tell me truthfully, Mr. Barnett,' Miss Perrine said, 'you don't have the phrase 'for a woman' left unsaid at the end of any of those sentences, do you?'

'Cecily,' Barnett said, 'a piece of paper with typewritten words on it is entirely without gender. When we cable a story to one of our client newspapers, I don't append a statement, 'done in a feminine hand.' You are a good writer.'

'Thank you,' she said. 'And thank you for calling me 'Cecily.''

'Well,' he said. 'It just slipped out I was afraid you'd think it forward of me.'

'I do,' she said.

The waiter brought their lunch, and Barnett busied himself with his salmon mousseline for a few minutes before looking up. 'Say,' he said, 'there was something I meant to tell you. We have a new writer.'

'Who?'

'Fellow named Wilde. Someone at the *Pall Mall Gazette* introduced him to me, and I talked him into doing a series of articles on understanding Britain for the Americans. Actually, I suppose, he'll write about whatever he chooses. These article writers always do. He's very good. We should have no trouble selling the series.'

She put down her fork. 'Oscar Wilde?' she asked.

'That's right.'

'He's brilliant,' she said. 'But he tends to be very eccentric and he seems to love to shock. We'll have to watch his copy.'

'I leave that to your immense good judgment,' he said. 'He's not doing it under his own name; maybe that will calm him down.'

'What byline is he using?'

'Josephus.'

'Why does he choose to disguise his name?'

'I asked him that,' Barnett said. 'And he told me — let me get it straight now — he said: 'Writing for Americans is like performing as the rear end of a music-hall horse — one does it only for the money and one would prefer to remain anonymous.''

212

'That sounds like him,' she said.

'He's either a natural genius at the epigram, or he spends large amounts of time in front of a mirror at home, rehearsing,' Barnett said.

They finished lunch and walked back to the office, chatting amiably about this and that. 'Who is this Professor Moriarty for whom you're doing the special assignments?' she asked him as they reached the door to the office..

'I'm not sure how to answer that,' he said. 'He is a former professor of mathematics, and a great scientist, if I'm any judge. He saved my life once. And, even aside from that, I have more respect for him than for any man I have ever met. But . . . ' he shrugged. 'Let me think on how to explain better who he is.'

★ ★ ★

It was after dark when a carriage pulled up to the door of 64 Russell Square and a tall man swathed in a light opera cape descended and rang the front door bell.

Mr. Maws answered the door promptly.

'Yes?' he said, surveying the gentleman expressionlessly.

'I would speak with the Professor Moriarty.'

'Whom should I say is calling?'

'I am Count Boris Gobolski, accredited representative of His Imperial Majesty Alexander the Third, Tsar of all the Russias, to the court of St. James.'

Mr. Maws nodded almost imperceptibly. 'Have you an appointment?' he asked.

'Your master will wish to see me,' Count Boris Gobolski said. 'Immediately. It is of utmost importance.'

'Come in,' Mr. Maws said. 'Please wait in the front room. I will inform the professor that you're here.'

Moriarty was wrapped in a blue silk dressing gown with a large red-embroidered dragon of menacing aspect curled over its right shoulder, was stretched out on his bed, propped up by a mound of pillows when Mr. Maws knocked and entered to announce Gobolski's presence. The bed curtains were tied off, and the bed was surrounded by chairs and footstools piled high with books. He had taken to his bed three days before, announcing that there was nothing further he could do until Trepoff made some move, and that he was not to be disturbed for trivialities.

Moriarty petulantly slammed closed the book he was reading. 'Probably wants a report,' he said. 'There was nothing in our agreement about reports. Tell him . . . ' He sat up. 'No, I had better go myself. I will give the gentleman to understand that there is nothing to be gained by incessantly pestering me.'

'He has never been here before, sir,' Mr. Maws felt obliged to state.

'That's no reason for him to start now,' Moriarty said. 'This must be nipped in the bud. I cannot work without a free hand.'

'Yes, sir,' Mr. Maws said. 'Shall I tell the gentleman that you will be down directly?'

'Yes, tell him that,' Moriarty said, pulling on his shoes. 'I suppose I'd better dress first. It wouldn't do to greet an ambassador in a dressing gown. Go and knock up Barnett on your way down-stairs. Tell him to join us in the study as

215

soon as he's presentable.'

'Very good, sir.'

Moriarty was dressed in ten minutes, and found Barnett waiting for him on the landing. 'Good to see you up,' Barnett said cheerfully.

'Bah!' Moriarty replied. He wiped his pince-nez and placed it over his nose, eyeing Barnett critically through the lenses. 'Our relationship,' he said, 'is somehow not what I expected.' Then he trotted down the stairs ahead of Barnett.

Mr. Maws was in the front hall, keeping a suspicious eye on the door to the front room. 'Show Count Gobolski into the study,' Moriarty directed him. 'Have you lit the lamps?'

'I didn't want to leave the hall, Professor,' Mr. Maws said.

'Of course,' Moriarty said. Taking a box of waterproof vespas from his pocket, he entered his study and performed the service himself, lighting the overhead gas pendant and the ornate brass gas lamp on his desk.

Count Gobolski entered the room, his opera cape still wrapped around him.

'Professor James Moriarty?' he asked.

Moriarty stood behind his desk. 'Count Boris Gobolski?'

Gobolski nodded nervously, and his gaze shifted to Barnett, who was standing by the small worktable across the room. 'Who is he?' he demanded.

'My assistant,' Moriarty said. 'Benjamin Barnett.'

'My pleasure, Count,' Barnett said, bowing slightly and smiling.

'I do not like this,' Gobolski said. His English was precise and perfect, and only a slight liquidity in the consonants marked him as a foreigner.

'Pray be seated, Your Excellency,' Moriarty said, indicating the leather chair by his desk. 'I would prefer Mr. Barnett to remain, but if you wish him to leave . . . '

'No, no,' Gobolski said, waving his arm vaguely at Barnett and dropping into the indicated chair. 'I did not mean — 'He paused and looked around the room. 'I believe I was followed,' he said. 'Coming here, I mean.'

'Ah!' Moriarty said. He reached behind

him and gave a slight tug on the bellpull. 'And what leads you to suspect that?'

'One develops a feel for such things,' Gobolski said.

Mr. Maws opened the door and stepped inside.

'Would you like a libation, Your Excellency?' Moriarty asked. 'A brandy, perhaps? I have a fine Napoleon I can offer you. Mr. Maws, see to it, will you? And send Tolliver out the back way to see if anyone is taking an interest in this house.'

Mr. Maws nodded and left, silently closing the door behind him.

'And now, Count Gobolski,' Moriarty said, 'what brings you calling at this late hour? And whom do you suspect of taking an interest in your affairs?'

'I am a diplomat,' Gobolski said, 'not a conspirator. But for a Russian today, that means little difference. One has to learn to live with being followed, threatened, terrorized. One lives in the shadow of assassination.' He smoothed his mustache down with a nervous gesture. 'Did you know,' he asked, leaning forward, 'that there is a police guard in front of my house twenty-four hours of the day?'

'It must be wearing,' Moriarty said.

'Nine of the members of my staff are nothing more or less than bodyguards,' Gobolski said.

Mr. Maws returned with the brandy glasses on a tray and distributed them, putting the tray with the bottle on a corner of the desk. Gobolski sniffed his drink suspiciously for a second and then drained the glass. 'Excellent,' he said. Mr. Maws refilled the glass.

'All of this,' Gobolski said, 'is the normal procedure.' He sipped at the second glass. 'Then I received a message from St. Petersburg today. Doubly encoded, so that when the code clerk was finished with it I then had to decode it again myself.'

'Yes?' Moriarty encouraged.

'There was a message in it — and instructions. The message was for Professor James Moriarty. The instructions were for me. I have never heard of you before, you understand.'

'I would not have expected you to have.'

'My instructions were to bring the

message to you myself, personally, and not allow anyone else to see it. That is unusual.'

'I'm sure.'

'The instructions further directed me to be careful,' Count Gobolski said. 'Be careful! When I already have twenty-four-hour policemen and nine armed guards.' He smoothed his mustache. 'I trust that the message holds some relevancy or importance for you. I confess that it conveys nothing of interest to me.'

'I haven't seen it yet,' Moriarty said, patiently.

'I tell you Mr. — Professor — Moriarty, there is enough to keep me busy in the diplomatic sphere without branching out into espionage. The External Branch of the *Okhrana* is responsible for espionage. It is not my job. The relationships between your country and mine — I assume you are British — are quite delicate. They require all of my time. I don't see why a man in my position has to act as a courier for messages of doubtful importance.'

'May I see the message?' Moriarty asked.

'Oh, yes. Of course.' Count Gobolski patted the pockets of his formal attire, and finally produced a slip of buff paper, which he passed over to the Professor.

Moriarty read it, and then reread it, looking puzzled 'This is all?' he demanded.

Count Gobolski looked slightly startled at the change in Moriarty's manner. 'All?' he said. 'Of course it is all. Then I was right — the matter is of no importance? I am missing Wagner for nothing?'

'On the contrary, my dear Count,' Moriarty said, 'it is of the gravest importance. But it is incomplete; the most significant facts are missing.' He held the slip of paper out. 'Barnett, what do you make of it?'

Barnett took the paper and stood under the gas pendant to read it. It was printed in a crabbed hand, presumably Count Gobolski's, and read in its entirety:

FOUR SAILORS FROM BLACK SEA FLEET HAVE LEFT SEVASTOPOL FOR

ENGLAND. JOINING TREPOFF SURELY.
TRAVELING AS GERMANS POSSIBLY.
EXPECTED JULY TENTH.

'Trepoff needs sailors,' Barnett said, handing the note back.

'So it would seem,' Moriarty said. 'And the tenth is only six days off.' He transferred his attention back to Gobolski. 'What do you know of Trepoff?'

'I?' Gobolski started. 'Nothing. I know nothing of Trepoff. I have heard rumors, of course. Who has not? But I know nothing of this madman. Nothing. It is said that he kills without warning. And that, although an agent of the Tsar, even the Tsar is afraid of him. Of course, that is not true. I know nothing of him.'

Moriarty leaned forward. 'Trepoff is in London,' he said, tapping the desk. 'He is real. You were sent with that message because of your exalted rank and station, because you could be trusted and no one else could. I thank you for coming. This is of the utmost importance, you must believe that. As important as any of your other work.'

'Trepoff is in London?' Count Gobolski shot a nervous glance around the room and wiped his mustache. 'Has your man ascertained yet whether my carriage is under observation?'

'He will inform us before you leave,' Moriarty said. 'But this message must be amplified.' He tapped the paper. 'You must send a reply requesting more detail, Excellency. I need to know the identity of the four men. I need to know their ranks and their specialties.'

'What for?' Gobolski said, honestly puzzled. 'They are only sailors. If they were officers it would have said as much.'

'But even sailors have specialties,' Moriarty said patiently. 'The may be deckhands, or gunners, or ordinance specialists, or artificers, or engine crew, or stewards, or any one of a dozen other jobs. If I know what they do, then I will have some idea of why Trepoff wants them. I need this information, Your Excellency.'

Count Gobolski nodded. 'Very clever. The specialties of sailors, I will send the message.'

'Thank you.'

There was a tapping at the study door, and Mummer Tolliver burst through. 'I've got 'em pegged right enough for you, Professor,' he said, coming to a halt in front of the desk.

'Then there is someone watching the house?' Moriarty asked. He looked pleased.

''Course there is, sir,' the mummer said. 'There's three of 'em, as a matter of fact.'

'Tell me about it,' Moriarty said, rubbing his hands together thoughtfully.

'Yes, sir. There's a chap bent over in the shrubbery in the square, behind the equestrian statue of Lord Hornblower. He's keeping a weather eye on the carriage what's parked outside the door.'

'My carriage?' Count Gobolski demanded.

'Right enough,' the Mummer agreed. 'And on the back steps of the British Museum, on Montague Place, there's a beggar with a horrible twisted lip selling pencils. Only it's a peculiar time to be selling pencils, says me, and he ain't no beggar, further.'

'That sounds like a certain consulting

detective of my acquaintance,' Moriarty said. 'I do hope he isn't too comfortable.'

'And then, around the corner of the next block, over on Gower Street, there's a hansom cab sitting, waiting for something.'

'A fare, perhaps?' Moriarty suggested.

'Funny time to be waiting for a fare on Gower Street,' the Mummer said. 'I went over to him myself and tried to engage him.'

'And?'

'He told me he was otherwise engaged. When I persisted, he told me several interesting things about my parentage that my father hasn't seen fit to mention. He spoke with an accent.'

'What sort?' Moriarty asked.

The Mummer shrugged. 'Wasn't French,' he said. 'German?'

'Could it have been Russian?' Moriarty suggested.

''Course it could,' Tolliver agreed. 'German, Russian — they all sound the same, you know.'

'Yes, I suppose they do,' Moriarty said. 'Anything else?'

'It is my opinion,' Tolliver said, 'that the gent lurking behind the statue and the gent atop of the hansom are working together.'

'Interesting,' Moriarty said. 'On what do you base this observation?'

'Their hats,' Tolliver said.

Barnett looked at his small friend. 'Hats?' he said.

'Yes. Caps, actually. They both have the same cap, and it's a queer one, it is. Long beak, coming to a point almost, in front. With a little strap in the back with a buckle. Never seen one like it before, and here's two in one evening. That's why I think they're related, those two.'

'Very good work, Tolliver,' Moriarty said. He turned to Count Gobolski. 'If you don't mind my asking, Your Excellency, where are you going from here?'

'To the house of — a friend — south of Kensington Gardens,' Gobolski said. 'Why do you ask?'

'Please write down the address and give it to Tolliver here,' Moriarty said. 'They will follow you when you leave here, but they will be prepared for someone attempting to follow them. That is, if it is the group I suspect. However, if Tolliver picks them up when you arrive at your friend's house instead of following them directly, we may catch them off guard. In that case we may be able to trace them back to their lair. Perhaps back to Trepoff himself.'

'You believe this is possible?' Gobolski asked. 'And you think this little man can do such a job?'

Tolliver grinned. 'I ain't perfect,' he said, 'but I'm good.'

Count Gobolski shrugged, unconvinced, but wrote an address down on the back of one of his cards. He handed the card to Tolliver.

'I wants to change clothes for this job,' the Mummer said, indicating his checked suit and high collar. 'This ain't a suitable disguise. Give me a moment.'

'We'll give you twenty minutes,' Moriarty said, 'ten minutes to change and a ten-minute head start.'

'Twenty minutes?' Count Gobolski pulled out his pocket watch and inspected its face. 'It is now ten twenty-five. I am already late.'

'Patience, Your Excellency,' Moriarty said, waving the Mummer out of the room, 'there is much at stake here. Perhaps I could interest you in a brief game of chess to pass the time?'

'Chess?' Count Gobolski looked interested. 'You play chess?'

'Barnett, hand down that board on the shelf behind you, if you will.' Moriarty said. 'And the Persian pieces in the box next to it.'

The game went on for forty minutes, with the two men engrossed in the board between them, and Barnett an interested, if not engrossed, spectator. Finally, Moriarty pushed a black pawn forward and straightened up. 'Checkmate, I believe, Your Excellency,' he said. 'A good game.'

Count Gobolski stared at the board. Then he took a small notebook from his pocket and jotted down the sequence of moves in a quick, nervous hand. 'Brilliant!' he said. 'So fast and so sure. And you an Englishman!'

'Thank you,' Moriarty said, taking the delicate ivory pieces and replacing them carefully in their box.

'Well!' Gobolski said, rising and putting his notebook away. 'Now I am incredibly late. I hope it is to the good.' He shook hands with Moriarty. 'I will send your list of questions to St. Petersburg tomorrow,' he said. 'Perhaps you would play chess with me again some time?'

Moriarty rose and bowed. 'My pleasure,' he said.

9

THE PUZZLE

Life must he lived forward,
but can only be understood backward.
— *Kierkegaard*

The cripple, squatting on his little body cart, pulled himself through the London streets with surprising speed, aided by his two short India-rubber-tipped sticks. Early risers on this Sabbath morning saw him pass and felt a touch of pity, a twinge of indefinable guilt — emotions his whole garb had been carefully designed to evoke — and more than one hand reached toward a pocketbook as he passed. He did not stop for alms, however, but pressed determinedly on, scurrying through the streets of Bloomsbury until he passed the British Museum and then hopping his cart dexterously up the steps of 64 Russell Square.

Mr. Maws opened the door upon hearing a persistent knocking, and looked stolidly down on the mendicant on the stoop. 'Yes?'

The cripple rubbed the side of his nose with his right forefinger.

Mr. Maws stepped aside. 'Enter,' he said. 'You may wait in the front room. He will be down directly.'

Ten minutes later Professor Moriarty strode into the front room and glared down at the mendicant. 'Well?' he demanded.

The cripple once again rubbed the side of his nose with his right forefinger. Then he ponderously winked at Moriarty, his face screwed up in an awful expression, and waited.

'Yes, yes,' Moriarty said impatiently. 'I already know that. Well?'

The cripple looked unhappy. 'The Kensington Wheeler, they calls me,' he said finally.

'And well they should,' Moriarty agreed. 'Why are you here?'

231

'Twist, 'e tells me right enough to come see the professor — you the professor? — and bring 'im a message.'

'I am the professor,' Moriarty said, as patiently as he could manage. 'What is the message?'

'Twist, 'e says as how you'll stand a quid for this 'ere message,' the Kensington Wheeler said firmly.

'I'll make it a guinea,' Moriarty said, reaching into his waistcoat pocket, 'if you'll get on with it.' He held some coins out, which disappeared in an indefinable manner into the mendicant's rags.

The Kensington Wheeler tucked his sticks under him and assumed a narrative stance. 'I 'as a spot,' he announced, 'to the right 'and side o' the doors o' the Church o' St. Jude on the south side o' River Thames, over in Lambeth. Sundays, that is. Rest o' the week I wheels about Kensington.'

Moriarty nodded. 'I see.'

'Well, sir,' the Kensington Wheeler continued, 'no sooner 'as I assumed my spot this 'ere morning when a growler pulls up to the corner and two gents gets

232

out dragging a third gent between them.'

'This third gentleman was unconscious?' Moriarty asked.

'No, sir. 'E were right lively. 'E didn't want to go with those other two gents no ways. But 'e were a little chap, and they was considerable bigger.'

'I see.'

'Well, sir, these two big gents they pays me no mind, like I was part o' the wall, which is a usual reaction what people 'as. But the little chap, 'e sees me, and right off 'e gives me the office, despite these other two 'olding 'is arms,. And 'e calls out to them — but really to me, dontcherknow — 'what you want to bother the Mummer for? The Mummer never 'urt you' — so I'd know who 'e is, like.'

'Ah!' Moriarty said.

'Well, sir, these other two gents, they gives me the once-over, but I makes like I'm part o' the wall, which is what they thought in the first place, so they leaves me alone. As soon as they is out of sight, I 'eads out for the guild-'all, even it being the start of the 'eaviest time o' the day for me, cause the little chap gave me the office. Twist tells me to bring the tale 'ere, and you'd make it worth my while.'

'Very interesting,' Moriarty said. 'You did well. You should have taken a cab here, though. I would have reimbursed you.'

'Ain't no cab going to stop for me, Professor, even if I waves the money at the jarvey. Which I 'as done.'

'I see. Well, you shall leave here in a cab. I'll have one here to take you wherever you wish to go. Can you tell me which way they took the Mummer as they left you?'

'Better 'n that,' the beggar said, 'I can show you what building they took 'im into.'

'Excellent!' Moriarty said. 'And so you shall. Go into the kitchen and tell Mrs. H to feed you. I'll be along presently, and we'll take a trip together. We must be quick about it, though.'

'I'll be quicker than quick, Professor,' the Kensington Wheeler said. 'I'm not much of a one for eating, but if I could 'ave a drop o' something before we leaves, it would restore my spirits like.'

'Whatever you like,' Moriarty said. 'Tell Mrs. H.' He crossed the hall to his study while the Kensington Wheeler propelled himself to the rear of the house. After ringing for Mr. Maws, Moriarty touched a concealed stud on the left side of the bookcase behind his desk, and it promptly slid forward. Moriarty swung the bookcase aside and opened the cabinet behind it.

'You rang?' Mr. Maws stood by the door.

'Yes. Have you seen Mr. Barnett this morning?'

'I believe that he has just come down to breakfast, sir,' Mr. Maws volunteered.

'Good,' Moriarty said. 'I shall require him — and you, Mr. Maws, if you would be good enough to accompany me.' He slid open a door in the cabinet and contemplated the row of revolvers contained therein.

'Is it about Mr. Tolliver, sir?' Mr. Maws inquired.

'Yes. The Mummer seems to have fallen into the hands of the opposition. I've no idea what they plan to do with him, but best not to give them the time to do too good a job of it.'

'Very good, sir,' Mr. Maws said. 'If we are to go armed, I would prefer one of the Webley-Fosbery .455-caliber revolvers.'

Moriarty handed over the requested weapon and a box of shells. 'Change clothes into something a bit less butler-like,' he said. 'And ask Barnett to step in here as you pass the dining room.'

'Very good, sir,'

A minute later Barnett came into the study. Moriarty quickly informed him of what was happening and handed him a Smith & Wesson hammerless revolver and ammunition. 'This is for self-protection,' he said, 'and, if necessary, a show of force. I don't know what we'll be coming up against, but if Trepoff is any part of it we'd best be prepared. He is a violently dangerous man.'

Barnett loaded the revolver and thrust it into his belt. 'Won't your London police object to gunplay of a Sunday afternoon?'

'It may require a bit of explaining,'

Moriarty admitted. 'We could always tell them we are rehearsing an amateur theatrical. On the whole, it would be best if we don't have to use these weapons. Besides, I would like to speak with Tolliver's captors in some detail, a task rendered easier if they are still alive.'

'And,' Barnett added, 'if we are.'

'True,' Moriarty replied, buttoning his jacket and selecting a walking, stick from the rack. 'Let us be on our way. Oh, there you are, Mr. Maws. See about capturing us a growler, if you will, while I retrieve the Kensington Wheeler from the kitchen.'

It was just past noon when the four-wheeler turned into Little George Street and pulled up at the Church of St. Jude. 'We'd best stop here,' Moriarty said. 'Mr. Maws, if you would help the Wheeler down, we'll make sure we have the right building.'

'I'll point 'er out to you, Professor,' the Kensington Wheeler said, 'but I ain't going inside with you. That there is your affair.'

'Good enough,' Moriarty said. 'Just

point the house out to Mr. Maws and you'll have more than earned your money.' He closed the door of the cab. 'Wait around the corner,' he told the driver. 'I don't know how long we'll be.'

The driver touched his whip to his hat, and the four-wheeler clattered off.

Mr. Maws walked off alongside the wheeler and was back in a minute. 'Fifth house down on the right, just as the gentleman described it,' he said. 'Far as I can tell there's no one at the windows. The blinds are drawn. How are we going to get in?'

'I've been giving it some thought,' Moriarty said. 'I could impersonate a gas man, but even a Russian wouldn't believe that if he remembered it's Sunday. Also, there may or may not be some urgency, depending on what plans they have for Tolliver. All in all, I'm afraid, the direct approach is the best.'

'Then let's go!' Barnett said.

'Remember,' Moriarty said, 'an absolute minimum of violence. We want prisoners.'

With that, the three of them walked at

a measured rate down the street to the fifth house and mounted the stoop. Moriarty knocked gently on the door.

' 'Oo's there?' a voice came through the closed door after a minute.

'It's Father Banion,' Moriarty said in a deep, melodious voice, his face pressed close to the door. 'I understand there's a sick man in there who requested my presence.'

The bolt was pulled and the latch lifted. 'There's no one sick in here, Father,' the man inside said, opening the door slightly to pass the word.

Mr. Maws hit the door solidly with his shoulder and sprung it open. In a flash Moriarty was inside and had grabbed the man and wrapped an arm around his mouth. 'There'll be someone very sick if you try to make a sound,' he whispered. 'I'll break your neck!'

The man struggled momentarily and then was still. His reaction was not one of belligerence, but rather of great surprise.

'Who are you?' Moriarty asked softly. 'Don't raise your voice!' He released his hold on the man's neck enough for him to catch his breath and reply.

'I'm the porter, sir,' the man squeaked. 'And who are you?'

'Scotland Yard,' Moriarty said. 'This house is surrounded.'

The man's mouth fell open. 'The p'lice!' he said. 'It's them foreign-looking gentlemen, ain't it?'

'What do you know about them?' Moriarty demanded in an undertone. 'Speak quickly!'

'Nuffin', sir. They been here about a fortnight, sir. I didn't do nuffin', sir, whatever they did. There's a whole bunch of them upstairs now.'

'I see,' Moriarty said, 'And how many to a bunch, my man?'

'I didn't watch them come in, you know. They don't like it if they think I'm watching them.' The porter sniffed and wiped the back of his hand across his nose. 'I'd say maybe a dozen, maybe a few more.'

Moriarty released the porter and turned to his two companions. 'We seem to have bitten off a hefty morsel,' he said.

'We could rush them,' Mr. Maws said,

flexing his shoulders.

'We could, indeed,' Moriarty agreed. 'Which would put us somewhat in the position of the fox rushing the hounds. But it is an option.' He turned to the porter. 'I'm afraid there's going to be some excitement here for the next little while. Have you a room? Good. Go to it now, and don't come out of it for the next half-hour.'

When the man had gone, Moriarty stepped to the foot of the stairs and listened. The sound of subdued conversation came from above. 'It doesn't sound like an interrogation,' Moriarty said. 'They probably have Tolliver locked up in one of the upstairs rooms while they discuss other matters.'

'Perhaps one of their number is heating the hot irons even now, while the rest of them talk,' Barnett suggested.

Moriarty shook his head. 'They've only had him here for a few hours,' he said. 'And this must be a specially scheduled meeting, since these people usually don't assemble in groups larger than three. But at any rate, it must have been set in advance of their capturing Tolliver.'

'It must be important, then,' Barnett said.

Moriarty nodded. He pulled his pince-nez glasses from one pocket and a cloth from another and began assiduously polishing the lenses. 'I'd give quite a lot to listen in on that conversation,' he added.

'I could sneak upstairs,' Barnett offered. 'Maybe overhear something.'

Moriarty shook his head. 'The chances of your being apprehended,' he said, 'are much larger than the chances of their speaking English.'

'I hadn't thought of that,' Barnett admitted.

Moriarty put his pince-nez back into his pocket. 'We could get reinforcements,' he said, 'but that would take longer than we can afford. They may decide to transfer Tolliver to a safer place, since this house is undoubtedly going to be abandoned after this meeting. Indeed, Tolliver may already have been taken away.'

'Then what do we do?' Barnett asked.

'We rush them, as Mr. Maws has

suggested,' Moriarty said. 'But in such a fashion as to create an air of moral, if not numerical, superiority. I see that this house is constructed with a back stairs. Ideal for our purposes.'

'How's that?' Barnett asked.

'We have to leave them a way out,' Moriarty said, 'or they'll come out over us.'

Mr. Maws pulled his revolver from under his jacket. 'Shall we go then, sir?'

Moriarty nodded and pulled a police whistle from his trouser pocket. 'When I blow this,' he said.

Mr. Maws smiled. ' 'Under the shadow of Death,'' he said firmly, ' 'Under the stroke of the sword, Gain we our daily bread'.'

Barnett turned to him. 'What's that?'

'Kipling,' Mr. Maws explained. 'Are we ready?'

'Don't shoot unless they fire first,' Moriarty instructed. 'What we're after is a maximum of noise and confusion, but preferably without gunfire.' He thought for a second, then: 'Mr. Maws, you take the stairs. Barnett, start on this corridor, but keep away from the back stairs. We have once again become Scotland Yard,' he said. 'And there are at least fifty of us. But somehow we've forgotten to cover the back exits.'

'How careless of us,' Barnett said.

At that instant an upstairs door opened and footsteps sounded over their heads. The murmur of voices grew louder.

Moriarty put the whistle to his lips and blew a triple blast. 'All right up there!' he yelled. 'This is the police. All of you come down with your hands over your heads. Resistance is useless!'

There was a moment of shocked silence from upstairs and then the murmur turned into a babble and the sound of footsteps increased in number, volume, and tempo.

Barnett started opening and slamming doors and shouting official-sounding instructions. 'Simmons,' he yelled, 'take your men around the back! Dwyer, check these rooms out!'

Mr. Maws stomped up the front stairs with the stolid tread of the invincible English policeman. 'You are all under

244

arrest,' he bellowed in a deep voice. 'It is my duty to inform each of you that anything you say will be taken down and may be used in evidence. Come along quietly, now!'

The milling footsteps upstairs broke into a panicked scurrying, as one of them found the back stairs and reported the fact to the others. A heavy sofa was pushed out into the upstairs hall facing the front staircase, and two men squatted behind it, pointing a brace of long-barreled revolvers at the advancing figure of Mr. Maws.

Mr. Maws dropped as someone's gun went off, and the bullet crashed through a print of Mercy Interceding for the Vanquished, which hung on the wall behind him. Mr. Maws's answering shot smashed into the door frame above the sofa.

There was a hurried whispering from behind the couch, and then a sliding sound, and then all was silent from above. Professor Moriarty climbed the stairs to where Mr. Maws lay and peered amusedly at the couch barrier. 'The birds have flown,' he said. 'And a good thing, too.'

Mr. Maws got up and dusted himself off. 'Disgraceful!' he said. 'I shall have to speak to that porter. I don't believe they clean this stair carpeting at all.'

Barnett came up to join them. 'Gone?' he asked.

'We have the building to ourselves,' Moriarty said. 'Except for the porter, and, I hope, Tolliver. You two go look for him. I wish to examine that meeting room and see if our friends left anything of interest in their haste.'

'I hope those shots don't bring the real police,' Barnett said.

'They may,' Moriarty acknowledged. 'In which case we are injured innocents. British stoic heroism. Saved a man from kidnappers — if Tolliver is here — but want no reward. After all, we didn't run away.' He went up to the landing and boosted himself over the sofa. 'But I'd better get a look at that room before they arrive.'

Mr. Maws searched the rooms on the floor they were on, while Barnett climbed the last flight to the top floor and checked those rooms out. It was Barnett who found Tolliver. The third door he pushed open led to a lumber room full of disused furniture. Tolliver was securely trussed up and tied to a bed frame, which rested against the far wall. Barnett cut the ropes with his pocketknife and released the brave little man.

'I heard the commotion when you arrived,' Tolliver said. 'What happened?' He sat on a trunk and rubbed his arms briskly. 'My hands are coming all over pins and needles,' he explained. 'They tied me a bit tight.'

'It's good to see you, Mummer,' Barnett said. 'But you're going to have to become a bit more proficient at the art of following people so we don't have to rescue you every time you go out of an evening.'

'I like that!' Tolliver said. ''Ere I am trying to bring a bit of excitement into the lad's life, and 'e's full of reproach. After all, it's not 'im what got trussed up like a capon.'

Barnett laughed. 'Come on downstairs,' he said. 'The professor will want to say hello.'

Moriarty was on his knees examining the floor in the meeting room when Barnett brought the Mummer down. 'Don't touch anything!' he snapped as they entered the room. 'I'm not through in here yet.'

'You might at least,' Barnett said reproachfully, 'tell the Mummer that you're glad to see him.'

'Nonsense,' Moriarty said, getting up and dusting off the knees of his trousers. 'We're here, aren't we?'

'Well, I'm glad you come,' Tolliver said. 'I was beginning to worry as to my future.'

Mr. Maws appeared in the doorway. 'Afternoon, Tolliver,' he said. 'Professor, I thought you might be interested to hear that I just glanced out a front window and noticed several large men taking up positions about the house.'

'Scotland Yard,' the Mummer said.

'Let us hope so,' Moriarty said. He sighed. 'No doubt they will remember about the back door. Ah, well. There doesn't seem to be anything of interest in this room, unfortunately. And to think, we had a whole room full of them here, and now they're all gone.'

'Leaving nothing behind?' Barnett asked.

'Nothing of consuming interest,' Moriarty said. 'There's that hat' — he pointed — 'and that picture, and a few cigarette butts of rather common brand.'

Barnett went over to examine the picture, which was tacked to the wall by the door. A full-color portrait of Queen Victoria looking stuffily regal, it had been carefully cut out of a recent edition of the *Illustrated London News*.

'Well, well,' Barnett said. 'A patriotic bunch of anarchists. What will they think of next?'

The sound of someone pounding violently on the front door came up from below. 'Open up!' an authoritarian voice bellowed. 'This is the police!'

'Go down and let them in, Mr. Maws,' Moriarty directed. But before Mr. Maws had reached the staircase, they heard the front door opening and the heavy feet of policemen treading on the stairs. 'The porter!' Moriarty said. 'I had quite forgotten about the poor porter. What must he think!'

Heavy footsteps sounded on the stairs, and a uniformed policeman came into view. ''Ere now, just you stand still there!' he commanded. 'There's three of them — no, four — up here, sir,' he called back down the stairs.

'Oh, officer,' Moriarty said in the concerned voice of a nervous schoolmaster, 'thank God you've come at last. We thought you'd never get here.'

That set the policeman back. Confusion reddened his already ruddy ears. 'What's all this, then?' he said.

'My young friend here,' Moriarty said, indicating Tolliver, 'has been imprisoned by a bunch of foreigners. We had just contrived to effect his release when you arrived. Surely it was our summons that brought you?'

'I don't know nothing about that, sir,' the policeman said. 'You'd better wait here, sir.'

'We'll just come downstairs,' Moriarty said. 'There may be more of them on the upper story. Tolliver, take your cap,' he added, indicating the piece of headgear hanging from the back of a chair.

'My cap?' said Tolliver. 'Oh, yes. Thank you, sir.'

They went downstairs, edging past the policemen who were gathering for the assault on the upper story. On the ground floor officers were going from room to room, while the porter stood with three plainclothes Scotland Yard men and Mr. Sherlock Holmes in the front hall.

'Holmes!' Moriarty said. 'Whatever brings you to Lambeth? And Inspector Lestrade, I believe.'

'Acting on information received,' Lestrade said stiffly, 'I obtained a warrant to search these premises. I was informed that you might be here, Professor, although, quite frankly, I didn't believe it. I'll have to ask you to explain your presence here, sir.'

Holmes pushed Lestrade aside and stepped forward, his fists clenched. 'Enough of this, Moriarty!' he snapped. 'We have you now. Where is she? The house is completely surrounded, you might as well give it up.'

Moriarty shook his head. 'Honestly, Holmes, I have no idea what you are talking about. You must have arranged this little raid, so I thank you. I was wondering why they gave up so easily. They must have looked out the window and seen you arriving. But I don't know what brought you.'

Holmes laughed. 'Really, Professor, you disappoint me,' he said. 'Who must have left? I came here expecting to find you, and I found you. Where is the Lady Catherine?'

'That again.' Moriarty took his pince-nez from his pocket and affixed them to the bridge of his nose. 'Holmes, please believe me. I had nothing to do with her abduction, and I have no knowledge of her present whereabouts. Is that what this is about? You followed me here, and decided that this is where I must have hidden her? Quite a piece of ratiocination.' He turned to the inspector. 'And on Sherlock Holmes's unsupported word you applied for a warrant? Giles Lestrade, I'm ashamed of you.'

Lestrade looked embarrassed. 'The

professor has been of some assistance to the Yard in the past,' he told Holmes. 'And I know of nothing against him except some unsupported rumor and your theories, Mr. Holmes. Not that you, yourself, haven't come to our aid on occasion.'

'Then you are not going to place Moriarty under arrest?'

'Now, Mr. Holmes,' Lestrade said, looking acutely uncomfortable, 'you know the law. If we find the young lady, and she accuses, ah, mentions the professor when she relates what happened, why then that'll be a different story. But as things stand . . . '

Holmes glared at Moriarty. 'Disgraceful!' he said. 'The greatest rogue unhung, and I can't even get him charged.'

Moriarty shook his head. 'Really, Holmes. And in front of witnesses, too. Actionable slander, I'd say.' He shook his finger in Holmes's face, which caused Holmes to take an abrupt step backward. 'As I've told you before, you must use your brain at all times, and never rely on preconceived notions. In this case, for example, if you would use your quite adequate powers of deduction and examine the premises, you would discover quite easily that I am speaking the truth. A group of Russian anarchists had the rooms upstairs. They had abducted my associate, Tolliver, here. I and my friends arrived to effect his release, and you were one step behind me.'

Holmes snorted. 'Anarchists!'

Moriarty turned to the porter, who was standing on the edge of the group, looking confused. 'Is that not so?' he demanded.

'Right enough,' the porter assented.

'And you have never seen me before today?'

'No, sir. Can't say as I have.'

'Very convincing,' Holmes sneered. 'I'm going upstairs to look around,' he told Lestrade. 'Hold them here until I return, if you don't mind. You can at least do that, can't you?'

'Now, Mr. Holmes — ' Lestrade said.

Moriarty smiled. 'I shall remain, willingly, until you return,' he said. 'I believe that the front room is empty. We shall wait in there until you are quite satisfied.' And pushing the door open with his stick, he strode into the room and settled into an overstuffed chair.

Fifteen minutes later the door opened and Holmes stalked in with Lestrade at his heels. 'The girl has not been in this house,' he announced.

Moriarty nodded.

'There were other people here,' Holmes conceded. 'Fifteen or sixteen of them. Russians, for the most part, although several of them have been in England for some time. Tolliver would seem to have been their prisoner for a matter of hours. They arrived at different times over a period of about one day. They were discussing plans of some sort, certainly illegal. Whatever they have planned is going to take place in the near future; at least a week off, but no more than a month. You would seem not to have been part of the group, Professor.'

'How do you know all that?' Lestrade demanded.

'Thank you for that,' Moriarty said. 'Don't look so disappointed, Holmes.

There are other criminals in the world.'

Holmes sat on the edge of the sofa and stared at Moriarty with a curious expression on his face. 'Then they have the girl,' he said. 'Tell me what you know about them.'

'Still the girl?' Moriarty said. 'Then you weren't following me?'

Holmes took a cigarette case from his coat and removed one. He started to return the case to his pocket, then paused and offered it to Moriarty. 'Try one,' he said. 'They're made for me by Drucquer's.'

Moriarty took a cigarette and returned the case to Holmes, who shoved it back into his pocket. Barnett noted the gesture and saw that, for these two men, there was no one else in the room at this moment.

Holmes struck a wax vesta and lit the two cigarettes, and the two men stared silently at each other as smoke gradually filled the room. 'The Duke of Ipswich received a note,' Holmes said.

Moriarty lifted an eyebrow. 'Finally,' he said.

'I was prepared,' Holmes said. 'The note was delivered in an ingenious manner, but I managed to follow the deliverer, and a chain of other underlings, until I was led to this house. The trail seemed to end here. I was sure that the answer lay here. That either the girl was here, or I could round up enough of the gang here to break its back and ascertain her whereabouts.'

'It's a good thing they got away, then,' Moriarty said. 'Had you captured those who were here, without the girl, she would surely have been killed.'

Holmes nodded. 'But you see,' he said, 'I thought it was you. And you are a fairly reasonable man. Whatever else you are.'

'What did the note say?' Moriarty asked. 'They didn't want money.'

'This is to go no farther than this room,' Holmes said.

'I pledge myself and my associates,' Moriarty answered.

Holmes looked at Lestrade.

'What, me?' the little detective asked. He took his bowler off. 'My solemn word,' he said.

'It is common knowledge in certain circles,' Holmes said in a low, clear voice, 'that the Duke of Ipswich is to become foreign minister when Lord Haider resigns, probably in a few weeks. The note informed the Duke that if he wished to see his daughter alive again, he was to perform certain actions in regard to a certain foreign power.'

'He could refuse the appointment,' Moriarty said.

'And assure the death of his daughter.'

Moriarty nodded. 'And, of course, the duke as a loyal British citizen has no intention of following these instructions, even if it means the death of his daughter.'

Holmes nodded. 'I must find the girl before he takes office,' he said. 'The first note, on the night she was taken, warned against publicity. The duke has complied with that. And now this.'

'What is he going to do,' Moriarty asked, 'if you don't find his daughter?'

'He is going to accept the portfolio,' Holmes said, 'and perform his job. On the day that he learns for certain that his daughter is dead, he is going to put a bullet through his brain.'

Moriarty nodded. 'That clever bastard,' he said.

'What?'

'I assure you I'm not referring to the duke,' Moriarty said. 'Unfortunately I can't give you too much information. Nothing, I'm afraid, that would be of immediate assistance to you. However, I can tell you this: the abductors of Lady Catherine have no intention of returning her alive. She may already be dead, but probably not. They knew the duke would not obey instructions. Indeed, they are counting on it.' He stood up. 'And I'll tell you something else; one of the benefits they looked for in this abduction, and the reason they waited until now to send these further instructions, was to set you against me. It kept you from looking for them, you see.'

Holmes thought about that for a moment, and then nodded. 'Who are they?' he asked. 'Surely you can tell me something about them. You can't have been here by accident. And the nation involved — we have both been there recently.'

'I can tell you nothing more at this time,' Moriarty said. 'In any event, I know nothing that would be of material benefit to you in your search beyond what you already know or can surmise. But I can tell you this, Holmes; in this matter our interests run together. If I discover anything of value to you, I shall convey it to you immediately. At any rate, come around to Russell Square in a day or two,'

'I'll do that,' Holmes said.

'Wear one of your less elementary disguises,' Moriarty suggested, 'for both our sakes.'

* * *

Moriarty spent most of Monday dissecting the cap they had picked up in the Lambeth house and subjecting the pieces to a variety of microscopic, physical, and chemical tests. By the time he went up to dress for dinner, he had filled several notebook pages with the results.

Barnett had to hold in his impatience

to hear what the professor had discovered as business was never discussed at dinner. They had coffee in the professor's study after dinner, and Moriarty produced the hat. 'I know a fair amount about it now,' he said. 'It is made of Egyptian long-fiber cotton, dyed with a vegetable dye not used in this country. It is of fairly recent manufacture, say within the past six months. Its owner is a healthy young man, under thirty-five, with a full head of dark-brown hair. In all probability he is of Eastern European stock, and under five foot six. He is interested in horse racing, or associates with people who are. He is a very neat, clean man. I think that is the best I can do for the time being.'

Barnett stared unbelievingly at the Professor. 'You got all that by staring at the hat under a microscope?' he asked. 'Are you joking?'

'Not at all,' Moriarty said. 'I assure you it is all either truth or reasonable assumption. But you see, Barnett, the problem is that it doesn't get us anywhere. I have spent a day at it, and furthered us not one bit.'

'Yes, but — ' Barnett said. 'The things you have pulled out of that hat . . . How do you know what the owner of that cap looks like?'

'I don't really know what he looks like, just hair color and a reasonable guess as to some other facts.'

'Hair color I can understand,' Barnett said. 'You found one of his hairs in the hat.'

'Several.'

'What about the other stuff; age, height, Eastern European, even horse racing. Don't tell me there was a horse hair in the lining.'

Moriarty smiled. 'No,' he said, 'in the brim. Used for stiffening.'

'Then how?'

'As to the age and general good health, that was marked by the condition of the hair — the human hair — I found in the cap. The length of the hairs — none longer than three inches — suggests a man. The hairs' diameter also affirms that they came from an adult male. The hairs were healthy, as a microscopic examination of the roots confirmed. This suggests that the owner of the cap also was healthy. The relative youth of the wearer I deduce from the lack of gray hairs among the thirty-six samples I found.'

'European stock?' Barnett said. 'Horse racing?'

Professor Moriarty tossed the cap on the table with a slight spin. 'Notice the shape it takes,' he said. 'That is comfortably. After repeated wearing it has taken up there because it has been blocked by the addition of a folded-up newspaper around the inner liner to make it fit more shape of the wearer's head. Which, you will notice, is long and comparatively slender. The man possesses a typically Slavic skull, from which I deduce that he is probably Eastern European.

'The size of the man I deduce from the size of the head. I could be quite wrong, of course, that there is an average about these things. The famous bell-shaped distribution curve shows up quite often in human affairs.'

'That leaves horse racing,' Barnett said.

'The paper folded up inside the crown,'

Moriarty told him dryly, 'is the turf odds page of the Sporting Times'

'Ah,' Barnett said. 'But is there nothing further?' Impressive as the professor's deductive display had been, he was right in saying that it didn't take them anywhere.

'One thing only,' Moriarty said. He took a piece of pasteboard from his desk and flipped it over to Barnett. 'This was stuck in the hatband.'

Barnett examined the fragment carefully. It was roughly square, about two inches on a side, and appeared to have been torn along one edge. There was a slight reddish tinge to it, but whether it was the natural color or the result of having been kept in a hatband, Barnett couldn't tell. One side was blank, and on the other two numbers and an unintelligible word were scrawled. The numbers were printed in the European fashion; in the upper left-hand corner was '1143' and toward the bottom was '2/5/0.' The word, which was between the numbers, was completely unreadable to Barnett and could have been English, French, Russian, or Arabic as far as he could tell. He was fairly sure it wasn't Chinese, but that was about the only possibility he could eliminate. The tear, with the billet held so that the numbers were readable, was along the right-hand side.

Barnett turned it over and over, 'what is it?'

'There are several possibilities,' Moriarty said, 'but the most probable is that it is a pawn ticket.'

'I see,' Barnett said.

'The top number,' Moriarty said, 'would correspond to the number of the item pawned in the pawnbroker's ledger. The bottom number is the amount loaned. The scrawl in the middle is certainly a description of the item, for those who can read it. I, unfortunately, am not among that favored few.'

'What pawnshop is it from?' Barnett asked.

'That is the problem,' Moriarty said. 'Most licensed pawnbrokers have their name and location printed or stamped on their tickets. But there must be thousands of unlicensed brokers in the city — small tradesmen who take a few items in pledge just as a sideline and don't want to pay the yearly licensing fee. The lack of a name on the ticket would indicate a more informal shop, but the high ledger number argues otherwise. The owner would appear to be from the continent, but that is small help.'

'It might be a clerk's handwriting,' Barnett suggested.

'Ah! You followed that,' Moriarty said. 'Good, good. No, it is probably the owner, judging by the size of the pledge. Anything over ten shillings is usually only given at the owner's discretion, although there's no hard and fast rule.'

'You want me to find the shop?' Barnett asked.

'Yes,' Moriarty said. 'See what you can discover of the pledger; he may be an acquaintance of the owner, or they may have taken down his name and address — although that's doubtful. Find out what the pledged item is. That may be especially helpful.'

'Okay,' Barnett said, putting the ticket carefully in his wallet. 'I'll start tomorrow morning.'

For the next week, Barnett wandered the streets of London, seeking out pawnbrokers and moneylenders. He had always thought pawnbrokers to be a secretive lot, but they became quite loquacious, he found, when you talked to them about something other than borrowing money. Unfortunately, none of them could identify the ticket or suggest whence it came. They did verify that the billet was, indeed, a pawn ticket, and an old man in Chelsea even translated the unreadable script. 'It's what we calls back-writing,' he said. 'Don't know why we do it. It's dying out now, but it used to be the custom in this here profession.'

'What does it say?' Barnett asked.

'Musical box, it says,' the old man told him. 'Must be something extraordinary in the way of musical boxes to pull two-pounds-five as a pledge.'

Barnett reported the translation to Moriarty that evening, received a grunt in reply, and continued the search the next morning. It was two days later, on Pigott Street in Limehouse, that Barnett succeeded in tracing the ticket to its originator.

Starkey & Sons, Money Lent on Pledge, looked like a small shop from the narrow storefront. But inside it went back for quite a long way. And there were two staircases, one leading upstairs and another down. The establishment was crowded with the most fanciful collection of items Barnett had ever seen. 'These are all pledges?' he asked, fingering a stuffed boar's head.

'Not at all, sir,' the aged proprietor said. 'The goods taken in pledge are all downstairs. We can't sell them in the shop, you see, even after the year-and-a-week. They have to be offered at auction. It's the law. These are all items we've picked up over the years at auctions, or the like, ourselves. My old father sir, bless his heart, had a sense of whimsy.' He pointed to a glass-fronted oak case along the wall. 'That contraption of leather tubing in the corner is called a serpent, sir. It is a musical instrument used at one time in military bands and the like. It fell out of favor during the reign of George the Fourth, I believe. Next to it is a stuffed and shellacked sand shark. On the shelf below is a collection of crocheted butterflies.'

'I take it your father was the original Starkey,' Barnett said, 'and you are the son?'

'My father,' the old man told him, 'was the original son. I am merely the original grandson. Feel free to look around, sir. Fascinating incunabula — and a dried lizard-skin collection — upstairs. If you see anything you like . . . '

'Actually,' Barnett said, 'as fascinating as I find this store, I came in to see whether you could identify this pledge.' He handed the old man the ticket

The old man looked up at Barnett suspiciously. 'Of course I can identify it,' he said. 'It's mine, ain't it?'

'I didn't know,' Barnett said, cautiously suppressing his feeling of elation. 'Are you sure it's yours?'

'I should know my own ticket, I suppose,' the old man said, adding hostility to suspicion. 'You have something to say about it?'

'Why isn't your name on it?' Barnett asked. 'I should think that an old, established firm like yours would have printed tickets.'

'My old father on his deathbed made me swear. Don't print the tickets,' he said. 'Dreadful waste of money,' he said. So what could I do? Anyway, we ain't had any complaints yet — present company excepted.'

'Don't misunderstand me, Mr. Starkey,' Barnett said. 'I'm not complaining. I'm delighted to find you. Could you tell me something about the pledge — a musical box, I believe — and the man that pledged it?'

'You're not claiming it yourself, then?'

'What, the musical box? No.'

'Ah!' the old man said, losing his suspicious expression. 'For a minute there I thought it was the old higgledy-piggledy. More than one man thinks that pawn-shops are fair game for all sorts of diversion. But they don't get away with that in here.'

'I'm glad to hear that, Mr., ah, Starkey,' Barnett said. 'Tell me, might I take a look at the musical box?'

'The box has been claimed,' Starkey said. 'Taken away.'

'Oh,' Barnett said unhappily.

'And as the gent didn't have the ticket, I thought that you — as you do have the ticket — were going to try to claim the item. It's an old game.'

'You mean you thought I was in collusion with the man who reclaimed the musical box?'

'It was not beyond the bounds of possibility.' the old man affirmed.

'It's nothing like that, I assure you,' Barnett told him. 'I am merely trying to find out who the man is so that I can return some property to him. There was no identification with the property, save this unlabeled ticket.'

The old man stared at Barnett silently for a minute. 'It must have taken you some time to locate this shop,' he said, speculatively.

'Days,' Barnett agreed.

'It must be impressive property for you to go to all this trouble to return it, and you must be an exceptionally honest man.'

'Well . . . ' Barnett said.

'Never mind,' the old man said. 'None of my business. Come to think of it, that was certainly an unusual musical box.'

'Really?' Barnett said.

'A square box, about eight inches on a side and two high, made of some hard, light wood. Put together with tiny ornamental brass screws and bands. On top of the box was a miniature grand piano some five or six inches wide with a small doll in a full dress-suit sitting before it, turned away from the keys. Exquisite work.'

'It sounds impressive,' Barnett said.

'Ah!' the old man said. 'But when you turn it on and it plays one of its sixteen selections — Bach, Beethoven, Rossini; a bit tinny, but real impressive — the doll turns to face the keys and begins playing. And its hand motions follow the music! Never seen anything like it.'

'I've never even heard of anything like it,' Barnett said. 'Where was it made?'

'France,' the old man said. 'In the twenties, I think. It is signed on the bottom by Jean Eugène Robert-Houdin, who served as court magician to Louis XVIII.'

'Court magician?' Barnett asked. 'In the eighteen-twenties?'

'Oh, yes,' the old man said. 'Houdin was famous for his clockwork mechanisms. My father told me about them, being something of a connoisseur, as the French put it. He once made a miniature carriage, pulled by four miniature horses. And, sir, it actually worked. But this was the first thing of the sort that I've actually seen with my own eyes.'

'What can you tell me about the man who pawned it?'

'Well, for one thing he wasn't French. Polish or Russian, I'd say. And he was very fond of that musical box.'

'But he pawned it.'

'But not for anything like its true value — even in pawn. He told me he did it just to keep it safe for the next few months.'

'I see,' Barnett said.

'But then he came back the day before yesterday and took it out again. Told me he'd lost the ticket, which I see was the truth. I told him I remembered him, which was so, and that I'd be sorry to lose the box.'

'Can you describe him for me? Was he short or tall?'

'Not too tall, I'd say.'

'Young or old?'

'If I had to put a finger on it, I'd say twenty-six or seven.'

'Did you happen to hear his name?'

The old man snorted. 'Better than that, sir; I have it written down.'

'You do?' Barnett wasn't sure he should believe this stroke of luck.

'Indeed! And his address, for that matter. You don't think I'm going to let anyone walk out of here with a pledged item and no ticket unless I get some proof of his identity, do you? I've been in this business for fifty years, and nobody has accused me of being soft in the head.'

'But I thought you said you recognized him,' Barnett said.

'And so I did. If not, I wouldn't have let him retrieve the object no matter how many papers he signed.'

'May I get a look at the paper you had him sign?'

'Gladly. In exchange for the pledge ticket. I hate to have them outstanding, you understand.'

'A fair deal,' Barnett agreed.

The exchange was made and Barnett copied down the information. Not that he had any real hope that the name and address were genuine, but it was certainly worth checking out. The name and address were block-printed on a buff card, PYOTRE I. AZIMOF: 7 SCRUTTON COURT. A scrawling signature was below.

'Good-bye, sir,' Barnett said. 'Thank you for your assistance. You have a fascinating shop here. I will have to come back and really wander through it someday.'

'It will be here,' the old man assured him. 'And, for so long as I have anything to say about it, so shall I.'

Barnett pulled his *Greene's Pocket Guide to London Streets & Thoroughfares* from his jacket and discovered that there indeed was a Scrutton Court, and that he was no more than seven or eight blocks from it. He resolved to scout out the building himself, without waiting to check with Moriarty, and try to get a look inside if he could think of a reasonably subtle way.

But first he would pause for a bit of lunch. While eating he would plan an approach that would be the least likely to raise suspicion. He felt it would not be wise, with Trepoff, to raise suspicion.

The Jack Falstaff Tavern on Cable Street had a pleasant grill room, and the proprietor, on hearing Barnett's accent, brought him a plate of lamb chops and grilled tomatoes, which he described for some reason as his 'American lunch.' Then, in a burst of Anglo-American friendship, the proprietor produced a pot of coffee, which had been boiled only briefly and was actually drinkable.

Barnett sat over the coffee and tried to pick an approach. Professor Moriarty would have seven acceptable schemes for getting inside the house, surely Barnett could come up with one. Barnett debated enlisting the professor's aid instead of proceeding on his own initiative, but then decided it would be more to his credit if he could prove himself an effective sleuth without help from the old master.

Barnett finished his third cup of coffee and got up. He'd check the house out from the outside. Maybe something immensely clever would occur to him as he walked by. Maybe there was no such house; the man had probably given a false name and address anyhow. Better check it out and see where to go from there.

Scrutton Court was a double row of two-story red brick buildings facing a narrow stone-paved street. Built early in the century as housing for the deserving almost-poor, so it had stayed for the past sixty or seventy years. Barnett had to walk the length of the street twice before he located the building numbers, which were painted in whitewash on the curb. A row of apathetic women watched him without interest from their porches as he passed, and then went back to hanging their wash from the lines that paralleled the houses.

Dingy white curtains covered the windows at number seven, and there was no sign of life from within. The house could be deserted, or there could be an army camped within, and the only way to tell was to get inside and look.

Barnett approached the woman on the porch directly across the street from number seven. 'Excuse me,' he said.

She looked up, her broad face expressionless. 'Aye?'

'Could you tell me if there's anyone living across the street? That building there,' he pointed.

'Couldn'a say,' she said.

'Well, have you seen anyone going in or out, in the past week, say?'

'Couldn'a say.'

'I see,' Barnett said. 'Thank you so much for your help.'

He crossed the street and stood in front of number seven. Then it occurred to him. The perfect approach! Old Mr. Starkey had told him about the musical box, and he wanted to see it with an eye toward making Pyotre Azimof an offer. He knew Pyotre wouldn't sell, but surely he couldn't resist showing the musical box off to an interested collector.

Barnett mounted the stairs and

knocked on the door. After some seconds, it was opened, and a burly man in rough nautical garb stared out at him.

'Good afternoon,' Barnett said. 'Does Mr. Pyotre Azimof live here?'

The man silently stepped aside, and Barnett walked in. 'Would you tell him someone would like to see him about his musical box?' he said.

The door slammed and Barnett was grabbed from behind. A rag with sweet-smelling fluid on it was held over his mouth and nose.

'Good afternoon, Mr. Barnett,' a soft, guttural voice said from further inside. 'It is a shame that your friend, Professor Moriarty, did not accompany you. But you will have to suffice.'

The room tilted and spun. Bright lights whirled around in Barnett's head, to be quickly replaced by harsh blackness. He struggled like a man submerged in quicksand, without really knowing what he was doing. Then nothing.

10

THE BIG BANG

And the night shall be filled with music.
— Longfellow

Barnett woke up slowly. A syncopated pounding thrummed across his temples, and a profound nausea replaced any other sensation. For a long time nothing else mattered. And then he was very sick.

Hands reached for him and held him up. A white basin appeared under his head, and he retched into it for what seemed several lifetimes. Then nothing more came up, and the retching changed to gasping, and the pounding of his racing heart overrode the pounding of his head. Slowly, very slowly, his heart calmed and his breathing slowed.

His eyes began to focus.

Guttural instructions were shouted,

and more hands pulled Barnett to his feet. A bucket of cold water was brought and dumped over his head, then another, and a third.

Barnett shook his head and opened his eyes. Slowly the room and the people in it came into focus: the thin man with the crooked nose holding the bucket and grinning; the heavy man who had let him into the house; a man in a black suit sitting in the corner, his face hidden under a black cotton mask; a man with wire-rimmed glasses who looked like a cobbler or tailor talking softly to a man with a small mustache, who looked like a radical student even to the two books under his arm. None of them appeared interested in Barnett, except for the man with the bucket and the man behind the cotton mask.

The man behind the mask barked out a new set of instructions, and the man with the crooked nose put down the bucket and yanked Barnett over to a wooden chair.

He pushed Barnett down and tied him quickly and expertly to the chair, his hands behind the back and one leg lashed to each of the chair's front legs. Barnett was too weak and sick even to protest out loud, much less resist the man who bound him.

The man behind the mask came over to glare down at Barnett. His eyes were hard behind the two thin slits. 'We meet again,' he said.

'Huh?' Barnett said weakly, still not sure what was happening. 'What' sat?'

'The last time, I struck you over the head with a brass monkey. One of that English lieutenant's treasured possessions, no doubt. 'Hear no evil,' or some such conceit.'

Barnett shook his head to clear his foggy vision and the pounding at his temples. 'So you're the guy,' he said thickly.

'I do apologize for your present condition,' the masked man said solicitously. 'I assure you you'll be all right in a few minutes. A pad saturated in chloric ether was applied over your nose and mouth to render you unconscious as you entered the house. But instead of

282

collapsing, you fought like a madman, which resulted in your absorbing much more of the vapor than is good for you. It's your own fault, really.'

'I fought?' Barnett remembered none of it.

'Those bruises on your arms were not gratuitous,' the masked man said. 'Nobody kicked you while you were down, Mr. Barnett.'

'I don't remember,' Barnett said. The brain fog was lifting and full awareness of his present position was creeping in to replace it.

'It doesn't matter,' the masked man said. 'No one here holds a grudge against you. We are the ultimately rational men. We do what we must, and we allow ourselves neither remorse nor pleasure at our actions.'

'That's very — sensible,' Barnett said, twisting at his wrists to test the rope that bound them. There was no give, and no stretch in the rope. He relaxed.

'I am glad you feel that way,' said the man behind the mask. 'Then you will understand that what we are about to do is not out of malice but merely political necessity.'

'What are you going to do?' Barnett asked. The headache was lifting, but he could feel the pain in his bruised muscles now, and the soggy chill of his clothing, soaked from the buckets of water dumped over his head.

'It will be a glorious event!' the masked man said enthusiastically. 'It will make the great sluggish mass of the British people aware of anarchy. It will be a new height. It will kill you, as you Americans so aptly put it.'

'You mean that literally, I suppose,' Barnett said.

'Oh, quite,' the man behind the mask assured him. 'We were hoping to get Professor Moriarty himself, but I'm afraid you will have to do. You and the girl.'

'This was all a setup,' Barnett said.

'When that gentleman over there,' the masked man said, indicating the man with the slight mustache, ' — let us call him — no, let him remain nameless — when that gentleman over there reported to me that he had lost his cap and that a pledge ticket was in the band, I at first castigated him severely. Then I realized that with proper management the pledge ticket would lead Professor Moriarty, or Sherlock Holmes — I had really hoped for one of the two — into my trap. It has at least produced you. I suppose it is too much to hope that the professor is going to attempt a rescue. I would like the chance to show him that I learn from my misjudgments.'

'Any minute now,' Barnett said.

The man behind the mask gave a derisive laugh. 'No, no,' he said. 'You have come here on your own. That is clear.' He paused thoughtfully. 'But you do have information of interest to me. How much Moriarty knows. What his source of information is. What his intentions are. You could tell me this.'

It was Barnett's turn to laugh. 'In return for what?'

'Your freedom.'

Barnett laughed again. 'How can you convince me that you will set me free once I've told you what you want to know?'

'My word, I suppose, isn't good enough?'

'Your word!' Barnett felt slightly hysterical. 'Why, you've got all these poor fellows believing that you're on their side! You — '

The masked man slapped Barnett across the face, and then again, and again. Slow, deliberate slaps, delivered with all the man's force. 'That is enough!' he said sharply. 'You will not malign these brave men with your talk. Shortly you will no longer talk at all! You two — take him to the upper room! We must complete our preparations here.'

The two men picked Barnett up, chair and all, one in front and one behind. They carried him up a flight of stairs and deposited him in a rear bedroom. Then they left, closing the door behind them.

'Hello!'

It was a girl's voice, and it came from behind him. Barnett tried to look around, but couldn't turn his head far enough. So he hopped the chair by jerking his body and applying torque to it, until he had turned enough to see. There was a young girl tied, spread-eagled, to the bed behind him.

'My God!' Barnett said.

'Who are you?' The girl's voice was quite normal, and well-modulated, but there was panic in her eyes.

'My name is Benjamin Barnett. And you must be the Duke of Ipswich's daughter, Lady Catherine.'

'Yes,' she said. 'Were you looking for me? Is anybody looking for me? What are they going to do with us, do you know?'

'Your abduction is not general knowledge,' Barnett said, 'but there are men — some very good men — out looking for you. What have they done to you? Why are you tied up like that?'

'I haven't been mistreated — beyond having been brought here in the first place, I mean. They've kept me locked up in a small room. They feed me twice a day. Usually bread, cheese, and wine. Once, for two days, they had hot food brought from somewhere. I tried leaving a message under the plate, assuming the service would be returned to whatever restaurant it came from. I heard nothing about it, but the next day I was back on bread, cheese, and wine. Then, a couple of hours ago, they dragged me in here and tied me like this. I have no idea what they intend to do. Do you? I've been imagining all sorts of horrid things.'

'I'd rather not try to guess,' Barnett said.

'A man with a great black mask over his face came in and stared down at me for a long time. Then he said that I was about to go down in the history of the struggle against bourgeois imperialist oppression, and I should be grateful to him. Then he laughed and stomped out of the room. What was he talking about?'

'I think I'm beginning to get the idea,' Barnett said.

'Why are you here?' she asked. 'Did they abduct you, too?'

'Sort of. Only I came and knocked on the door and practically invited them to.'

The girl twisted on the bed. 'These ropes are cutting into my wrists,' she said. 'I don't think this is very funny. My poor father must be worried to death about me. He gets positively furious if I go anywhere alone, as though I were still quite a baby. You're an American, aren't you?'

'Quite right,' Barnett said. 'Is it that obvious?'

'I like Americans,' she said. 'What are they going to do to us? They're not going to let us go, are they? I mean, ever.'

'I don't know what their plans are,' Barnett said, trying to sound cheerful, 'but don't lose hope. We'll get out of here somehow.'

'I've been here for weeks. You just arrived. I hope you have something in mind, Mr. Barnett, to get us out of here. Because the Lord knows I've tried everything I could think of. And I wasn't even tied up. But now I am, and they put you in here. And you're tied up, and we can't even move, so how can we possibly ever get out of here?' And she turned her face away and sobbed quietly into the pillow.

'I'm sorry if I upset you,' Barnett called softly. 'I was trying to cheer you up.'

The girl sniffed, stifled her sobs. Then: 'What do you do, Mr. Barnett, when you're not tied up?'

'I am a journalist.'

'How did you get here?'

'I knocked on the front door, and here I am.'

'Oh, dear,' the girl said, twisting her head on the pillow. Her nose was itching, and she tried to twist around far enough rub it against the pillowcase, but the ropes holding her arms were too tight. After fighting her bonds futilely for a minute, she gave up and burst into tears.

'Those people — they're going to kill us! They've kept me here for six weeks, cooped up in that little room. And now they're going to kill me. It isn't fair! And you, too.'

Barnett didn't know what to say. He couldn't argue against it without her thinking him feebleminded, and he couldn't agree to it without depressing her even more.

Further speech was rendered pointless when the man behind the mask came into the room. 'Greetings,' he said.

'What do you want with me?' the girl sobbed.

'Patience, woman,' the man said. 'In five minutes it will be seven o'clock.'

'Thanks,' Barnett said sarcastically. 'I had been wondering.'

The man behind the mask gestured behind him and the man with wire-rim glasses came in carrying the musical box that had lured Barnett to that house. 'This is somehow fitting,' the man with the mask said. 'I hope, Mr. Barnett, that you enjoy classical music, and that you don't mind the rather tinny sound of the musical box.'

'Why?' Barnett asked.

'Because it will be the last thing you hear on this earth,' the man told him.

The other man placed the musical box on a table and, taking a large brace-and-bit from his belt, drilled a hole in the floor by that table.

'What's happening?' Barnett demanded.

'I think you should know,' the man behind the mask told him. 'In the room directly below this one there are several hundred pounds of explosive. Much more than we need, actually, but we can't cart it away with us anyway.'

The bit went through the flooring and the man with the glasses knelt down and peered through the hole.

'The explosives,' the man behind the mask said, warming to his subject, 'are tightly packed around a central core in such a fashion as to direct the main force of the explosion up, rather than out. With any luck we shouldn't demolish more than two or three buildings on either side of this one.'

The man with the wire-rim glasses said something in a guttural foreign language and left the room. The man behind the mask snapped something at him in the same language as he went, and then pulled out his pocket-watch and shook his head in annoyance.

'A problem there, Trepoff?' Barnett asked.

The man behind the mask looked up at him. 'No man may say that name and live,' he said. 'Which, in your case, is not the most powerful threat I can imagine.'

A muffled shout sounded from the room below, and Trepoff walked over to the drilled hole and thumped his cane on the floor by the hole. 'They have to drill a hole in the ceiling below to line up with the one in this floor,' he told Barnett. 'Although why they couldn't have thought of that before . . . This is liable to put us off schedule.'

'There are incompetents in every line of work,' Barnett told him. 'Even in yours.'

Trepoff turned to him. 'A shame you won't be able to write this up in your best humorous style, Mr. Barnett,' he said. 'A companion piece to your miraculous escape from the Turkish prison.'

'You are going to kill us!' the girl cried, twisting in her bonds to face Trepoff. 'Why? What have I ever done to you?'

'You were born,' Trepoff said. 'Think of it this way, woman: your death is to be useful in a great cause. How many people go through their entire dull, drab lives and die meaningless deaths without ever having been useful to anything beyond themselves? But you, mademoiselle — '

There was an impatient rapping from below, and Trepoff broke off to bend down and grasp two wires that had appeared in the newly drilled hole. He pulled the wires up through the hole and attached them to two brass screws that had recently been screwed into the wood of the musical box.

'You are about to participate in a great experiment,' Trepoff said. 'When I start the musical box, the little pianist on top will turn to his piano and play sixteen tunes, each one precisely three minutes and forty-five seconds long. Thus, in exactly one hour he will be finished, the machine will turn itself off, and the pianist will once again turn away from the piano. In doing so, he will complete an electrical connection between these two wires, and a current will pass from the galvanic batteries in the room below through a voltaic arc apparatus inserted into a tube of compressed guncotton. This will serve to detonate the explosive mass. At that moment the two of you will cease to exist. Have you any last words?'

'It does seem a shame, Mr. Trepoff,' Barnett said, 'to destroy that beautiful musical box.'

'Ah, yes,' Trepoff said. 'But let us

console ourselves with the thought that art must die so that ideals may live.' He thumped his cane on the floor three times and received a three-thump reply from below. 'It is time to leave you now,' he said, turning back to the musical box and releasing a catch on the side. The metallic notes of J. S. Bach's Well-Tempered Musical Box wove a pattern of sound around him as he left.

'He's gone,' Barnett said.

The girl did not reply. Barnett turned to her and saw that she had her face turned away and was crying softly into the pillow.

Bach faded away, to be replaced by Handel, and the girl screamed, putting into that one sound all the fear, frustration, and anguish of six weeks of imprisonment ending in an afternoon of death.

'Here, now!' Barnett cried, hopping his chair closer to the bed by jerking his body forward. 'You mustn't — ' Suddenly he realized what he had just done. He had moved the chair! If he could do it to go three inches closer to the bed, then, with work, he could do it across eight feet of floor to get to the two wires.

Very slowly he hopped the chair around to face the wires. He had to be extremely careful not to tip over; if he fell on his face he might not be able to get up again.

Slowly he hopped his way across the floor. Handel gave way to Couperin, and he had gone almost two feet. Couperin was replaced by Liszt, and he had gone four feet. His shoulders and pelvis ached from the strain.

There was a banging from below, and the sound of running on the stairs, and Trepoff reappeared in the doorway. 'Something was nagging at my mind,' he said. 'And I see that I was right! Inexcusable carelessness on my part.'

He stepped aside and two men entered the room and dragged Barnett back to the bed. Using a length of thick rope, they tied him and his chair securely to the heavy post at the foot of the bed. Then they left.

Trepoff stood in the doorway for a second, surveying the room. He nodded. 'Adieu,' he said. And then he was gone.

The miniature pianist atop the musical box continued running his doll-fingers over the keys, and composition after composition was rendered in tinny tones. Barnett lost count. The girl was now silent. Perhaps she had fainted. It would be a good thing, Barnett thought, if she had. He twisted and struggled until his arms were raw under the jacket, but the ropes held.

Suddenly, as a Rossini overture began either the fourteenth or fifteenth piece, a pounding noise sounded faintly and far-off from below. Someone was at the front door.

Barnett yelled, but to no effect. Nobody outside on the street could hear him from upstairs. Shortly the pounding stopped.

Rossini ended with a click and whirr, and Scarlatti began the fifteenth — or sixteenth — selection.

The pounding at the front door began again. It was too late now. Even if someone did get in, they would never make it upstairs in time if this were the sixteenth selection.

But if it were only the fifteenth, there might be time. 'Help!' Barnett yelled. 'Help! Upstairs!'

The door flew open and Sherlock Holmes strode into the room, a great revolver in his hand. 'Well,' he said. 'What have we here?'

'Quick, man!' Barnett screamed. 'There are two wires affixed to that musical box. Unfasten one of them immediately. And, for the love of God, don't let it touch the other wire!'

Holmes raced over to the box and pulled one of the wires from its screw. As he did so, the Scarlatti drew to a close and, with a whirr and click, the little doll-figure turned away from the piano. Silence.

Barnett looked from the musical box to Holmes and, for once, words failed him. His lips moved but no words came out.

'You have just saved all our lives, Mr. Holmes,' Barnett managed to say at last. 'I don't know how to thank you.'

'If that young lady on the bed is Lady Catherine,' Holmes said, 'I am sufficiently recompensed.'

'She is,' Barnett said.

'Is she all right?'

'I believe she has just fainted.'

Holmes took a clasp knife from his pocket and severed their bonds.

'How on earth did you find us?' Bennett asked Holmes, as his hands were freed.

'I traced a brougham that they had used in the abduction by the tyre-marks and had it kept under observation. When next it came out my agent followed it to that house and sent for me. When he told me that he had seen seven people depart in the last ten minutes, I decided to break in.'

'And thank God you did,' said Bennett.

'That music that was playing,' Homes said, 'Scarlatti, wasn't it?'

'I believe so,' Barnett said. 'I was rather preoccupied.'

Holmes nodded. 'Scarlatti.' He eyed the musical box. 'An exquisite thing, that.'

The banging on the front door began again, and Holmes looked up. 'If you'll excuse me for a second,' he said, 'I will go downstairs and admit my colleague, Dr. Watson. While he revives Lady Catherine, we can talk.'

★ ★ ★

Two days passed before Sherlock Holmes came to Moriarty's front door and demanded entrance. Mr. Maws showed him into the study. 'You're to wait,' he said. 'The professor is expecting you.'

Ten minutes later Moriarty entered the study and crossed to his desk. 'Good afternoon, Sherlock,' he said.

'You expected me?' Holmes demanded, turning from the cabinet he was examining.

Moriarty glanced up at the complex face of the brass chronometer, which hung over the door. It was six twenty-nine. 'Not quite so soon,' he said. 'I apologize for leaving you in here alone, and thus putting temptation across your path. The drawers and cabinets, as I'm sure you found, are all locked.'

'I had never imagined anything else, my dear Moriarty,' Holmes said, moving over to the high-back chair and sitting down.

300

'Still, one can always hope.'

Moriarty leaned forward over his desk, his deep-set gray eyes contemplating Sherlock Holmes unblinkingly for many seconds. Then he shrugged slightly and leaned back in his black leather chair. 'The girl is all right?' he asked.

'The duke had two of Harley Street's most lettered specialists to examine her,' Holmes said. 'She didn't seem to need them. An amazingly resilient creature.'

'You spoke to her?'

'A bit. Not as much as I would have liked. It is clear that you had nothing to do with the abduction.'

'Thank you.'

'You expect me to apologize?'

'I expect nothing.'

Holmes struck his right fist into his open left hand. 'I am mortified, Professor,' he said. 'Not for having suspected you; we both know that you are capable of any act.' He looked earnestly at Moriarty, who did not change his expression in the slightest, but merely waited patiently. 'No, I am mortified at having allowed this suspicion to become an overwhelming obsession. It is true, I admit it. I allowed my emotion to color my rational processes, without which I am nothing. I should have known almost immediately that you were not involved. There was no demand for money.'

'The first communication?' Moriarty suggested.

Holmes nodded. 'It was indicated in the first note the duke received that money would not be required. I confess that rather than come to the proper deduction, I formulated fifteen different schemes you could have been devising.'

'Ah, Holmes. After all this time. Surely you should know me better. I won't pretend, here in this room, that I don't satisfy my incessant need for funds by abetting, or even indulging in, acts you might term criminal. But you must know that I would see a difference between quietly emptying a safe and abducting a seventeen-year-old girl.'

'An apparent difference in scale, yes,' Holmes said. 'But you cannot measure the results of either act. And they are both against the law. Who are you to decide which is right and which wrong?'

'And who, pray tell, is the state to decide for me?' Moriarty demanded. 'If I steal fifty pounds from a safe, I may go in for seven years' penal servitude. If I steal fifty thousand pounds by selling watered stock, I may make the honors list. If I murder a man on the streets of London and take his watch, I will be hung by the neck until I am dead. If I murder a hundred men on the Gold Coast to take their land, Her Majesty's government will send a gunboat to bring me back in triumph.'

'I do not claim that the laws are uniform or just,' Holmes said. 'But they are what we have. They are better — infinitely better — than the chaos that would result without law.'

Moriarty stood and began to pace behind his desk, his chin sunk onto his chest. Then he stopped and laughed. 'We argue law and we argue right and wrong,' he said, 'yet we are what we are, you and I, for reasons that lie deeper in us than can be reached by writs of the court or by statutes. I think it is good that we are both satisfied with what we are, for I do not think argument will change us. And I must say that this discussion, enjoyable as it is becoming, is drifting off the subject.'

'The subject?'

'Trepoff.'

'Ah, yes; Trepoff. The masked man.'

'Yes,' said Moriarty.

'He is planning some major outrage?'

Moriarty nodded. 'So I believe.'

'He told Lady Catherine something to that effect,' Holmes said. 'Her abduction was to be prefatory to the main abomination.' Holmes shook his head. 'The murder of innocents to draw attention to the plight of anarchists.'

'So he would have you think,' Moriarty said.

Mr. Maws knocked on the study door and then stuck his head in. 'Count Gobolski,' he announced.

'Ah!' Moriarty said. 'Show him in. Count, how good to see you. You have something for me? Allow me to introduce Mr. Sherlock Holmes. Holmes, His Excellency Count Gobolski, the Russian ambassador to St. James.'

Gobolski shook Holmes's hand firmly. 'The inquiry agent,' he said. 'I have heard.' He turned to Moriarty. 'He can listen? No matter, I have nothing to say. I have a paper for you from St. Petersburg. Here. I am no longer being followed. Good day.' He thrust his hat back onto his head and stalked out of the room. At the door, he stopped and turned back for a second. 'We will play chess again some evening, Professor,' he said. 'I will be in touch. You owe me a return match.' With the merest hint of a bow, he was gone.

Moriarty stared at the slip of paper and then dropped it on his desk. He rang for Mr. Maws. 'Barnett should be returning shortly,' he told his butler. 'Please inform him that I would like to see him when he arrives.'

Mr. Maws nodded and left

The slip of paper held one word, block-printed, and Holmes easily read it where Moriarty had dropped it.

SUBMARINERS.

'What does that signify?' Holmes asked.

Moriarty looked at him. 'It concerns Trepoff,' he said. 'What is your interest?'

'Trepoff must be stopped! I intend to do so.'

'I, also,' Moriarty said.

'Then I must ask you, in turn,' Holmes said, 'what is your interest? Surely not pure beneficence.'

Moriarty smiled. 'Like you, Holmes, I am for hire.'

Holmes frowned. 'The Duke of Ipswich is naturally not satisfied to let matters rest now that he has his daughter back. He has commissioned me to apprehend her abductor, although I would almost certainly continue the investigation anyway. Who has employed you, and why?'

'I would like nothing better than to discuss it with you,' Moriarty said. 'But first I must know that we are working together.'

'You are suggesting that we pool our talents?'

Moriarty nodded. 'We haven't much time, I'm afraid. If we both arrive at the same solution, from two separate paths, fifteen minutes late, it would be the height of folly.'

Sherlock Holmes rose and slowly walked over to the great bookcase that filled one wall of the study and stared absently at the titles. 'To work with you — ' he said. 'You would expect nothing from the duke?'

'Nothing.'

'The miscreants are to be turned over to the authorities?'

'Assuredly.'

Holmes strode back to the desk and put out his hand. 'Done!'

Moriarty and Holmes shook hands solemnly. 'I pray that this is indicative of the future, Holmes,' Moriarty said.

'I fear that this is unique, Professor,' Holmes replied.

Moriarty sighed. 'What a shame,' he said; 'what a waste.' He took his pince-nez from his breast pocket and thrust them onto his nose. 'Let's get on with it,' he said.

For the next hour Moriarty told Holmes the Trepoff saga in its entirety, omitting no detail, however trivial. Holmes made no notes, but merely stared intently at the professor as he

307

spoke. Twice he interrupted to ask brief questions and nodded in satisfaction at the answers.

During this monologue, Barnett came in, and was silently waved to a corner chair by Moriarty.

When Moriarty had finished, Holmes recited what had happened to him since the Duke of Ipswich had sent for him on the night of his daughter's disappearance. It was a tale of false clues, dead-end leads, and provocative accidents. Several of the clues had pointed directly at Professor Moriarty before disappearing in a labyrinth of complications and misdirections. 'Of course, the whole occurrence was an elaborately staged misdirection,' he said. 'I can see it now.'

'It is, in a way, a compliment,' Moriarty said.

'Excuse me,' Barnett said from his corner chair, 'but what are you two talking about?'

Holmes swiveled around. 'The abduction of Lady Catherine was arranged for our benefit,' he said. 'Not the act itself, but the way it was done. Trepoff wanted to keep me busy chasing Moriarty, and the professor busy avoiding me. So he planted clues. And, because they accorded with what I expected to find, I did not examine them too critically. As a result, I wasted a lot of time.'

'You sure showed up in the nick of time the other night,' Barnett said.

Holmes smiled. 'I am not altogether incompetent,' he said.

'Those sailors Trepoff sent for were submariners,' Moriarty told Barnett. 'From where could he acquire a submarine?'

'Not from the Royal Navy,' Barnett said, remembering Lieutenant Sefton's story. 'They don't use them.'

'There is one,' Holmes said, 'at the Thornycroft yards at Chiswick. It was dredged from the bottom of the Thames after sinking three times in three trials. Not submerging, you understand, sinking. It is not in working order.'

'Holmes!' Moriarty said. 'You never cease to amaze me. I had no idea you were interested in submersibles.'

'I'm not in the least,' Holmes said. 'My

brother, Mycroft, however, is a fount of such information. Among other things, he does some work for the Admiralty. Only last week — no, two weeks ago — he was after me to take on a case involving the theft of some whitehead torpedoes.'

'Ha!' Moriarty said, taking his pince-nez glasses off and polishing them with a small rag. 'A case that you were unable to take up because of your involvement with the abduction.'

'That's correct,' Holmes said.

Moriarty fixed Barnett with his gaze. 'If I remember correctly,' he said, 'you told me that one of the features of the Garrett-Harris submersible was its ability to release Whitehead torpedoes while submerged.'

'That's right,' Barnett said. 'But it blew up. Do you think there's another one?'

Moriarty waved a hand at Holmes. 'There's your misdirection,' he said. 'They didn't want you investigating the theft of those torpedoes.'

'An intuitive leap,' Holmes sniffed.

'Not at all,' Moriarty said. 'Barnett, your knowledge of coming events must be copious. What event is coming up in the next week or so involving the sea? Something major.'

'The sea?'

'The launching of a new battleship, perhaps. I don't suppose the Tsar is coming for a state visit by ship? Something of that sort?'

'Nothing,' Barnett said. 'Of course, I might have missed something. I can go to the office and check the file.'

'Nothing nautical?' Moriarty said.

'Not on the scale of battleships,' Barnett said. 'There's the regatta tomorrow, but they're small private yachts.'

'What regatta?' Holmes demanded.

'The Queen's something,' Barnett said. 'I don't remember. Wait a minute and I'll get the evening paper. I'm sure the *St. James Gazette* is covering the story in full.' He left the room and was back in less than a minute, riffling through a newspaper.

'Yes, here it is,' he said. He creased the paper back. 'The annual regatta for the Queen's Cup is to be sailed Saturday, August first — that's

311

tomorrow — between ships of the Royal Yacht Squadron and ships of the Royal West of England Yacht Club. Her Majesty will give the cups out herself. There are actually several cups, apparently. Let's see; there will be one winner in each class, and a special cup for the club with the highest point average.'

'Fascinating,' Holmes said.

'Go on,' Moriarty said.

'I don't know what else you want,' Barnett said. 'The Prince of Wales is the Commodore of the Royal Yacht Squadron, and H.R.H. the Duke of Wessex is Commodore of the R.W. of E. Yacht Club. The course, something over fifty miles, is laid in the Solent. It begins at Cowes, goes eastward to the Nab lightship and around, back past Cowes to Lymington, and then back past Cowes again to Portsmouth, finish line lying between the block house and the *Victoria and Albert*, the Queen's own yacht, from which she will be watching the affair.'

'That's it!' Moriarty said.

'Could be,' Holmes admitted.

'What?' Barnett asked, folding the paper.

'The Garrett-Harris submersible,' Moriarty told him, 'was not destroyed. I should have realized it weeks ago. It is a fatal error to make assumptions based upon facts not in evidence.'

'But I saw it blow up!' Barnett said.

'Did you?' Moriarty asked. 'What exactly did you see?'

'Well,' Barnett thought back, trying to recapture the moment in his memory. 'It was going through the water, just submerged, leaving a phosphorescent wake, the slight 'V' of foam from the periscope imposed over that. Then it sighted its prey — a sloop — and began stalking it. The submersible sank beneath the sea until it was totally invisible and moved forward to line itself up for the torpedo launch. As it launched the torpedo, it exploded. A great geyser erupted from the sea, drenching the ship I was on, and the two broken halves of the submersible appeared briefly on the surface before going to their final resting-place in the mud below. It seemed to me that I saw the body of a man in one of the sections. At any rate, neither of the operators was ever found.'

'A wonderfully concise description. And it shows that you saw nothing.'

'I saw the whole thing!' Barnett protested.

Holmes clapped his hands together. 'It has always fascinated me,' he said, 'how people will swear to have seen something when an analysis of their own description clearly shows that they didn't and couldn't have.'

'It's the principle of most sleight-of-hand,' Moriarty said.

'What didn't I see?' Barnett demanded.

'You didn't see anything,' Moriarty told him, 'from the time the submersible disappeared under the sea.'

'If you mean I didn't have the craft directly in my sight the whole time,' Barnett said, 'then you're right; I didn't. But the inference of the following events is certainly valid.'

'Is it?' Holmes asked, chuckling.

'I offer you this scenario, Mr. Barnett,' Moriarty said, speaking clearly and distinctly as one explaining the obvious to a child. 'Let us suppose that Trepoff, for whatever reason, wanted a submersible . . . So, hearing that the Turks are testing one, he went to Constantinople. It would be a coup to get one from Russia's traditional enemy, the Ottoman Empire. He went to where the submersible was docked and managed to get access to it.'

'How?' Barnett demanded.

'Three or four methods occur: forged papers, bribed guards, stealth, or some combination thereof. We may never know which method he adopted. Once there, he determined that he would need some time to effect the removal of the craft. I assume it had to be hoisted aboard some freighter, disguised as a large piece of machinery.

'What better way to gain time than to make it appear that the craft has been destroyed? Trepoff quickly acquired a large metal structure of the approximate size — I suggest a large boiler of some description. He towed it to the appropriate spot the night before and sank it, along with a powerful bomb. Trepoff is good at bombs. Possibly he planted a body on the boiler.'

'What about the two Americans who ran the ship?' Barnett asked.

'One of them was undoubtedly the body that you saw. The other was kept alive. Somebody had to run the craft. That he was subsequently killed is shown by Trepoff's need for the four submersible-trained sailors.'

'Possible,' Barnett said.

'And then they took it out and ran it for the sea trials that you saw. Up to the point where the craft submerged. At that moment it turned away from the show and headed back toward the freighter, which was to pick it up and take it to England. The explosion a minute later blew the boiler and the murdered American submariner to the surface for one brief appearance, which was enough to convince the onlookers that it was the submersible.'

'And Trepoff,' Holmes said thoughtfully, 'returned to England with the Garrett-Harris submersible, which is capable of releasing Whitehead torpedoes while submerged.'

'That is my theory,' Moriarty said.

'And a pair of Whitehead torpedoes was stolen from the naval establishment at Devonport a fortnight ago. Each of them, according to Mycroft, possessed of several hundred pounds of the latest explosive.'

'And Her Majesty Queen Victoria, whose picture I found gracing the meeting hall of Trepoff's no-name society, is going to spend tomorrow on board her yacht, the *Victoria and Albert*,' Moriarty said. 'And if I were an anarchist, the queen of the largest empire in the world would certainly be a tempting target.'

'They'd never dare!' Barnett exclaimed. 'The public revulsion would set their cause back a hundred years.'

'Exactly Trepoff's aim,' Moriarty said.

'We must get to Portsmouth without delay!' Holmes said.

Moriarty stretched out his hand for his Bradshaw's. 'Let us see what the British Railways have to say about that. It is fourteen minutes past nine, and the next train to Portsmouth . . . ' He riffled through the pages thoughtfully, then put the guide down. 'It appears that we cannot get to Portsmouth by any scheduled train any earlier than eleven-oh-four tomorrow morning. Which will never do.'

'Intolerable!' Holmes said. 'What shall we do?'

'Hire a Special,' Moriarty told him. 'I'll send out Mr. Maws now to arrange it. If you'd like to go back to Baker Street and pack, Holmes, I'll meet you at Waterloo Station in an hour.'

'Very good,' Holmes said, getting up. 'A Special. If you don't mind, I shall bring my companion, Dr. Watson, along. He is a good man to have at your back.'

'By all means,' Moriarty said. 'Barnett, will you join us?'

'You couldn't keep me away!' Barnett exclaimed.

★   ★   ★

It was eleven twenty-six before way clearance was obtained for the trip, and the Special — one ancient engine and two cars — pulled out of Waterloo Station. Sherlock Holmes and his taciturn friend Dr. Watson joined Moriarty and Barnett in the compartment farthest from the engine, where it was quietest, and discussed the situation.

Dr. Watson was a portly, ruddy-faced, handsome man with a well-trimmed mustache. Barnett had met him briefly when he and Holmes had come to Barnett's rescue in the house of the explosive musical box. Now Barnett took the opportunity to study him more closely. He was the epitome of the Victorian Englishman, and the perfect foil for Holmes. Stolid, slow, without Holmes's incisive mind or ready wit, he was nonetheless brave, loyal, and as tenacious as an English pit bulldog. He contributed little to the conversation, but seemed content to sit back and appreciate every word uttered by Sherlock Holmes.

'We must decide upon a course of action,' Moriarty told Holmes, modulating his voice to be easily heard over the clacking of the wheels. 'We will have precious little time.'

'If we are right,' Holmes said.

'I admit that the probabilities are only slightly better than half,' Moriarty said, 'but it is on the strength of that half that we are all aboard this Special, puffing through Guildford at a quarter past midnight.'

'I thought you were both convinced that you were right,' Barnett said.

'It was not the conviction that we were right, but rather the fear that we might be right that has compelled us to this trip,' Moriarty said. 'And now we must proceed as though we had no doubts.'

'We will have to alert the authorities,' Holmes said.

'Police or naval?' Moriarty asked. 'And tell them what?'

'Nevertheless the attempt will have to be made.'

Moriarty shrugged. 'As you will,' he said. 'The most important thing is to locate the submersible. We will, of course, attempt to capture Trepoff as well, but stopping the submersible must have the first priority.'

'Consider that the submersible may be

already submersed,' Holmes said. 'Sitting on the bottom, awaiting the proper moment.'

Barnett shook his head. 'No chance,' he said. 'There are two problems: air and fuel. When the craft is submerged it runs on electrical storage batteries, which give off noxious fumes when in use. As a result the air must be purged every two hours, which is also when the batteries expire and must be recharged.'

'Let us suppose,' Holmes suggested, 'that the craft merely rests on the bottom and does not call upon the batteries for motive power. How long then?'

Barnett shook his head. 'I'm no expert,' he said. 'I'm just remembering what I was told by Lieutenant Sefton — the man I was supposed to have murdered — before the trials. I believe that the air does foul, but at a slower rate. The oxygen in the air gets used up by the occupants' breathing, in any case.'

'Trepoff will need all his submerged time to make good his escape,' Moriarty said. 'The submersible will remain in its hiding place until Trepoff is ready to strike. Then it will proceed directly to its target, blow up the *Victoria and Albert* with the queen aboard, and leave the harbor. Somewhere in the Solent a ship will be waiting to pick up the submersible — or at least its crew — and remove them from the area.'

'What makes you think Trepoff will be so solicitous of the welfare of his agents?' Holmes asked

'He may well be aboard himself,' Moriarty said. 'And although certainly a brave and daring man, he tends to be careful of his own welfare. Besides, he couldn't afford to have four Russian sailors, clearly not anarchists, captured. Killed, perhaps; but not captured.'

'That brings us to an interesting question,' Holmes said, thoughtfully pressing the tips of his fingers together. 'How is Trepoff planning to make it clear that this is an anarchist outrage? Surely he isn't going to leave it to be supposed.'

'Somehow anarchists are going to be apprehended for this crime,' Moriarty agreed. 'Probably in such a state that they can't reveal too much.'

'Dead,' Barnett said.

'Quite probably,' Moriarty said.

'Dastardly plot,' Doctor Watson said.

As the Special chugged and clanked its way across the quiet English countryside, the four men in the compartment looked silently at each other. This was not the proper setting for such horrors. They should take place in an alien clime, not in damp, stolid, virtuous Victorian England.

'I don't see that we can accomplish anything useful tonight,' Moriarty said. 'We won't arrive until about half-past two. I suggest we get a few hours sleep and start fresh in the morning.'

'I agree,' Holmes said. 'Creeping around in the dark in a city one is not familiar with would not be overly productive.'

'My feeling is that Trepoff will pick the moment of the awarding of the cups as his prime moment to attack,' Moriarty said. 'It will create maximum effect and confusion. The area will be full of boats going in all directions. That should maximize his chances of escaping.'

'What time is that, Professor?' Watson

asked. 'When is Her Majesty presenting the cups?'

'The newspaper estimated that it will take place around six in the evening,' Moriarty said. 'If we start looking at six in the morning, that will give us twelve hours to find the submersible before it is employed.'

'God grant that it is enough time,' Holmes said.

'All the inns in Portsmouth are most probably filled this weekend,' Moriarty said. 'I have taken the liberty of adding a sleeping car to our special, as, fortunately, one was available.'

'I was wondering what the extra car was,' Barnett said.

'We shall each have our own compartment,' Moriarty said. 'Not exactly the ultimate in luxury, but it will serve.'

'The expense for the sleeping car must have been considerable,' Holmes said. 'Surely this was an extravagance.'

'I believe the Tsar can afford it,' Moriarty said.

The special pulled into a siding in the Portsmouth yard shortly after two in the morning, and the group separated to get what sleep they could.

Barnett would have been willing to swear that it was no more than a few minutes after he lay his head on the small pillow that a fully dressed Moriarty was poking him awake. Barnett groaned and sat up. 'What time is it?' he asked.

'Ten past six,' Moriarty told him. 'I've let you sleep late.'

'I don't know how to thank you,' Barnett said.

'Get dressed as quickly as you can,' Moriarty instructed him. 'Holmes and I have been studying a map of Portsmouth. We've decided to make the Royal Standard public house our base of operations, and it's a two-mile walk.'

'Any particular reason why the Royal Standard?' Barnett asked.

'Yes. Two. It's fairly centrally located along the docks, and the guidebook says it sets a fine breakfast table.'

'I'll be right with you,' Barnett said.

After a brisk walk to the Royal Standard, they consumed a hasty breakfast, selecting from a buffet table that groaned with solid English fare.

'Now we begin,' Moriarty said. 'Two south toward the Battery and two north toward Whale Island, and we somehow contrive to inspect everything that touches the water or floats on it that is large enough to conceal a Garrett-Harris submersible.'

'The Navy may object to our poking around some of their docks,' Barnett said.

'Well, we'll have to assume that they object just as strongly to Trepoff concealing his submersible there,' Moriarty said.

'We must notify the authorities,' Holmes said.

'I doubt if you will be able to convince them of anything,' Moriarty said. 'But feel free. I shall come with you if you like. It will be interesting to hear you accusing someone other than me of unspeakable misdeeds and evil acts.'

Holmes stood up. 'Very well, then,' he said. 'Come along. There is a police station three blocks from here.'

Moriarty nodded. 'Barnett,' he said, 'why don't you and Dr. Watson walk south along the harbor and see if you can determine anything of interest. After we speak to the authorities, Holmes and I will proceed north.'

'Very good,' Barnett said.

'We shall meet back here in, let us say, four hours to compare notes. And by the way, Barnett, do not try to be a hero all by yourself this time. If you find the craft, do not attempt to do anything whatsoever on your own. Come back here for reinforcements. If it makes you feel any better about it, we shall do the same.'

'Okay,' Barnett said.

Watson looked to Holmes for instructions and Holmes nodded. Watson beamed. 'We'll find the little sinker for you if it's there, eh what?' he said, looking very pleased with himself. With that, he clapped his bowler on his head and left with Barnett.

Holmes and Moriarty walked to the police station, and Holmes strode up the stairs and through the oak door.

'Good morning, Sergeant,' he boomed at the blue-coated man behind the desk. 'Who is in charge here today?' Moriarty stood quietly by the door.

'Good morning, sir,' the sergeant said. 'That would be Inspector Peebles, sir.'

'And may I speak with him?'

'May I inquire as to the nature of your business, sir?'

'My name is Sherlock Holmes, Sergeant,' Holmes said. He waited a second for a reaction, and when he got none, he continued, 'I have some information which will be of interest to Inspector Peebles.'

'Yes, sir. Might I inquire as to the nature of that information?'

Holmes sighed. 'I really don't want to go through it twice,' he said. 'Time is limited. It concerns a plot against the life of Her Majesty the Queen!'

'Yes, sir,' the sergeant said. 'Another plot against the life of the Queen. Very good of you to come in and warn us about it. I can assure you, sir, that proper precautions are being taken.'

Holmes rapped his stick against the desk. 'This is not a joke, Sergeant!' he said. 'I insist upon speaking to the inspector.'

The sergeant sighed. 'Yes, sir,' he said.

'If you will excuse me for a second sir, I'll tell him he's wanted.' The sergeant left his desk and disappeared into the back.

Holmes looked over to Moriarty and saw that he was silently laughing. 'This is not amusing!' he rasped.

'No,' Moriarty agreed. 'Of course it isn't.'

Inspector Peebles, a plump, smiling man, entered the room with the sergeant. 'Now, now,' he said, chuckling happily, 'what's all this?'

'My name is Sherlock Holmes, Inspector,' Holmes said, 'and I have information regarding an attempt that is going to be made against the life of Queen Victoria.'

'Now, that's very serious,' the inspector said, still smiling. 'Just how is this attempt going to be made?'

'By submersible boat.'

'By what, sir? What was that?' A puzzled look replaced the smile.

'By submersible boat. Submarine. We have reason to believe that a foreign agent has smuggled a submersible boat into the harbor and is planning to blow up the *Victoria and Albert*.'

'Now, now, that's quite serious, sir,' the inspector said ponderously. 'Just where is this submersible located now, sir?'

'I don't know,' Holmes said.

'I see, sir,' the inspector said. He turned to Moriarty. 'Is this gentleman with you?'

'That's right, Inspector,' Moriarty admitted.

'Well, why don't you and your friend just go out and find this submersible for us. As soon as you have found it, you be sure to come back here and tell us where it is.' The inspector's smile returned. 'Then we'll take care of it for you.'

'Yes, Inspector, we'll certainly do that. Thank you, Inspector. Come along now, Holmes.'

They left the station together, Moriarty silent and Holmes fuming. 'They didn't believe me,' he said, the line of his jaw rigid with fury. 'They treated me as though I were mad!'

'Well, it is a rather incredible story,' Moriarty said. 'I'm sure that if Lestrade were here you could convince him, however. You seem to be able to convince him of anything.'

'We've got to find that boat by ourselves,' Holmes said.

'Yes,' Moriarty agreed. 'And I think we'd best be about it.'

They proceeded north along the waterfront, poking into and exploring every wharf and jetty they passed. Gradually, Holmes regained his good humor as he became intrigued with the problems of the search. Moriarty stopped in fascination at a clearing by the Naval Barracks where two great balloons were slowly puffing up on the ground.

They were being filled with hydrogen gas, generated by a complex self-contained apparatus resting in two wagons by the side of the field. Canvas pipes, treated with gutta-percha, connected the generator with the balloons.

'What's happening here?' Moriarty demanded of a frock-coated man who was directing the operation.

The man turned to him and took off his stiff top hat. 'Balloons, sir,' he said. 'Observation balloons.'

'I can see that,' Moriarty said. 'I have some small knowledge of aerostatics myself.

My name is Professor James Moriarty and this is Mr. Sherlock Holmes.'

'I am Hyman Miro,' the man announced. 'Scientist and inventor and developer of the Miro-graphy system of wet-plate photography.'

'Ah, yes,' Moriarty said. 'I am somewhat familiar with the system. It employs a reversal process using a collodion plate and the bromide of silver. The developer, if I remember correctly, is largely pyrogallic acid.'

Miro beamed. 'That is correct, sir. Pyrogallic acid and ammonium carbonate, with potassium bromide. You have employed my system?'

'Yes, sir,' Moriarty said. 'The photography of celestial bodies requires rapid, fine emulsions. Yours is quite adequate.'

'We, ah, have business, Moriarty,' Holmes said, tapping his foot.

'Patience, Holmes,' Moriarty said. 'Meeting Mr. Miro may prove very useful. You are,' he asked Miro, 'planning to use these balloons as tethered observation platforms for the purposes of photography?'

'I am,' Miro said. 'If the weather remains fine, I should be able to expose my plates for no more than the tenth part of a second and still get a complete image. I will be able to stop the motion of the ships on the water, sir. A wonderful thing.'

'And you are going to be up in them all day?'

'Up and down, sir. Up and down. The wet plates must be developed within minutes of being exposed or they lose detail. The darkroom will be erected between the two balloons, which will be lowered and raised on command by a powerful winch.'

'Very clever, sir,' Moriarty said.

'Until six o'clock, sir,' Miro said.

'Ah?' Moriarty said.

'Yes. The P.L.R.F.C. is taking over the balloons at six to prepare for their fireworks display. Can you imagine, sir, fireworks from a hydrogen balloon? It's the height of idiocy!'

'The P.L —' Holmes said.

'Yes, sir. The P.L.R.F.C. The Portsmouth Library and Recreation Fund

333

Committee. They are in charge of the evening's festivities. Fireworks!'

'Really, Moriarty,' Holmes said.

Moriarty raised his hand. 'Mr. Miro,' he said. 'I am about to entrust you with a grave responsibility.'

'Sir?' Miro said.

'We have reason to believe that an attempt is going to be made to blow up the *Victoria and Albert*.'

'The Royal Yacht?'

'Correct. A madman who has stolen, and has in his possession, a submersible craft, is going to use it to approach and destroy the Royal Yacht, with Her Majesty on board. We are trying to apprehend him now, but if we fail, then in a matter of hours he will carry out his plan.'

'Well, sir,' Miro said, 'what can I do about it?'

'A submerged craft is much more readily visible from high above than from the side. It is a matter of the angle subtended. The craft has to be within a hundred yards of the Royal Yacht to release its Whitehead torpedo. You'll have a fine view.'

Miro's eyes lit up. 'What a photograph!' he said. 'But you can't mean that you want me to spend the day searching for this undersea craft? I wouldn't be able to get any photographs.'

'No, sir,' Moriarty said. 'What I'd like is to send my assistant up with you. Not this gentleman,' Moriarty said quickly, as Miro eyed Holmes, 'but another.'

'What good will that do?' Miro asked. 'We'll be up there, and you'll be down here.'

'You said something about fireworks,' Moriarty said. 'My assistant could take some up with him, and let off a colored rocket if he spots the craft.'

Miro thought for a minute. 'Sounds crazy to me,' he said. 'But . . . you say you've used my process for astronomical photography?'

'I'll be delighted to show you my plates,' Moriarty said.

Miro clapped his topper back on his head. 'Send your man over,' he said. 'It doesn't matter when: I'll be up and down all day.'

'Thank you, sir,' Moriarty said. 'You're

doing a great service for your country — and your queen.'

'I'll be in touch with you,' Miro said, 'about viewing those plates.'

Holmes and Moriarty continued their northward quest, examining the Filling Basin and the Rigging Basin of the big naval shipyard, and on to Fountain Lake, the tide pool where the frigates were moored. Whale Island, with its great Gunnery School, thrust out into the commercial harbor beyond. They walked slowly around each pier and mooring, looking for a place where a forty-foot-long submersible could be hidden. There was no such place.

'Well, Professor,' Holmes said, as they scrambled back from examining the inside of a closed boathouse through a window overhanging the water, 'at least this had the negative virtue of eliminating most of the inner harbor. When we get back to the pub, we'll know hundreds of places where the craft is not.'

'Perhaps our companions had better luck,' Moriarty suggested. 'It's about time to head back now, anyway.'

'Right,' Holmes said. Then he grabbed Moriarty's arm and pointed. There, in the sky in front of them, the great bulk of a tethered hydrogen balloon slowly filled the sky as the device rose higher and higher at the end of its cable.

'Interesting,' Moriarty said. 'Note the unusual ratio of the height of the balloon to the chord of the diameter. I would think it would cause a loss of stability, but perhaps not. I'll have to speak to Mr. Miro about that.'

'That's the wave of the future, Moriarty,' Holmes said, staring up at the balloon with an intent expression on his face.

'If so, it's taking a long time waving,' Moriarty said dryly. 'The Montgolfier brothers made the first balloon ascent one hundred and two years ago, on June fifth, seventeen eighty-three.'

'Someday,' Holmes said, 'passenger-carrying balloons will be crossing the oceans at unheard-of speeds, linking the peoples of the world into one great hegemony, led by a just and powerful nation that flies a flag quartering the

Union Jack with the Stars and Stripes.'

'Why, Holmes,' Moriarty said, tapping him gently on the back, 'that's almost poetic.'

'Come,' Holmes said, 'we'd better get back to the public house.'

Twenty minutes later, they arrived back at the Royal Standard to find Barnett and Dr. Watson waiting for them. Over a hasty but excellent lunch, washed down by a fine cider, Barnett told the tale of the unsuccessful search to the south. 'No submersibles,' he said, 'no Russians, no inaccessible areas on the dock; nothing but a lot of people enjoying the spectacle of hundreds of sails crisscrossing the bay.'

'We've been going about this wrong,' Holmes said.

'How's that?' Moriarty asked.

'We've been on land trying to search the sea. We should be on the sea. We should hire a boat. A steam-launch.'

'Excellent, Holmes!' Moriarty said. He thumped on the table. 'Landlord! I say, landlord!'

The portly proprietor of the Royal Standard hurried over. 'Is something the

338

matter, gentlemen?' he asked, drying his hands on the towel tied around his ample waist.

'Not at all,' Moriarty said. 'A fine establishment you have here. Excellent food.'

'Why, thank you, sir. Food is important to me, so I always assume it's important to my customers, too.'

'And right you are,' Moriarty assured him. 'Now tell me something, sir; I'm sure you know what goes on in these parts better than anyone. Where could we hire a steam-launch at this particular time?'

'That's a hard one, sir,' the proprietor said, screwing his face up into an attitude of concentration. 'Captain Peterson's rig has been let to a party of journalists. Lowery's is still in repair; busted boiler, it has. The *Blue Carbuncle* is over in Cowes for the day. Hired out to a photographer, I believe. The *Water Witch* — why, that's right! Captain Coster was in here this morning. He's the skipper of the *Water Witch*. Complaining, he was, that his party what chartered the boat for the day had as of yet not shown up. That was some hours ago, but if they've not appeared yet, I'm sure he'd take you out. Are you gentlemen from a newspaper?'

'You might say,' Barnett said.

'Could you direct us to this Captain Coster?' Moriarty asked.

'Nothing easier,' the landlord said. 'To the left as you leave and then to the right at the second crossing. The *Water Witch* is white with black trim and a broad red stripe on the funnel. You can't miss her.'

'Thank you, sir,' Moriarty said, rising from the table. 'Come, gentlemen; this might be just what we need.'

As they left the inn, Moriarty gave Barnett his new task. 'Miro is expecting you,' he said. 'Try to make yourself useful to him, but not at the expense of failing to search for the submersible. Take signal rockets up with you, and make sure you have an igniter. If you sight the craft, set off a rocket. Use different colors for different directions. Let us say red, white, blue, and green for north, east, south, and west.'

'Yes, sir,' Barnett said. 'I'll keep a

careful lookout. Is the direction to be from the balloon or from the *Water Witch*?'

'What an excellent thought,' Moriarty said. 'You'll be able to keep us in sight, of course. From the *Water Witch*, then.'

'You'd better stay with us,' Holmes said, 'until we're sure we get the craft.'

The *Water Witch* was still at its mooring, and Captain Coster was only too happy to take them out. 'Want to go out and watch the regatta, do you?' he asked. 'I can get you in a good position for that, although I daren't get too close. They'll have my license for sure if I interfere with the race.'

'We just want to stay in the harbor for now,' Moriarty told him. 'There's a particular boat we're looking for and we want to cruise around and see if we can find her.' He swung around to Barnett. 'We're settled here. You'd better go off to Miro. We'll be looking for your signal.'

'Okay,' Barnett said. He trotted off down the wharf.

Captain Coster built up a head of steam in the *Water Witch* and they

341

headed across the harbor toward Gosport Town on the far side. There they gradually made their way around the curve of the shore, pulling alongside every wharf and jetty to peer into boathouses, hulks, sheltered moorings, and anything else that looked like a possible hiding-place for the forty-foot steel cigar.

After two hours' futile searching, they crossed back and resumed the hunt on the Portsmouth side. Captain Coster pulled the *Water Witch* as close as he could to the various objects they wanted to examine, and Holmes and Moriarty took turns leaping aboard a variety of boats, barges, and assorted flotsam that graced the harbor and could provide shelter, however unlikely, for the Garrett-Harris. What Captain Coster thought of this, he didn't say. He was obviously used to the odd requests of his paying passengers.

It was five o'clock when the *Victoria and Albert* steamed into the harbor and stopped at its spot at one end of the finish line. Several small Navy steam cutters took positions around the Royal Yacht, presumably to fend off overenthusiastic sightseers. On the upper deck, a stout somber woman dressed in black sat alone under a canopy and wrote in her diary.

There was no sign of the submersible.

11

EARTH, AIR, FIRE, AND WATER

Speed bonnie boat,
like a bird on the wing.
— *Harold Edwin Boulton*

'Disgraceful,' Captain Coster said, puffing away on the thin black rope he called a cigar.

'What's that?' Moriarty asked.

'Them barge captains. They have no regard for any of the rest of us. They're so used to being pushed about they can't even take the responsibility of properly mooring their barges. Look at that one now, come adrift. I'll have to notify the port director when we dock, and he'll have to send a tug to pick her up.'

'Does it happen often?' Moriarty asked, staring speculatively at the drifting barge.

'All too,' Captain Coster said.

'Although usually only when the beggars are empty. This one has a full load of coal, I notice. Some colliery is going to be delighted if she smashes up on the Head or beaches herself.'

Holmes, who had been considering the barge carefully, came over to Moriarty. 'Look closely at that craft,' he said. 'Does anything strike you?'

'Yes,' Moriarty said. 'I've been thinking the same thing.'

'That's it, then?'

'The probabilities would so indicate.'

'What is it, Holmes?' Watson asked, staring at the barge.

'Captain Coster,' Holmes said, 'please look carefully at the barge. Does it seem to you that it is riding too high on the water? Compare it with those barges at the pier to our left, which are also fully loaded with coal.'

'Why, yes,' Coster said. 'That had been bothering me, but as I couldn't think of anything to account for it, I decided I must be mistaken.'

'Pull alongside that barge, Captain,' Moriarty directed. 'Carefully, very carefully, if you don't mind.'

Slowly the *Water Witch* edged along-side the coal barge. Moriarty took a small self-loading pistol from his pocket and worked the slide to chamber a bullet. Dr. Watson pulled his old service revolver from his belt, and Sherlock Holmes produced a smaller, silver-plated revolver from an inside pocket of his traveling cape.

Captain Coster did his best to look calm and unconcerned at his passengers' odd behavior. 'This person you're looking for,' he said. 'I take it he's not a friend of yours.'

'Hush!' Holmes said, putting his finger to his lips. 'Keep your ship alongside. We'll be back.'

The three of them, Holmes in the lead, leaped across the two feet of water separating the two craft and scrambled up the rough wooden side of the barge. The craft was nothing more than a huge rectangle full of coal from front to rear. At the very stern was a small wooden superstructure resembling a shed with windows cut in it. Black curtains shielded the windows from the inside, and there was no sign of life.

Slowly they worked their way to the stern. 'It seems unlikely that we haven't been seen — or perhaps heard,' Moriarty whispered. 'We had best be ready for a warm welcome.'

Holmes smiled grimly. 'It occurs to me,' he said, 'that if we're mistaken, some poor bargee is about to experience the shock of his life.'

Holmes and Watson lay prone on a bed of coal, their weapons pointed at the door, while Moriarty snapped it open with a well-placed baritsu kick and ducked aside. It swung wildly back and forth with a clatter that echoed off the water. Still nothing moved.

After a cautious moment, Moriarty dropped to the deck and carefully peered around the doorway. Then he stood up and dusted himself off, looking disgusted. 'Come here, gentlemen,' he said, 'Look at this.'

Inside the cabin were three men. Two of them were sprawled opposite each other across a small table and the third was crumpled on the floor halfway to the door. The two men at the table each had a hole in his chest, a great, ugly gaping hole of the sort caused by a large-caliber handgun fired from close range. The man on the floor had three such holes in his back. He lay in a clotted pool of his own blood, his face turned up, eyes opened, wearing a surprised expression. On the table was a small mound of anarchist literature, now covered with dried blood.

Stepping gingerly to avoid the blood, Holmes bent down to examine the body on the floor. 'Dead for some time, I should say,' he said. 'What do you think, Watson?'

Watson stooped over and pressed his fingernail into the flesh of the wrist and then opened the dead eye and peered at it. 'Four or five hours, as a quick estimate,' he said. 'Nasty way to go — not that any death is pleasant. Still, the massive trauma of a half-inch piece of lead pushing its way through the human gut must rank as one of the less desirable ends.'

'Well,' Moriarty said. 'Trepoff has his

dead anarchists. Now what has he done with the submersible?' He knelt down and began tapping on the deck, to be rewarded almost immediately with a dull thumping. 'Down here,' he said. 'There must be a trap door.'

Holmes joined him and, together, they pried and tapped and examined and pushed and prodded at the boards of the cabin floor. It took them five minutes to find the catch, hidden between two floorboards. Moriarty pushed at it, and it dropped a pair of hinged doors to reveal a three-foot-square hole. Holmes went over to the table for a candle, which stood between the two dead anarchists and lighted it.

'He's gone, of course,' Moriarty said.

'But we'd best check,' Holmes said.

'Of course,' Moriarty said. He swung himself over the side of the trap and climbed down the ladder affixed to the edge. When his head was level with the floor, Holmes handed him the candle, and then he disappeared below.

A few moments later he was back. 'Come down here,' he called to Holmes.

'This is impressive. You should see it. Bring another candle or, by preference, one of the oil lamps.'

Holmes and Watson removed two oil lamps from the gimbals that tied them to the cabin walls, lighted them, and clambered down the ladder to join Moriarty. The whole interior of the barge proved to be a vast, empty chamber. A board and beam load-bearing ceiling roofed it over, and provided support for the one or two feet of coal above, which disguised and concealed the chamber. Along the two sides and the aft section where they stood ran a wooden platform. Water came up to about three feet below the platform, filling the whole center of the chamber.

'Here,' Moriarty said, 'is where the Garrett-Harris was moored.'

'There must be a hole in the bottom of the barge,' Holmes said, 'just large enough for the submersible to come in and out.'

'At the moment,' Moriarty added, 'it is out. We can investigate this later, but right now we'd best get back to the *Water*

Witch and see if we can determine where that blasted steel cigar is lying in wait.'

They had no sooner reached the upper cabin than they heard Captain Coster hallooing for them. Moriarty raced out on deck and over to the side. 'What?' he yelled.

Captain Coster pointed up. Moriarty turned. There, in the air above them, was the fading light of a blue signal flare. Suddenly a second flare arced up to join the first. This new one burst forth with a brilliant white ball of light.

'Blue, then white,' Moriarty said. 'Southeast. Very clever of Barnett.' He scrambled over the side of the barge and onto the steam-launch, with Holmes and Watson only a few steps behind. 'Southeast,' he told Captain Coster. 'Head southeast. Holmes, get forward and see if you can spot the thing.'

'What can we do if we find it, now it's submerged?' Watson asked.

'Ram it!' Moriarty snapped. 'It won't be more than four or five feet down.

We should be able to split it open like an eggshell.'

'Here, now!' Captain Coster said. 'What is it you're talking about ramming with the *Water Witch?* Her hull is none too strong, you know. Besides, I can get into an awful mess of trouble if I go about ramming other boats.'

'Don't worry about that, Captain,' Moriarty said with firm authority. 'Just make your course, and quickly! We're on the Queen's business. If any harm comes to your boat, you shall be completely reimbursed for damages.'

'The Queen's — '

'Get a move on, Captain,' Moriarty said. 'There's a submersible out there somewhere stalking the *Victoria and Albert*, and we have to stop it!'

'Yes, sir,' Captain Coster said, snapping him a firm salute. 'Aye, aye, sir.' He grabbed the wheel and headed the *Water Witch* around.

The sea was cluttered with small pleasure-boats — a thousand Sunday skippers all out to cheer their favorites as the great race drew to a close. The first of the big yachts were now coming into sight in the distance, tacking into the bay and lining up on the *Victoria and Albert* and the finish line.

The *Water Witch* cut a line due southeast, passing to the left of the Royal Yacht and heading into the Solent. 'We'll pass well to the lee of the yachts,' Captain Coster said, 'so that's all right. But where is this submersible?'

'Perhaps your associate saw a partly submerged tree trunk,' Holmes suggested.

'I say!' Watson called from the bow. 'Look!' he pointed to a rocket trail streaking into the sky about them. As they watched, it burst into a shower of green sparks cascading over their heads.

'Green,' Moriarty said. 'West.'

'Perhaps it merely signifies the start of the evening display,' Holmes suggested sourly.

'No,' Moriarty said. 'Barnett is sending the best information he can with but four colors as a language. Captain, turn this craft due west.'

'As you say,' Captain Coster said,

swinging the ship around.

Moriarty climbed up to the top of the cabin and stared about him, examining the positions of the ships in the bay. Then he jumped down. 'Of course!' he said, snapping his fingers.

'What?' Holmes demanded.

'The submersible is circling the *Victoria and Albert* from the west,' Moriarty said. 'Trepoff wants to have nothing between himself and the Solent channel after he makes his shot. Barnett must have estimated that we couldn't catch up with him in direct pursuit, so he sent us around this way.' He turned to the captain. 'Cut in closer to the *Victoria and Albert*,' he directed.

'Those Navy steam cutters surrounding her will stop us,' Coster said.

'We'll take that chance.'

'We'll be cutting across the finish line in front of the yachts. The commodore won't like it.'

'We'll live with that too,' Moriarty said. 'Cut it close, there. And open up that engine!'

Captain Coster yelled instructions to

his one-man crew, who was down below stoking the boiler, and the *Water Witch*, engine racing, moving in to cut across the side of the *Victoria and Albert*. Two Navy cutters came to life and sprung out to intercept her. The nearer one was alongside in a minute, just as the *Water Witch* came parallel to the side of the Royal Yacht. A skinny young man in a full-dress uniform with the thin, curled stripe of a sub-lieutenant on his sleeve was leaning out from the prow of the cutter, his gold sword flapping against his leg.

'Ahoy there!' he yelled, cupping his hands against the wind, 'Heave to, you men!' Captain Coster shrugged and started to comply.

'There!' Watson suddenly yelled. 'There it is! I can see it. Off to the left there!'

Moriarty peered out and saw the barely visible submersible, a menacing cigar-shaped shadow beneath the waters. Suddenly, a streak of white foam detached from the bow in an upward arc and sped toward the *Victoria and Albert*;

a Whitehead torpedo with a two-hundred-pound nitrocellulose warhead creating its destiny, racing to meet the monarch of one-third of the world's people.

'It's now running on the surface!' Moriarty yelled. 'Quick, kick that engine in and get off this boat!' He grabbed the wheel and spun it around, as Coster, who had shut down the throttle, slapped it full open again.

'Here, you!' the sub-lieutenant yelled, 'where the deuce do you think you're going? Stop or we'll fire!'

'Holmes, Watson, get off this boat!' Moriarty yelled, swinging the *Water Witch* onto a path that would intercept the Whitehead torpedo. 'Captain Coster, jump!'

Holmes swung himself over the aft rail. 'Leap for it, Watson,' he yelled, before cutting the water with a clean dive toward the Navy cutter. Watson spun his bowler toward the horizon and joined Holmes in the water. The ship's one crewman appeared from somewhere below and leaped overboard.

'My boat, man!' Captain Coster

screamed, trying to grab the wheel from Moriarty. The professor picked him up by the front of his pea jacket. 'Victoria will buy you a new one,' he said savagely, and with seemingly superhuman strength he lifted Coster high and threw him over the stern rail.

Moriarty made a final adjustment in the course of the boat, lashed the wheel in position, and then raced back to the stern rail. Making one last check on the closing trajectories of the boat and the torpedo, he decided that the *Water Witch* would intersect a full ten yards before the torpedo reached the *Victoria and Albert*. Then he stripped off his jacket and dove, a long, flat dive, into the bay.

He was in the water no more than a few seconds when the Whitehead torpedo punched into the *Water Witch*. It drove through the scantling on the port side, all the way through the boat, and out the starboard side before it exploded. A great geyser shot up, cresting a hundred feet in the air, and fell back across the bow of the *Victoria and Albert*, causing the big yacht to rock ponderously in place. A moment later the concussion wave reached Moriarty, throwing him out of the water and putting a deep trough under him when he fell back down. Then the water closed over him and he had to struggle hard to reach the surface before his lungs gave out.

The *Water Witch* took on water rapidly, settling by the bow. The deck was already awash, and only the small cabin was clear of the sea. Then the stern lifted clear of the water and the bow plunged. It stood frozen in that position for a long moment before sliding, bow first, to the bottom.

A moment later the Navy cutter reached Moriarty, and two seamen pulled him from the water. Holmes, Watson, Captain Coster, and his crewman were already on board. Holmes was deep in discussion with the young sub-lieutenant.

'Oh, my God,' Watson suddenly screamed, pointing across the water to the Royal Yacht. There, etched by the rays of the Western sun, the clear wake of a second Whitehead torpedo could be seen cleaving a path toward the bow of the *Victoria and Albert*.

One of the guarding Navy steam cutters, now on the lookout, raced to intercept it. For a moment it seemed as though the cutter would be too late, but then, scant feet from the bow of the Royal Yacht, it crossed the line of the torpedo. The sailors on the cutter scattered, jumping overboard in every direction; but the young officer at its helm stayed motionless behind the wheel, calmly steering the craft into the torpedo.

And then the cutter was gone, and an exploding cloud of white water marked where it had been. A second later the crump of the explosion reached them, rocking and shaking their boat. Then the cloud of water fell back, obscuring the *Victoria and Albert* for a moment and drenching its decks. A large concussion wave spread out from where the launch had been, and the Royal Yacht bobbed up and down like a rowboat for a few seconds. Of the cutter and the young officer, there was no sign.

The sub-lieutenant, his face white, turned to Moriarty. 'Mr. Holmes has been telling me what this is all about, Professor Moriarty,' he said. 'I am Lieutenant Simms. How can I help?'

'Find that damned submersible,' Moriarty said.

'Has it any more Whitehead torpedoes?'

'I think that's the lot,' Holmes said.

'It can't fire more without surfacing at any rate,' Moriarty said. 'I'd like to get him before he has a chance to reload.'

'You think he's going to try?'

'No. I think he's going to leave as expeditiously as possible. He — look there!'

A red starburst lit the sky above them. 'North,' Moriarty said. 'Barnett is still on the job. Trepoff has decided not to run the Solent.'

Another red burst spread its crystal light, followed by a white ball of fire.

'North-northeast,' Moriarty said. 'Have you a compass?'

'Don't need one,' the officer said. 'It would be, let's see . . . ' He looked around and sighted along his arm. 'Just that way.'

'Right back toward Miro's tethered aerostats,' Moriarty said. 'Trepoff may have a land vehicle concealed somewhere about. We must try to beat him to the shore.'

Lieutenant Simms leaned over to a brass speaking-tube by the wheel and blew into it. 'Engine crew!'

'Aye, sir?' came a thin voice out of it.

'I want you men to shovel coal into that boiler until you redline the gauge. That's an order.'

'Aye, aye, sir.'

'Kelly,' the lieutenant said, turning to the young seaman at the wheel, 'make a straight course for that great tethered balloon abaft the fitting station. As straight a course as you can without running us aground or hitting anything.'

'That balloon's coming down, sir,' the sailor pointed out.

'It's pretty big,' the lieutenant said. 'I don't think it will descend from sight. But if it does, then make a course for where it was.'

'Aye, aye, sir.'

In a minute the sturdy cutter was

plowing through the water in a mechanical frenzy, the tie rods from the double pistons clanking madly in their housing. In two minutes the escape valve for the boiler was whistling and burbling as it released some of the tremendous pressure that had been built up.

'Is this safe?' Watson asked the young officer, looking nervously at the escaping steam.

'They don't usually blow up,' Lieutenant Simms said. 'They are supposed to be built for a twenty-five percent overload. Of course, this is an experimental model. We shall see.'

'Umph,' Watson said, and he made his way to the bow.

Holmes stood on top of the wheelhouse, clutching the small signal mast for support. 'There,' he said. 'Look! It has surfaced.'

Moriarty peered over the water in the direction of Holmes's pointing finger, but he couldn't make out anything, so he climbed up to join Holmes. 'Where?'

'Over there!'

'Oh, yes,' Moriarty said. The thick

metal cigar was moving rapidly through the water dead ahead of them, with its small conning tower completely above water. 'On the surface, with air for its engine, it can make surprisingly good time.' He pulled out his watch and timed the closing distance between the cutter and the submersible against the submersible's approach to the shore. 'It will beat us ashore,' he said. 'But only by a minute or so.'

'Ashore or not,' Holmes said, 'he will not escape me. I will get this man.'

'We,' Moriarty corrected, 'will get this man.'

Holmes turned a bleak eye on him. 'Did you see the Queen?' he asked.

'What do you mean, Holmes? When?'

'After the *Water Witch* exploded — you were still in the water — I saw Her Majesty come forward on the upper deck of the *Victoria and Albert* to watch what was happening. The wave from the second explosion washed right over her.'

'Was her Majesty hurt?'

'I don't believe so. But, dammit, Moriarty, that was the Queen of England!

That man was trying to assassinate the crowned head of the English people merely to accomplish a political end in a country two thousand miles away from here.'

A sudden gust of wind blew salt spray in Moriarty's face and he took out his handkerchief to wipe it. For a moment he was surprised to find that his handkerchief was soaking wet already. 'True,' he said.

'She is not perfect, Moriarty,' Holmes said, clenching his fist. 'I'll admit that, dammit, she is not perfect. But I've never known England without Victoria, and I have no desire to. She stands for decency and morality and everything that's good in this imperfect world.'

'I don't want to argue with a man in the grip of a patriotic passion,' Moriarty said, doing his best to wring his handkerchief out. 'Besides, you may be right. At any rate, we saved her life. Doesn't that make you feel good?'

'You saved her life,' Holmes said. 'You and the officer at the wheel of that cutter. What a strange thing fate is that it should twist so: Moriarty saving the life of his queen. Surely one of the great ironies of our time.'

They had gained greatly on the submersible in the past minute, and it was now clearly in view. But it was also much closer to the shore by now. Even with the great difference in speeds, the submersible would reach the shore ahead of the cutter. The only question was by how much.

Silently, impotent in the hands of the immutable laws of physics and mechanics, Holmes and Moriarty watched the submersible ground itself on the rocks of a small strip of beach, even as the cutter halved the distance between them. Three men popped out of the forward hatch of the submersible and ran off up the rocks.

'She's beached!' Lieutenant Simms yelled. 'The sub is beached. We'll reach her in less than a minute. I'll run the cutter right in alongside her. Probably rip the bottom out.' He whistled into the speaking tube. 'Stop shoveling! Prepare to run aground!' Then he turned to his wheelman. 'Kelly, I'll take the wheel. You stand by that strain valve and be ready to release the pressure on my command. Instantly, you understand, or we'll all be blown into the next life.'

'Aye, aye, sir,' Kelly said, taking a firm grip on the strain valve rope.

Lieutenant Simms artfully headed the launch into the same small strip of rocky beach that the submersible had found, aiming for a spot immediately to the right of the submersible. Holmes and Moriarty went forward to join Watson, and the three of them braced themselves against the coming shock of running aground.

At the last possible second Simms threw the engine out of gear and yelled: 'Now, Kelly!'

The cutter slid smoothly up on the beach in a screaming, billowing cloud of steam that pierced the ear and obscured all vision for fifty yards in every direction. As soon as the cutter jammed to a halt, Moriarty and Holmes leaped off and raced over the stony beach, with Watson close behind them.

Once clear of the billowing steam, they paused to look around. Holmes grabbed

Moriarty's arm and pointed. 'Look!'

In the clearing ahead of them the two hydrogen balloons had been winched down and had their gondolas resting on the ground. The three men from the submersible had commandeered the near balloon, and were keeping its crew away with large wicked-looking revolvers. Two of the villains had boarded the gondola, and the third was hacking it free of the heavy rope tether with an axe. Miro and his assistants were standing with their hands high over their heads, looking startled and frightened out of their wits.

Holmes and Moriarty raced toward the clearing, but before they arrived the balloon was free. The axe man dropped his axe and clambered aboard, pulled up by the other two, as the great balloon bounded upward, lofting into an English heaven.

'Here! Over here!' someone called as Moriarty and Holmes reached the clearing. 'Quickly!' It was Barnett, who raised his head from where he had been hiding — in the gondola of the second balloon — and beckoned to them. 'I've almost got it free,' he called. 'Come on. Climb in and we'll go after them.'

Moriarty and Holmes raced across the field to the second gondola and climbed in. Watson puffed up to them a couple of seconds later.

'Don't get in, Doctor,' Barnett said sharply. 'If we're too heavy — or too light — we won't be able to match velocities with them.'

'Notify the Navy, Watson,' Holmes said. 'We'll be heading out to sea. Get a ship to follow us if you can.'

And with that, they were free. 'I'll do my best, Holmes,' Watson yelled up at them as they pulled away from the field.

'How'd you do that?' Moriarty asked Barnett. 'They had to hack that other balloon loose.'

'There's a release for the tether in the bottom of the gondola,' Barnett said. 'In case the balloon begins to drag on something, I suppose. Nobody told Trepoff. I assume that was Trepoff?'

'I certainly hope so,' Holmes said.

'You've done very good work,' Moriarty told Barnett.

The balloon was already more than a hundred feet above the ground and rising rapidly. Their quarry was a hundred yards ahead of them and several hundred feet higher. 'They seem to be pulling away from us,' Holmes noted.

'There is a steady wind of about twenty knots at roughly the five-hundred-foot level,' Barnett said. 'They must be in it already. When we reach it, we'll keep up with them.'

'Keeping up isn't enough,' Holmes said, fingering his revolver. 'We must catch them.'

They were heading generally south-west across the bay. Below them the white sails of the regatta yachts were circling the *Victoria and Albert*. Ahead of them, the town of Gosport, a mile or so of land, and then the Solent and the Isle of Wight. 'They'll have the steam cutters out to support us,' Moriarty said. 'If we can force Trepoff down in the Solent, he'll be picked up by the Navy.'

'Perhaps we can shoot him down,' Holmes suggested, still clutching his silver-plated revolver.

'Too far for pistol shooting,' Moriarty said. 'Besides, a pistol bullet passing through the fabric of the balloon would merely cause a minor gas leak which would have no discernible effect on the performance of the aerostat.'

'We must do something!' Holmes declared.

They passed over Gosport and the mile-wide strip of land, steadily gaining altitude. Trepoff's balloon was now several hundred yards ahead of them and holding that distance. They were over water now, and the ships below looked like precise toys, built for some hobbyist's bathtub lake.

A spark appeared in the gondola of the forward aerostat, which grew into a rapidly approaching arc of flame reaching out for them. It burst into a myriad of sparkling colors somewhere over their balloon. Then a second spark shot toward them, to dissolve into a cascading ribbon of red flame directly before their eyes.

'Trepoff has found the fireworks!' Barnett cried. 'They were being loaded when he and his men appeared.'

'Dear me,' Holmes said. 'This is liable to prove embarrassing.'

'I don't suppose we have any similar cargo?' Moriarty asked, looking around the surprisingly spacious interior of the wicker gondola.

Barnett pointed to three wooden crates on the floor. 'There,' he said. 'I would like to point out, however, that they are very dangerous. Miro gave me a long lecture about the folly of firing off rockets from the basket of a hydrogen balloon. He was not happy about the signal flares, and they're only half the size of these skyrockets.'

'We must be careful,' Moriarty agreed. 'Let us get these crates open.'

As he spoke a rocket burst over their balloon and released four brightly burning blue flares, which descended on silk parachutes, slowly passing in front of them. One of them hit the side of the balloon, sliding along the fabric for a few moments before bouncing off.

Holmes released his breath. 'I have never,' he said, 'felt quite so helpless.

Well, Professor, Barnett — dangerous as it may be, I vote for an answering fireworks barrage from this gondola.'

They ripped the crates open. A new assault of colored balls popped toward them from the other aerostat, twisting and glowing madly, falling only a few feet short.

The first crate contained three boxes marked 'gerbes,' and the illustrations on the box covers showed colored balls popping from a tube. 'I think we've just seen those,' Holmes said. 'Next crate.'

The second crate held finned skyrockets, packed in firing tubes. 'This, I think, is what we are looking for,' Moriarty said. 'How many are there?'

'Fourteen,' Barnett said.

'Not so deep as a well,' Moriarty said, 'or so wide as a church door, but that should suffice.' Three points of red suddenly appeared in the sky above them and burst into a shower of sparks which cascaded over the balloon and fell on all sides of them. 'Indeed,' he added, 'it had better suffice.'

He took one of the skyrocket tubes in his hand and examined it. 'How ingenious,' he said. 'The fins are on tiny springs which push them open after they pass through the tube.'

'Perhaps,' Holmes suggested, 'it would be wiser to examine the contraptions later. For now let us concentrate on shooting down that balloon before its passengers succeed in doing the same for us.'

'Take your jacket off,' Moriarty told Barnett. 'Be prepared to extinguish fires started by flame-back from the skyrockets.'

'There's a damp horse-blanket here,' Barnett said, producing it from a wicker basket built into the side of the gondola. 'Miro had it soaked for the same purpose. I'll use it.'

'Excellent,' Moriarty said.

Holmes propped one of the skyrocket tubes against the side of the gondola and sighted along the top. 'This should put it in the general vicinity,' he said. 'Here, I'll stand aside and you light the fuse.' He stood to one side, holding the skyrocket tube firmly at arm's length, propped against the side of the gondola.

Moriarty ripped a length of fuse from one of the gerbes and lit one end with a waterproof vespa, which he carefully waved out and tossed over the side. 'Ready?'

'Ready,' Holmes agreed.

Moriarty applied the burning fuse to the short fuse of the skyrocket, which sputtered and smoldered and disappeared into the tube. Eight seconds later a blast of flame came out of the rear of the tube, and the skyrocket shot out the front. It arced across the sky, over Trepoff's balloon, and released a series of colored balls before exploding in a shower of red and green sparks.

An answering salvo from Trepoff put a rocket between the gondola and the balloon, but it passed harmlessly through the shrouds before disintegrating into a crowd of flame-snakes that spiraled to the sea below.

Holmes corrected his aim and Moriarty touched off the next skyrocket. This one fell short and exploded in a puff-ball of blue light that was quickly extinguished by the sea.

Suddenly a spark appeared in Trepoff's gondola, and a flame curved upward. And then, in a moment that etched itself in the minds of all the onlookers for miles up and down the Solent, a tracery of flame worked over the fabric of Trepoff's balloon, creating fiery designs in the rounded sides. Then it burned off, and for a second seemed to have gone out, when all at once the balloon erupted and a plume of flame spurted out the side and enveloped the whole craft.

Barnett saw a white, frightened face at the side of the gondola before the craft fell from the sky, a fiery comet tail streaming out behind it.

'Miro was right,' Moriarty said calmly, as the flaming mass struck the water far below. 'This is a dangerous business.'

'I only hope they find the bodies,' Holmes said, 'or we shall never know if that was Trepoff.'

Moriarty shook his head. 'Only the future will tell us whether Trepoff was in that aerostat,' he said. 'Remember, we have no idea of what he looks like. Barnett, can you get us down?'

Barnett reached up and untied a rope that valved hydrogen out of the top of the gasbag. 'It will be a slow descent,' he said.

'Good,' Moriarty remarked. 'I have just seen a fast descent.'

By the time their aerostat reached the water, a cutter was standing by to pick them up. The lieutenant in command saluted them as they came aboard. 'Good evening, gentlemen,' he said. 'I have orders to take you to the *Victoria and Albert*. Her Majesty would like to have you presented. At your convenience, of course.'

12

THE UNWRITTEN TALE

On earth there is nothing great but man;
In man there is nothing great but mind.

— *Sir William Hamilton*

'You are going out?' Moriarty asked.

'I am having dinner with Miss Perrine,' Barnett told him.

'Ah, of course,' Moriarty said. ''*Jedem nach seinen Bedürfnissen,*' as that strange little fellow at the British Museum put it.'

'This is to be a business dinner,' Barnett said stiffly.

'Could it be otherwise?' asked Moriarty blandly. 'Incidentally, I meant to remark on your deft handling of the Trepoff affair in your article for the popular press.'

'Well,' Barnett said, 'I figured if I didn't write it, then someone else surely would. As it is, I preempted the story and selected the facts to be told.'

'Excellent,' Moriarty said.

Barnett looked pleased. 'Thank you.'

'You kept my name out of it,' Moriarty said. 'And I thank you.' He looked at the ship's chronometer above the study door. 'You'd best go to dinner,' he said. 'Business before pleasure, after all.'

'We are meeting Mr. Bernard Shaw at Covent Garden after dinner,' Barnett said. 'Cecily — Miss Perrine — is trying to talk him into doing a series of articles for us.'

'Shaw,' Moriarty said. 'I have read some of his criticism. A great talent. Not a genius, as he thinks, but a genuine talent. A well-developed second-rate talent with a first-rate Irish ego.'

'Speaking of Irish egos — ' Barnett said.

'Go to dinner!'

Barnett allowed himself a slight smile. The next two years promised to be quite interesting. Donning his black silk topper, and adjusting it carefully on his head, he hurried off toward the British Museum.